# OFF SEASON

CHICAGO THUNDER HOCKEY

## JODI OLIVER

Cover Design by Kari March Designs

Photography by Wander Aguiar

Editing by Leticia's Edits

Proofread by Rachel Rumble

*Content Warning: mentions of past death of parents and grandparents, on-page bereavement, mentions of past bullying, mentions of past child abandonment, on-page anxiety. Please take caution if any of these may be triggering for you.*

*For those who take comfort in seeing a robin.*

## Chapter One

*Ethan*

The puck sails over Elliot's left shoulder, into the back of the net, and the arena practically vibrates as the visiting fans cheer and applaud in celebration. The LA bench clears and players swarm the ice to revel in their victory, and while my heart is thumping hard against my chest from the adrenaline, my head drops in defeat.

We came so fucking close.

Game seven.

Double overtime.

We were so close to clinching the Western Conference Champions title. We had the Stanley Cup Finals within touching distance, but we couldn't grasp it. All we can do now is watch as Los Angeles celebrates.

Bending at the waist, I rest my stick over my thighs and focus on my breathing. It's like there's an invisible band squeezing my lungs, and an ache rooted deep in my chest as a million and one emotions rush through me.

Frustration. Anger. Sadness. Envy.

But there's still pride among all the negative feelings. Even though I'm fucking distraught, I'm proud that we fought so hard, even if it wasn't enough to get the W.

Our goaltender, Elliot Olsen, skates over and sniffs, trying to contain the emotions bubbling beneath the surface. His eyes are filled with unshed tears behind his cage, the protective padding doing nothing to hide how his body is trembling from his ragged breathing.

I stand to full height and bring him in for a hug, knowing nothing I say or do will be able to soothe the heartbreak he's experiencing.

I've been here before—many times—but this was his first playoff experience, and it hurts more when we were *this* close to making it.

"You gave it everything you could, El," I say reassuringly. "You played your heart out, and I'm so proud of you."

And he did. He played fucking amazingly and made some incredible saves.

"But if I didn't let in that g-goal—" he hiccups, sucking in another sharp breath. He's trying his damndest to hold himself together.

"No," I interrupt, shaking my head as I pull away to look into his glassy eyes. I remove my glove and place my hand on his shoulder pad, giving him a slight shake. "This isn't on you, okay? There's a lot of things we could have done better, but you can't think like that. This isn't on you."

It's easy to be consumed by the ugly emotions that follow a big loss. To allow disappointment to rush through our veins and focus on the mistakes. The what-ifs and could-have-beens.

We'll work together on how to improve, and we'll bounce back.

We always do.

He gives me a shaky nod. I know he doesn't believe me right now, but he will in time.

It's all part of the game.

Highest highs and lowest lows.

I've been in the league long enough that I'm used to the emotional rollercoaster it brings, but some of these guys? It's their first playoff. Hell, for some of them, it's their first year in the NHL.

Elliot turns to lean on Blaine, his twin brother and our teammate, who's also trying to hold back his emotions.

This fucking sucks.

Raising my hand, I rub the hollow spot in my chest over my pads and skate to center ice when it's time to shake the opposing players' hands.

"Great series, Parkes." Edwards, LA's captain, brings me in for a bro-hug, slapping my shoulder with his gloved hand. "It's been a great run."

"Good luck, man. I hope it works out for you."

And I mean it. We were drafted in the same year, and this is his final shot at the cup because he announced his retirement a few weeks ago.

*That'll be you soon.*

Fuck off, conscience; give me a break. I'm trying to keep it together here.

Once I've shaken hands with every player and staff member, I head back down the tunnel and return to the locker room. I sit down in my cubby, resting my elbows on my knees before dropping my head into my hands.

These guys worked so hard this season and played some of the best hockey of their careers. Even when we were hit with injuries, we kept pushing harder every game. We stepped onto the ice with determination and hunger to win.

We wanted this win.

We *deserved* to win, and as captain, I feel responsible for our loss. I feel like I've failed my team.

I've failed our fans.

I've failed myself.

And I'm fucking devastated.

What could I have done better?

*Ugh.* For fuck's sake.

There's nothing I can do now except move forward: study tape to see what can be improved, train hard during the off-season, and channel our energy into making next season *our* season.

My jaw clenches, and I quickly blink away the burn from my eyes at the sound of someone hitting their cubby in anger.

I need to get my shit together.

I need to be the strong one for the team. The one guy they can depend on to help ease the weight of their own emotions.

The atmosphere is somber when the rest of the guys filter in. Some just sit and stare at nothing, lost in their own heads, while others undress without a word. There's no post-game playlist. No rogue socks being thrown or asses slapped with damp towels.

Just this painful silence and heaviness in the air.

I don't move. I just lift my head slightly, resting my chin on my steepled fingers, and watch this great group of guys for the last time.

I've been playing in the NHL since I was drafted by the Thunder nearly twenty years ago, but time doesn't make it any easier. It doesn't matter if you've been in this game for one year or almost two decades. You spend more time with these guys than you do with your family. You build connections and lasting friendships, and while trades and retirements are all part of the game, it doesn't make knowing I'll never play with this group again suck any less.

Coach Harris walks in. His hands are shoved deep into the pockets of his pressed pants, exhaustion clear on his face. He takes a moment to look at all of us individually before running a hand down his face with a heavy sigh.

"I'm really proud of every single one of you. I'm proud of this team and what we've accomplished. You guys worked so fucking hard this season. The time and commitment you've put in has been incredible. You deserved this win, and I'm disappointed for you all that the season ended this way. Unfortunately, you know it's the way it goes sometimes in hockey, but I want you all to know you should be proud of yourselves, and we'll come back fighting next year."

I clench my jaw again as my chin wobbles slightly. Normally, I would follow up with a few words of my own, but tonight I can't speak. The words are lodged in my throat. All I can do is nod and grunt, agreeing with every word Coach says.

Blaine gives me a sad smile, squeezing my shoulder before disappearing into the showers. One by one, they give me a fist bump or shoulder squeeze as they move to the showers until I'm the only one left in the room, still sitting fully dressed, staring at the mountain of jerseys in the laundry hamper. I haven't even unlaced my skates. I'm frozen in time with nothing but a dull fucking ache deep in my chest. Twisting like a knife.

Is this loss hitting me harder because the dreaded R-word keeps filtering more frequently through my mind? It's fairly common that once a player hits the big three-oh, the imaginary timer begins to count down the years you've got left in the league. Recovery takes longer, aches and pains become more regular, and younger guys keep getting faster.

*So much faster.*

I'm not naive enough to think I have many seasons left, but fuck, this loss is hitting me harder than ever.

And not just emotionally.

Sucking in a deep, shaky breath, I squash my emotions down and start to undress. This isn't the time or place for me to feel sorry for myself. After I carefully place each piece of equipment in its designated place in my cubby, I head into the showers.

"Ethan, you're up for interviews in ten!" I hear the team's public relations coordinator, Colleen, call out as I rinse the shampoo from my hair.

That's another thing I dread. The press.

I don't want to answer questions about how I feel, or what we can do better, or what the morale is like in the locker room, or what I will miss most about this group of guys.

Sometimes I think they purposely ask stupid questions to see if they can get a rise out of me.

Once showered, I throw on a team-branded dry-fit t-shirt and athletic shorts and slip my feet into my slides. I follow Colleen out to the press area, where there are at least two dozen reporters looking at me with sympathetic faces.

I want to tell them all and their sad-looking faces to fuck off, but I don't. I can't. I've been trained better than that, and I know they're not really sad. They're vultures waiting to strike at the first sign of weakness.

Instead, I sit down at the table behind a microphone and cast a sideways glance at Colleen, trying to tell her without words that I don't want to be here. The anguish must be evident on my face because she sends a genuine apologetic smile my way.

I don't need to harp on about how shitty this feels, because while the pain is immeasurable right now, I know losing is only temporary.

Thankfully, they accept my grunts and grumbled answers—*yeah, it sucks we lost. I'm proud of the team. I'm disappointed our season ended this way. Yeah, we'll review tape in a couple of days. This group has played some great hockey. Yeah, the morale is low, but we'll bounce back stronger next season,* blah blah fucking blah, and finally, after a long, torturous hour, I'm parking my car in the underground parking lot beneath my apartment building.

The door to my apartment slams behind me, and I let out a heavy sigh into the empty space. The only sounds I can hear are sirens in the distance and the blood rushing in my ears. After tossing my bag on the floor and my suit jacket on the kitchen island, I pour myself two fingers of scotch before throwing myself onto the couch. I stare aimlessly out of the window, zoning out as the sea of car lights on Lake Shore Drive rush beneath me.

It's moments like these that make me wish I wasn't alone. That I had someone to come home to, someone to talk to. Someone I could lose myself in to stop my brain from drifting into those negative spaces I told Elliot to resist.

*Do as I say, not as I do.*

I didn't say I was good at taking my own advice.

My phone vibrates in my pocket, and another sigh escapes my lips at the sight of my mom's name on the screen.

"Why won't anyone let me be miserable in peace?" I grumble, but because I'm a good son and would never dream of ignoring my mom, I swipe my finger across the screen to answer.

It's not that I don't want to talk to her. It's more to do with not wanting to talk to *anyone* right now.

"Hey, mom," I say as her face fills the screen.

She swipes her fingers under her tired, watery eyes, giving me a shaky smile. "Hey, honey. I'm so sorry about the game. I'm so bloody proud of you, though."

The emotions that have been simmering inside me since the buzzer sounded begin to bubble to the surface. My mouth twists from the tangy, bitter taste that travels up the back of my throat. My mom is the only person I allow to see me like this. To see the raw, vulnerable feelings that I keep locked away from everyone else.

"Don't blame yourself, Ethan. You were amazing out there. You all were. I think it came down to pure luck that they scored. You'll see it when you review the tape, but please, *please* don't let this eat away at you."

A choked noise gets trapped in my throat as my resolve

begins to crumble. Of course she would know what I'm thinking.

"We were so close, Mom." My voice cracks in that last word.

Throwing my head back against the couch cushions, I glare up at the ceiling. Willing the burning in my eyes to subside. The muscles in my jaw begin to ache from the tension of grinding my molars.

I don't know why I'm beating myself up so bad; it was the fucking conference final, not the Stanley Cup Final. I know we played amazingly, and I *know* sometimes it's just the way it goes. That's how it is in hockey.

It can love you, or it can hate you. There's always going to be a loser, but it fucking sucks that it was us tonight.

It's an open wound that'll take a day or two to heal.

"I know, sweetie, and I know this isn't what you want to hear, but there's always next season." I open my eyes at her soothing voice. There's kindness and pride in her brown eyes. She knows not to blow smoke up my ass, even if she is my mother.

When I was playing in the juniors, I told her not to feed me lies or false hope. To only tell me things she genuinely believes in. I'd had enough lies from my dad to last me a lifetime.

"You've got such a strong team around you. I know it's only words, and nothing I can say or do will make it any easier right now, but you've had an amazing season."

I drag my free hand down my face and groan into my palm. "I feel like time is ticking for me, you know? I'm getting old. I'll be thirty-eight in a few weeks. I don't have many seasons left in me."

She scoffs. "You are not *old*, Ethan, so quit thinking like that! You've got plenty more in you. You see legends playing into their forties, and that will be you, too! But I know you." She rolls her eyes adoringly. "You need some time to lick your wounds before you can come back fighting, but don't you dare for one second think you have failed anyone, and that includes yourself."

I raise my eyebrow at her glaring into the camera. She knows me so well.

"Promise me," she demands when I don't respond.

"I promise," I grumble.

"Good." She smiles. "On a lighter note, it means I get to see you sooner." She does a little dance in her seat. The excitement in her voice eases some of the ache in my heart.

My mom's originally from England. She moved to Toronto for work when she finished university, where she met my dad and fell pregnant with me. Then, when I was seven years old, he left, and we haven't heard from him since.

She stayed in Toronto until I turned twenty, when I bought her a house in England with my first big paycheck, and she's been living there ever since.

She gave up everything for me so I could play hockey, so the least I could do was make sure she had everything she could ever need or want in life.

"I'll look at flights once I'm done with team stuff."

"I've missed you so much. I can't wait to see you!" She beams at me. "And that means you'll be here for Samantha's wedding!"

"Fuck, don't remind me." I grimace, downing the rest of my scotch.

It's not that I'm not happy for my cousin. I'm over the fucking moon for her that she's finally getting the wedding she's dreamed about since we were kids, but her groom? Her groom happens to be my ex-fiancé's brother.

The same ex-fiancé who left me at the airport on the way to our own wedding without even as much as a goodbye.

It was a heartbreak I've never fully recovered from. I built my walls up stronger than ever after that, and I've made sure nobody has broken through my defenses since.

I can handle difficult questions from the press and even people invading my life from every angle.

But I'm not sure how I'll handle seeing him again.

# Chapter Two

*Jacob*

"That's it, we're all sold out," Daniel announces, appearing from around the corner sporting a wide grin.

My jaw drops in disbelief. "What? Are you kidding me?! Didn't we bake twice as much as usual?"

He chuckles, carrying the empty trays to the sink for cleaning. "Time to get your thinking cap on, boss. We clearly need more. The people of Chicago are demanding their sweet treats."

I shake my head at the "boss" endearment, trying to fight the smile from my lips. It's still very surreal for me. I don't think this feeling will ever get old, because never in my wildest dreams would I have expected my small business to boom the way it has. What started as a hobby in my grand-parents' kitchen—baking cakes for aesthetically pleasing social media posts and custom celebration cakes for friends and their families—ended up with my name above a shop front and selling out at twelve thirty on a Monday.

Yep. A *Monday.*

Who would have thought? But it's not always been this way.

The reason behind our recent success is the guy who swept my brother, Alex, off his feet. He started dating Blaine Olsen, a hotshot hockey player for the Chicago Thunder, six months ago. When I got the flu just before Christmas, leaving Alex to take care of the shop on his own, Blaine surprised us both by stepping in and helping out. He didn't bat an eye at putting on an apron and serving baked goods.

We didn't realize the impact his showing up would have on the business at the time, but ever since, we've had people lining up outside—literally.

This city really does love its hockey team.

But the luck didn't end there.

Shortly after, the team approached us and asked to use the premises to film a segment for their social media channel, where some of the team decorated and sold their creations to adoring fans. It put *Jacob's Delicious Desserts* right on the map for being one of the top bakeries in Chicago and made us the sole dessert caterer for their VIP boxes on game nights.

How is this my life?

It's safe to say it's been an overwhelming whirlwind since, but a good one. I'm thankful for the unexpected fortune every day, but there's still a part of me that worries I'm going to wake up one day in the nightmare that was my life only a few months ago.

Surely no one can be this lucky without a catch.

Daniel and I are just getting to work on finishing the custom orders that are due to be picked up later today to then get a head start on prep for tomorrow when my phone begins to ring. I slip it out of the pocket of my apron and swipe my finger across the screen to answer.

"Hi, Alex," I greet my brother.

"Hey! How's it been today?"

He usually works with us, but with Blaine's season being over, he's taking a few days off.

Plus, they're both taking a trip to California soon, so he's been getting ready for that.

"Busy." I rest the phone between my ear and shoulder, allowing me to finish doing the decorative pink swirls on the princess-themed birthday cake I'm working on. "We sold out just after lunch."

"Wow. Do you think we need to start upping the quantities?"

"You sound just like Daniel," I answer with a laugh, looking at the guy in question. He smirks, brushing off an imaginary piece of lint from his shoulder.

I'm so glad we hired Daniel. He's been a lifesaver, along with Aria, who helps us out on the weekends. We're not at the point of expansion, but having two more people to help me and Alex has been such a relief.

Still, if we continue to grow at this rate, we'll need to look at hiring another person or three. And maybe find a bigger store.

That's a scary thought.

"I was wondering if you could do me a huge favor," Alex asks.

"Sure, what's up?"

"Could you bring some cupcakes over later for the guys? They're all sad, and I don't have enough ingredients here to make anything."

I scrunch up my nose. "They're sad because of the hockey game?"

The Thunder lost a big game on Saturday night. Alex has been telling me for weeks how important it was, trying to teach me the playoff format and what it all means, but I'll admit—I'm not a hockey fan.

Actually, I'm not a fan of any kind of sport thanks to some douche canoes in high school, but I've been trying to make a conscious effort since Alex and Blaine's relationship became serious.

He's good for my brother. He treats him like a prized treasure, so the least I can do is try and learn about his job.

Alex lets out an exasperated sigh. "Yes, Jacob. They were so close to advancing to the Stanley Cup Finals. It was game seven, double overtime in the conference finals. They were one goal away from getting into the Finals. It's gonna be a sore subject for a while."

Double overtime? Ouch. Even though I'm a novice, I know that must sting.

"How's Blaine taking it?" I ask, carefully carrying the cake I've finished into our fancy new fridge—thanks to a certain amazing man who helped us upgrade all the equipment after yet another oven broke down on us a couple of months ago—and take the second cake out.

"Tough," he says. "He's been like a shell of himself, but I managed to cheer him up by su—"

"I don't want to hear about your sexcapades, thank you," I quickly interrupt.

He snickers. "Well, let's just say I soon had him smiling and forgetting all about the game, but he's been…" He trails off, lowering his voice to a whisper. "He's been overly affectionate this morning. He's being a little needy."

"That's because he's a big, sappy goofball."

"I know," Alex lets out a dreamy sigh. I can hear his smile in his voice. "I love it, though."

When I first met Blaine, his cocky, self-assured attitude made me want to tell Alex to run for the hills. His energy screamed *I'm gonna break your heart,* but thankfully he proved me wrong. Because behind the arrogant and egotistical facade was a guy who was afraid of getting his own heart broken and who became the cheesiest, sappiest guy I've ever known. And my brother has never been happier.

It's all I could ever ask for.

I just hope one day I can find it for myself, too.

A couple of hours later, armed with a box of a dozen strawberry and vanilla cupcakes, I walk into Blaine's living room.

"I come bearing cake!" I sing, but my smile wobbles slightly at the sight of the three larger-than-life men looking forlorn. There's a fourth one I don't recognize, but he doesn't look as sad as the others.

Alex extracts himself from the octopus hold Blaine's got on him and heads over to me. I hold the box out to the side and return his hug while his rescue puppy, Ernie, bounces over and starts tugging on the shoelaces of my Converse.

"Thank you, I'm sure the boys will appreciate it." Alex whispers in my ear.

Right on cue, Blaine's big, gentle giant of a teammate, Zach Reid, unfolds himself from the couch and walks over to us. He waits until I've placed the box of cupcakes on the kitchen island before enveloping me in a bear hug. I stiffen for a brief moment on instinct, then relax, sinking into his embrace. He's nearly a foot taller than me, so my face presses into his solid chest.

"Thank you for the cupcakes, Jacob," he says quietly when he releases me, a soft smile on his face.

I like Zach. He's a regular in the bakery, as he has an immense sweet tooth, and his presence is kind of soothing. How he remains so fit blows my mind considering what he eats.

He picks up two cupcakes from the box and takes them back to the couch, handing one to the dark-haired guy I don't recognize. He's the biggest guy in the room. He reminds me of the boys from school, and my blood pressure instantly spikes. My body goes on high alert—spine stiffening, stomach churning. I sway slightly as black dots cloud my vision.

My breathing falters, and Alex places a hand on my forearm, bringing my attention back to him.

"That's Carter; he's Zach's childhood best friend. He lives in Denver." Alex lowers his voice, adding, "He's nice, really kind, I promise."

Carter raises his hand in a wave, unaware of my spiraling thoughts. "Hey, man."

I force a smile, tipping my head in greeting, but my heart is still beating wildly in my chest.

Jocks make me nervous, and it's not because of the ones sitting in this room. High school was hard for me, and the repercussions have wreaked havoc on me since.

Kids don't realize the impact their words or actions can have on someone until it's too late and the damage is irreparable. It's been over ten years, and I still get anxious. I tense up, like I'm waiting for the push and shove that used to follow whenever they were around. It's taken a little while for my brain to catch up to the fact that these guys are good people. They're not going to hurt me.

Alex makes me coffee, and we take a seat in the living room. Blaine instantly drags him back onto his lap and hides his face in the crook of Alex's neck.

"I'm sorry about your game." I give him a sad smile.

I have no idea what to say to these guys. Their faces are long, their eyes filled with sadness. Even Blaine's twin brother, Elliot, who is usually the epitome of bright and bouncy, looks miserable. He's slumped in the corner of the couch, combing his fingers through the soft fur on the sleeping puppy's belly. "I feel like it's all my fault."

"No, it's not, El!" Blaine answers sternly. He lifts his head and glares at his twin. "You were fucking awesome out there. It just wasn't our time."

"That's very diplomatic of you," Alex says, kissing Blaine's temple. "You played amazing—you all did. You can scrutinize your game all day long, but you can't beat yourself up over it." He leans over and gives Elliot's shoulder a squeeze.

"How's everyone else holding up?" I ask.

I don't want to ask outright because Alex has already

been teasing me endlessly about it, but I want to know how Ethan's doing.

Ethan Parkes, aka the amazing man who helped replace our broken oven and saved me from drowning financially not too long ago, also happens to be the captain of the Chicago Thunder.

At the start of the year, I was living a nightmare. Alex and I were up to our eyeballs in debt. Equipment broke that was no longer covered under warranty, rates became higher than expected, and along with things going wrong in the house our grandparents passed down to us, credit cards and loans became a savior.

We were caught in a vortex, living paycheck to paycheck as we tried to pay it off. Then, one gloomy February day, Ethan approached me about a deal: he would pay off all our debt, and I would pay him a realistic amount every month, without interest.

I was skeptical at first. Who wouldn't be? We were virtually strangers, with Blaine as a mutual connection. Alex and Blaine's relationship was still fairly new at that point, too. It seemed too good to be true, and I was convinced there was an ulterior motive for his offer. But then Ethan explained how his mom worked three jobs when he was growing up to keep him in hockey, a roof over their heads, and food on the table. It made sense.

He didn't want to see us struggle or drown under a mountain of debt like his mom had, especially when he had a solution.

So, it was an offer I couldn't refuse, and ever since, a rather unusual friendship blossomed between us.

*And somewhat of a crush.*

Yeah, let's not go into that.

I mean, we're not talking every day, but he stops by the bakery at least once a week to check in and see how I am. His attentiveness hasn't helped the crush I have on him, but those moments have become the favorite part of my week.

"Just say it. I know you're talking about Ethan." Alex smirks.

I narrow my eyes.

"Nobody's heard from him," Blaine replies, ignoring Alex's teasing tone. "He'd usually be in our group chat sending motivational texts, but there's been nothing… It's like he's—"

"Disappeared," Zach adds.

"Maybe he's just taking some time to process? I always need a bit of downtime to gather my emotions after a big loss," Carter suggests with a small shrug of his wide-set shoulders.

I eye him warily out of the corner of my eye. I didn't think it was possible for anyone to be bigger than Zach, but wow, Carter is huge. Between the two of them, they make the large sectional look tiny.

"No, I don't think that's it." Elliot shakes his head, bringing my attention back to him. "As much as he's a grumpy, grizzly bear, he wouldn't just go off the radar, especially after a loss like this. He's our support beacon. He's the glue that keeps us all strong."

My chest constricts as worry pools in my stomach. Is Ethan alone? Or hurt? He's a natural caregiver, always wanting to protect those he cares about and make sure they're okay, so knowing he hasn't even reached out to his teammates makes the hair stand up on the back of my neck.

This isn't like him.

"Maybe you could go and check on him." Alex nudges my thigh with his socked feet. "He likes you, and it might do him some good to see someone outside of hockey."

I scoff, trying to hide how much I like the idea. "Why would he want to see me?"

"Why wouldn't he?" he retorts.

*Because while I would love to see him, what if he turns me away?*

I know my crush on him is completely inconvenient, especially since we have a business agreement, but I don't know if I could handle any form of rejection from him. I'm already annoyed at myself for having a crush on a hockey player, of all people.

"That's a good idea, actually." Zach nods in agreement.

Blaine lifts his head, his eyes sparkling with mischief as a wide smile spreads across his face.

"No," I say, pointing my finger at him before he can speak.

"What? I didn't say anything!" He feigns innocence.

I glare at him. "You didn't need to; your face said it all, and whatever you're thinking—no."

"Stop winding him up about it! That's my job." Alex swats his chest with the back of his hand.

Blaine idly rubs the spot over his chest, his mouth curving into a grin. "It's nothing, I just had an idea. Nothing to worry about."

With Blaine, that means I definitely need to worry.

# Chapter Three

*Ethan*

"I've already told you—I'll look at flights when I'm done with team stuff," I grumble. I'm trying not to lose my patience because it's not my mom's fault I'm dragging my feet over booking my flights to England.

Every time I tried to sort it out, I ended up balking and slamming my laptop closed. I want to go because it's been nearly six months since I've seen my mom, but I know the second the airplane lands in Heathrow, my stomach is going to be churning at the thought of seeing *him,* and nobody likes nausea.

"Ethan, stop being such an idiot and just book them already. You're coming to Samantha's wedding whether you come on your own or I have to fly to Chicago and drag you by the hair," she threatens in her stern mother tone, like I'm a petulant child instead of an adult nearing their forties. "I know you don't want to see him, sweetie, but it's been ten years. You should count yourself lucky you've not bumped into him before now."

Fuck. I know she's right, but it doesn't make it any easier. Every time I allow myself to think about it, my blood boils with anger.

Am I over Ian? Yeah, a million percent, but I never had closure. I don't know *why* he left so abruptly, without rhyme or reason, and that's what makes me so fucking mad. It's like a wound that hasn't fully healed, which also pisses me off.

Taking a sip of my coffee, I kick my feet up against the opposite chair and gaze at the lake from my balcony. The sun bounces off the water, causing it to sparkle like glass. It's calm. Tranquil. The polar opposite of how my muscles are currently vibrating from the anger bubbling away in my veins, like they do every time he crosses my mind. I fucking hate it.

I close my eyes and take a deep breath through my nose, focusing on the summer sun warming my skin and soothing away the tension.

"When are you going to be done with team stuff?" she asks again for the fifth time since she called.

"In a week or so." The lie tastes bitter on my tongue. We're going to be finished in the next few days, but I need to give myself a bit more time.

"Okay, well, you better make sure you book your flight as soon as you can. I want to see my boy. I miss you."

I pinch the bridge of my nose as guilt ripples through me, settling in my chest. I don't mean to be an asshole, especially not to my mom. She means everything to me. She's the only family I have aside from my teammates, and I know she's doing this out of love.

She is the only reason why I agreed to go to this goddamn wedding and come face-to-face with my past.

"I miss you too, Mom. I'll sort out my travel soon, I promise."

There's a beat of silence before her voice turns soft. I don't miss how her words are hinted with sadness. "I hope you find your person one day. Someone you can open up to. Who loves you, and adores you, and appreciates you for who you are."

I swallow the lump in my throat.

"There's nothing wrong with having feelings, Ethan, whether they're happy or sad. It's what makes us human, and you, my son, are my favorite human."

*Fuck.* Squeezing my eyes closed, I'm at a loss for words for the second time in days. I simply grunt before we say our goodbyes.

Ever since my dad left, I've struggled to deal with my emotions. He used to get so angry at me, telling me I was "too emotional". Even with him gone, his words would play like a broken record in my head, and I didn't know how to handle everything I was feeling. So, I squashed it all down and poured all my energy into being the best hockey player I could be. Whenever the weight of it all became too heavy to carry, I bottled it up and channeled every ounce of it onto the ice.

That hasn't changed, and these days, when it becomes too much to bear, I find an excuse to get into a brawl on the ice.

I've sacrificed so much of my life to the sport. I didn't

get to play outside on my bike, or go to sleepovers, or attend birthday parties at Pizza Hut. I didn't get to go to prom or the drive-in theater to make out with the boy I had a crush on.

Hell, I didn't even have time to develop a crush.

I was the kid who was on the ice every waking minute that I wasn't in class perfecting my craft. That hasn't changed much either, which means relationships—both romantic and platonic—aren't easy for me.

I'm not like Blaine or Elliot, who can spill their hearts out about whatever is on their minds. I'm always consciously aware that I could open the door just a fraction too far and allow someone to slip through my defenses, only for them to tear me up and leave me in a broken mess.

I can't allow that to happen.

Not again.

It's safer not to let them in. To just give them enough to know that I care, but not enough to risk getting hurt.

A loud pounding against the door snaps me out of my dark mental cloud. I slowly get to my feet, stretching out my back before making my way to it, only to be greeted by Elliot's Cheshire Cat grin when I open it.

"Hello, Mr. Grouchy Pants," he says as he pokes me in the pec with his finger before pouting comically. "You've been ignoring us and me no likey."

I bat his hand away.

"Yeah, man. Where have you been?" Blaine peers over his brother's shoulder.

"We thought you might have left for England without saying goodbye." Zach frowns from behind both of them.

I rub my palm over my chest. The sight of their stupid

faces thaws the ice that surrounds my heart. "You know I wouldn't leave without saying bye. I just needed a few days."

*To feel sorry for myself. To mope around.*

"Well, you've had a few days, my delightful ray of sunshine, and you're not allowed any more." Elliot pushes past me and heads into the kitchen. "I'm hungry, have you got any snacks?"

I roll my eyes, stepping aside to let the other two through.

"Do you guys want a drink?" I ask, turning the corner to see Elliot already raiding the fridge.

"He's got water, soda, wine, and some weird green juice stuff." He brings the bottle of kale, spinach, and celery juice to his nose and sniffs it. Gagging, he quickly puts the bottle back and looks at me, his face screwed up in disgust. "Dude, that's vile. How can you drink that? It smells like grass."

"It's good for you." I roll my eyes again and nudge him out of the way.

"It's a big nope from me." He quickly grabs a bowl of fruit and some cheese and moves to the pantry to grab the potato chips I only buy for him. I don't know what he's planning to make with the random mix of food, but I've learned not to question him. Elliot tends to march to the beat of his own drum.

"So, what's going on? Why have you been ghosting us?" Blaine presses, crossing his arms over his chest.

Zach's face falls. "You're not retiring, are you?"

I sigh, closing the fridge door with my elbow, and pass them both a bottle of water. "No, but I'm not going to deny that it's been on my mind a lot recently. I've probably got at least one more season in me, maybe two if my knee doesn't act up again, but this loss hurt a bit more than normal."

My jaw clenches at the pity in their eyes. It makes me want to tell them to get out. It's fine for them. They're still in the prime of their careers.

But I don't, because I know they care.

They don't want me to stop playing any more than I do.

"Let's go sit outside," I suggest, needing to break away from their pointed stares.

We take a seat on the balcony. Blaine is still looking at me with concerned eyes like he's trying to find the right words to say. I feel like a bug under a microscope with their inquisitive eyes boring into me.

"Your bad mood isn't just about the game, though, is it?" Zach asks once he folds himself into the chair beside me. "We've had losses before. When we lost in the final two seasons ago, you didn't retreat like this, so there's got to be something else bothering you." He pauses for a moment. "Is it something to do with you going to visit your mom?"

I've never told the guys about Ian.

It was before most of them joined the team anyway. The only ones who know are Adam Kendrick and Jonathan Peyton, and I didn't think it was necessary to rehash my humiliation for these guys. I didn't want the additional wave of sympathy from being jilted.

At the time, Ian didn't really make an effort to get to know my teammates. We didn't have a boys' night like we do now, but he always made an excuse for not attending team events or going to the Kendricks' for dinner with me.

I wasn't sure if it just wasn't his thing or if he was

ashamed of me. He didn't give me anything. In retrospect, I should have asked. I should have made him tell me.

I've kept that bit of my history under lock and key for ten years, and I don't plan on sharing it now.

"Do you remember me mentioning my cousin's wedding?"

The three of them nod.

"Well, I don't want to go. There's going to be a lot of people there asking questions about my relationship status, and I'm dreading it."

Which is only somewhat true.

Yes, people will be questioning why I'm still single when I'm a professional athlete and have a lot of money. They never seem to fathom that sometimes being in the limelight and having wealth can be one of the loneliest places of all because people rarely want you for *you*. But there will also be a lot of people waiting to see how I react around Ian.

"Can't you take a fake boyfriend?" Blaine suggests.

Elliot snaps his fingers. "Yes! That's a genius idea!"

"No." I shake my head. "That's a ridiculous idea. Plus, who would I take? It's not like I can just find someone to take with me across the Atlantic for a couple of weeks."

"Take Jacob," Blaine quips, grinning, his gray eyes gleaming.

*Uh… What?*

"Think about it. He needs a break, right? You know him. I'm sure you somewhat trust him because you fucking paid off his debt, and you go and see him in the bakery all the time."

My eyebrows shoot up, surprised. How does he—

"Oh yeah, Alex tells me how you drop in without even buying anything." He lifts a brow in amusement.

"How can you leave without buying anything?" Zach gasps. "That's like—"

"Blasphemy to the bakery gods, is what that is. Is there a god of cake? I'm gonna google it," Elliot says before getting his phone and typing away as he throws some chips into his mouth.

"But you guys are leaving for California soon. Who will take care of the shop?"

I'm grasping at straws here because his point is valid. It *is* a great idea.

We've only gotten to know each other in the last few months, mostly by exchanging texts and my weekly visits to the shop. We know each other enough for him to understand my need for privacy. He doesn't seem phased by me being guarded, and when I think about the kind of person I see myself with in the future, he's it.

He's independent, he's caring, and he's fucking gorgeous.

Dark blond hair, cornflower-blue eyes, delicate features, and a lithe body.

He's like my filthiest fantasies come to life.

And the business agreement we have in place will ensure that no lines can be blurred, making it the perfect arrangement.

Blaine waves me off. "None of your concern. Just think about it—Jacob would be perfect. You get your fake boyfriend, so people don't ask questions, and he gets a vacation. It's a win-win for both of you."

Now that he's planted the idea in my head, I can't stop thinking about it.

I'm a strong guy. I can intimidate people with just one look. Guys often fear me on the ice, but having Jacob at my side at the wedding will bring me a sense of security. Because while I don't need him to protect me in a literal sense, I need him to ground me. I need the wave of calm being around him always gives me.

Now all I have to do is convince him to go along with it and come to England with me.

# Chapter Four

*Jacob*

Alex is chewing on his bottom lip, brows drawn tight in concern, and it's taking all my effort not to reach out and smooth out the crease with my thumb.

"Are you sure you'll be okay?" he finally asks.

"Yes, I'll be fine," I drawl. "Stop worrying about me and go enjoy your vacation."

He runs a hand down his face and sighs. "I know, I'm just..." he trails off. "I feel weird leaving you. We haven't been apart since I was in college, and even then, I was only a short bus ride away. I've never been so far away from you, and I'm not quite sure how I feel about it, and what if it gets busy and you need me?"

There's a pang in my chest.

Placing the piping bag down, I round the counter and stop in front of him.

He's a few inches taller than my five-foot-eight frame,

having been blessed with our father's genes. Alex has always been the sensitive soul of the Lowry family; he has always cared for both people and animals around him. Like when he was eight years old and saved a baby bird that had fallen from its nest in the backyard. He made a new nest, safe from the neighbor's cat and any other predators that might want to get it, and he fed it and watched it from the kitchen window every day until it was strong enough to fly.

He's a caretaker, so it comes as no surprise that he's getting himself worked up over being so far away from me.

"San Diego is only a four-hour flight away. If I need you —which I'm sure I won't because I'll be fine—then you can jump on a plane and be with me." I reach up on tiptoes and wrap my arms around him, bringing him in for a hug and squeezing him gently. "Alex, we're okay now. *I'm* okay now, so you can stop worrying and go enjoy yourself. Heck, I'd love to go to California. The sunshine, the beaches. The Navy SEALS training on the beaches? Yummy." I grin.

He laughs, then his face softens. "Sometimes it doesn't feel real."

"That we're no longer living a nightmare?"

"Yeah."

"I get that. Sometimes I have to pinch myself to know I'm not dreaming too, but it *is* real. You don't need to worry anymore."

"It's pretty crazy how much our lives have changed in the last six months, huh?"

"Yep! It's pretty wild, but we would've gotten there in the end. Ethan just came into our lives at the right time and got us out of it sooner."

He nods with a small smile.

It's been me and Alex against the world for just over three years, since our grandparents passed away within weeks of one another. They had raised us ever since that knock on the door from the police, letting them know our parents had been in a fatal accident. I was ten years old, and I still remember it vividly. My grandma's sobs, my grandpa's choked voice as he thanked the police. Alex was only seven. He couldn't understand what was going on or why they weren't coming home, and it was that night I vowed to my parents, wherever the afterlife had taken them, that I would take care of him and ensure he was always happy.

I've always prioritized Alex, even now that he's twenty-five and more than capable of taking care of himself. He'll always be my baby brother.

My lifeline. My anchor. My purpose.

I might put on a brave face and pretend that everything is sunshine and roses, but I refuse to let him see the grief that often rocks me to my core.

"Also, remember, Aria is helping out a few extra days, and I've got Daniel," I reassure him. "Between the three of us, we'll manage just fine."

Alex chews on his bottom lip, eyeing me with a hint of suspicion. Thankfully, Daniel inadvertently saves me by calling for Alex to help him out front.

"You promise me you'll tell me the second you need me?" he pleads.

"Of course; you have my word." I nod, although it would take something drastic for me to call him back from his vacation.

He's already missed out on so much in his life; I won't be the reason he misses out on anything else.

"Jacob!" Alex calls out an hour later. "Someone's here to see you."

I glance up as Ethan appears in the doorway, wearing a somewhat sheepish smile on his face. A rush of excitement washes through me at the sight of him, like it always does. I allow my eyes to roam over his wide-set shoulders, noticing the way his broad chest is testing the fabric of his olive green t-shirt. When he shoves his hands into the pockets of his blue jeans, my gaze instantly falls to those tree-trunk thighs.

It should be illegal for someone to be so hot. He should come with a warning label—*I may scowl, but I'm hotter than the sun.*

His hulking form makes the kitchen feel tiny.

I swallow, trying to dampen my suddenly dry mouth to speak. "Hey, Ethan."

"Hey, Jacob." He smiles, taking a step forward, and leans against the counter. The way he says my name in that deep baritone voice causes goosebumps to ripple across my skin.

"Can I get you a drink?"

He shakes his head.

"Something to eat?"

"No, thank you."

I frown.

He always does this—shows up out of the blue, never wanting to eat or drink anything. Not that I'm complaining, but being around Ethan frazzles my brain cells. All the blood rushes to my extremities whenever I'm in his presence, and I become a fumbling disaster.

I want to shake him and demand he tell me why he's

here before I lose my mind. He isn't usually one for small talk, which can only mean…

Shit.

"Did I miss a payment?"

He shakes his head again, his lips twitching with a smile. "No, you didn't, and even if you did, I wouldn't come knocking."

"True." I scrunch up my nose.

Ethan shifts from foot to foot, clearly nervous. The uncertain body language is so uncharacteristic that worry begins to bubble in the pit of my stomach. The frown line between his brows grows a little deeper, and when he speaks, my heart plummets into my stomach. "Maybe you should sit down."

Wait, *what?*

A chill runs down my spine. Is he going to tell me our agreement is over? My palms start sweating. I wipe them over the front of my apron, and I hate how shaky my voice is as I say, "Ethan, you're kinda making me nervous."

I do as I'm told, though, and take a seat on one of the stools. Folding my hands in my lap to stop him from seeing the effect he has on me, I press my lips together and stare at him. Willing him to hurry up and speak.

"I need to ask you a favor."

"Uh, okay. What's up?"

"I'm heading to England soon, and there's this wedding I need to attend." He exhales, glancing up at the ceiling in contemplation before he continues. "Thing is, I don't want to go, but I have to because it's family."

I blink at him. "O-kay, so where do I come into this?"

"I need you to come with me and pretend to be my boyfriend."

My jaw hits the floor. My eyes widen in disbelief because there's no way I heard that right.

Maybe I'm dreaming, or the iced coffee I've just had is making me a little delusional, and I've landed in some alternative universe. It sounded like Ethan, the guy I've been crushing on for the last five months, just asked me to be his boyfriend.

Okay, I may be purposely ignoring the "pretend" part, but whatever. That's a minor detail.

"I'm sorry, what?" I ask.

He rolls his eyes, and if it weren't for the deep creases on his forehead, I'd probably think I'm annoying him. Not this…situation. "I knew this was a stupid idea. I shouldn't have listened to Blaine," he grumbles.

My shoulders slump at the sound of Blaine's name. The little bubble I was floating in bursts, and I quickly crash back down to earth.

*This was someone else's idea?*

I try to ignore the weight of rejection on my chest.

"Blaine suggested that I go to England with you and pretend to be your boyfriend in front of your family?"

"Pretty much, yeah." He squeezes his eyes closed before shaking his head and finally saying, "This was a dumb idea. I'm sorry, forget I mentioned anything."

Running a hand through his hair, he doesn't look at me. He simply spins on his heels to leave. I'm only able to move when I see him almost reaching the door. Rushing over to him, I wrap my hand around his inked forearm to stop him.

"Ethan, wait," I plead.

He turns his head and looks down at me.

"I'm just…surprised, is all. I wasn't expecting you to ask me that." I look at where my hand is wrapped around his arm. How would it feel to have those arms wrapped around me? Holding me up against a wall while he—

*Not the time or place for that!*

I mentally shake it off as I feel the heat rising up my neck.

"Can I have some time to think about it? I can't just up and leave. I have this place to think about, and Alex is off to California tomorrow."

"And I can cut my trip short." Alex suddenly appears, his head bobbing into view between Ethan and the door. "From what Blaine's told me, Ethan isn't leaving for another week?" His eyes shift to Ethan for confirmation.

Ethan nods, his brows furrowed in confusion.

"So that means I can have a week in California, and you can go to England. We can always visit Blaine's parents again when you come home, but you should go. Who knows if you'll ever have the chance again." Alex reaches through to poke me in the shoulder, his voice lowering. "Do you remember what you told me when I was worried about going on a date with Blaine?"

I close my eyes as I remember that awful night.

I had just received the latest bank statements, and the amount we owed seemed to be increasing. I ended up in tears because I felt like a failure. After endless hours, days, and even years, of pouring blood, sweat, and tears into my business, seeing it in black and white in my hands had been soul-destroying.

Yes, I made mistakes. I suppose a lot of small businesses

do during their first year as they learn the ropes, but I had also been struck with bad luck. Everything that could go wrong had gone wrong. Alex suggested bailing on his date with Blaine so he could throw the hundred bucks we had set aside for his date back into the pot, but our debt was so much more than that. It wouldn't have even touched the surface.

And if he hadn't gone on that date, they wouldn't have fallen in love. We wouldn't have had the success we did when Blaine saved our asses that gloomy December morning, and he wouldn't have introduced me to this gorgeous hunk of a man, who now wants to whisk me off to England with him and play pretend.

Yep, the coffee must definitely be playing tricks on me.

"Go and enjoy yourself. Don't let it pass you by; you will only live to regret it," my brother repeats my own words back to me and winks before giving Ethan his best scowl. "If you don't take care of him, though, I'll set Blaine on you."

"Oh, I'm quaking in my boots," Ethan deadpans, but his lips curve in a smile. "I will, don't worry."

Chewing on the corner of my lip, I mull it over. It's too big of a decision for me to make here and now, but there's something in my gut telling me to go. I can't remember the last time I did something so…adventurous.

I turn to Ethan. He's looking at me with a mix of apprehension and hope. I want to say yes so badly, but I need to be sensible.

"I'll think about it and let you know. I need to make sure everything will be okay here."

He nods understandingly.

"I understand, thank you."

As he moves to leave, we both realize my hand's still on his arm. I forgot all about it, and I rush to remove it as Ethan just smirks, looking at me.

I instantly miss touching him, and from the look in his eyes, I'm pretty sure he knows it.

✕

"You!" I point an accusatory finger at Blaine. "What did you do?"

"Me?" A sly grin spreads across his face. "I have no idea what you're talking about."

Placing my hands on my hips, I walk further into the apartment, narrowing my eyes with every step. "You know very well what you did."

Alex snorts behind me as I stalk closer toward Blaine, causing him to scramble to his feet and shift behind the couch. His eyes dart between me and where Alex is in the kitchen, slight worry lining his forehead.

"You're gonna have to fill me in because I haven't done anything." He nudges Ernie, waving his hand in my direction. "Ernie, protect me."

"If you haven't done anything, why do you need Ernie to protect you?"

We end up circling the couch. Ernie follows us, bouncing excitedly across the cushions, his pink tongue lolling to the side.

I scowl at Blaine, then look at the dog. "Ernie, get him."

Blaine trips on the corner of the rug, and that's all the encouragement Ernie needs. He pounces off the couch and starts tugging on Blaine's sock.

"Ernie! You're supposed to be protecting me, not taking his side!" Blaine whines. He tries to shove the puppy away, then yelps when Ernie's tiny puppy teeth catch his toes.

"Ernie knows not to interfere in things." I cross my arms over my chest.

Alex chokes on his water, coughing and spluttering between fits of laughter. "Trust me," he croaks. "He interferes a lot."

I cast a glare at my brother before looking back at Blaine. He picks himself up off the floor, scooping the puppy into his arms and tickling his belly.

"I'm assuming a certain cranky captain came to see you today."

"Yes, he did. He told me all about your *brilliant* idea. I was doing fine crushing on him in secret, Blaine! Why'd you have to go and put ideas in his head?"

"Look, I thought it was a good idea. Ethan needs help. You need a vacation. Throw in the fact you have a crush on him, and ta-da!" He does one-handed jazz hands. "You've got yourself a British summer romance. It'll be like in that movie, *The Holiday*, but set in summer instead of Christmas, and neither of you are British."

"It's nothing like the movie at all," Alex laughs.

With zero fight left in me, I drop onto the couch and cover my face with my hands, letting out a silent scream into my palms.

I hate the fact that he's right. I can't even remember the last time I went on a vacation. It was probably when I was in high school and our grandparents took me and Alex to a cabin in Wisconsin.

Hell, I've never been on an airplane before. I only have

a passport because I applied for one when I opened the bakery.

I don't even know why. There was just something in my gut telling me I'd need it one day.

*Well, would you look at that—divine intervention.*

I feel the couch dip as Blaine sits down next to me. Ernie wriggles his way onto my lap, weeding his face between my hands, and licks my face. I cuddle the bundle of fur to my chest and hide my face in his fluffy neck.

"For what it's worth, I think it would be good for both of you." Blaine's voice takes on a softer tone.

"What makes you say that?" I ask, turning my head slightly to look at Blaine.

"Ethan is one of my closest friends, but he's very… private. I've been playing hockey with him for six years now, and I've never met his mom." He gives me a pointed look. "There's obviously something between you, especially if he's suggesting introducing you to his family. I don't think any of the guys have met his mom either, except maybe Kendrick and Peyton—and probably Coach—but that's because they're old timers."

"Why is that?"

"Who knows." Blaine shrugs. "Ethan is an enigma, but maybe you can help him come out of his shell a bit more. We all feel like he's keeping us at arm's length on a personal level. As a captain, we're under his wing. We can trust that he has our backs no matter what on the ice, but personally? Off the ice and away from the rink? Nobody knows him. His apartment is sparse. There's no hint of who he is away from hockey. I think he's lonely, but no matter what we do, he won't let us in."

That doesn't surprise me at all. He is the definition of a grump, but I think it's more of a protective shield than his actual personality. Plus, there's got to be a reason behind his need for a fake boyfriend. What could he be hiding? Or who does he need protection from?

*And why do I want to protect him from whatever it is?*

Alex's words play on repeat in my mind—about living in the moment and taking the chances I'm given with both hands. I know he wouldn't push me to go if he didn't think he could cope. He's proven time and time again that he's more than capable.

I trust him with every ounce of my being.

I'm wary because, while I would only be in England for two weeks, it would be enough time to fall for Ethan.

Being in close proximity, meeting his family, and seeing a side of Ethan Parkes that is unknown to most?

It's my damn heart that I don't trust.

## Chapter Five

*Ethan*

I sneak a glance at Zach before focusing back on the road, my fingers tapping an incessant beat against the steering wheel. "Do you think it was a stupid idea to ask Jacob to come with me to England?"

It's been a few days since I visited Jacob at the bakery and dropped the bomb of a question on him. He's sent a few texts here and there, letting me know he's still thinking about it and trying to finalize some things at the bakery, but the growing sense of rejection in the pit of my stomach is starting to make me feel uneasy.

Especially now that I know how his skin feels against mine, and how stunning he looks when he's been caught red-handed.

*Don't go there.*

"I wouldn't say it's a stupid idea, because what better way to shut down any relationship status questions than showing up with a boyfriend on your arm. But you've got that business agreement, right?" Zach asks.

I nod.

"You've just gotta make sure that no lines get blurred. From what I know, this loan you've given is vital to Jacob and Alex…" He trails off, the unspoken *don't fuck this up for them* coming across loud and clear.

"Right," I grumble.

My hands grip the steering wheel a little tighter, not liking the underlying accusation in his tone. It's not like I would pull the plug on my deal with Jacob if he ends up saying no. No matter what his answer is, nothing is going to change.

This is completely separate.

Plus, I would never do that.

"What are you trying to say, Zach?"

When Zach mentioned his trip to Hawaii with his childhood best friend Carter, I quickly offered to drive them to the airport, thankful for the distraction.

Zach is my voice of reason. He's quiet, observant, and has a much more rational head on his shoulders than some of the others.

But now I'm starting to regret my offer.

He sighs, his dark brows furrowing over the bridge of his nose. "He likes you. I can tell by the way he watches you and the way he lights up around you. He seems cautious about it, though, like maybe he doesn't want to like you the way he does."

Frowning, I turn my head to look at him again as traffic comes to a halt.

"Don't be ridiculous."

He rolls his eyes. "Dude. People think that because I don't say much, I don't see shit, but I do. I see *everything*, and the way he looks at you?" He sighs. "He looks at you like you've hung the moon."

"It's probably some hero complex for helping him out."

"Nah." He shakes his head. "It's more than that. I see the same look in Kendrick when he looks at Maria, or in Blaine when he looks at Alex. It's like he's…enchanted. All I'm saying is, if he says yes, just be careful with him, okay?"

I can't deny I'm drawn to Jacob. Who wouldn't be? His bright energy is magnetizing, and I've become addicted to the warmth that rushes through my body whenever he smiles at me.

It's like he sees *me*. Not my career accolades, the name on my back, or my salary that's plastered all over the internet. I don't think he even cares about hockey. Despite us only knowing each other for a few months, I like that he isn't afraid to call me out on my moods. He doesn't take my shit, and I *really* like that sassy personality burning inside him.

Blaine called me out the other day for being a regular at the bakery, and it's not to fulfill some kind of sweet fix, unlike the guy sitting next to me. It's all to do with Jacob.

He's like sunshine personified, and I'm a lazy street cat seeking his warm rays.

But I can't say I've witnessed the look in his eyes that Zach's referring to. He's always been kind and welcoming, but I've always put his behavior down to politeness, maybe even gratitude for helping him out in a time of desperate need.

Maybe the walls I've built around myself have become so high I can no longer see over them.

Like I've unconsciously placed an imaginary blindfold over my eyes because my heart can't get hurt that way.

"Would you be open to that?" Carter asks, leaning forward from where he's sitting in the back seat.

"Open to what?"

"Dating Jacob," Carter clarifies. "He seemed nice enough the other day when I met him."

"He is a good person. He's very kind and caring; I think he would have a lot to offer someone in a relationship," Zach adds.

"I'm not looking for a relationship right now. I'm married to hockey, and that's the way it's gotta be until the day comes."

In the corner of my eye, I catch Zach rolling his eyes again. "Until the day comes, really? That's a bullshit excuse, and you know it."

I raise my brows at his annoyed tone but stay quiet.

"Kendrick and Maria work. Hell, look at Blaine and Alex. Never in a million years would I have put money on Blaine being the one to become a major simp, but he's making it work, and guess what?" He leans across the center console, his long, dark hair falling around his face. There's challenge in his eyes. "He still plays hockey. I think you're just scared, and you're using hockey as an excuse. You don't need to wait until retirement to find your man. Don't you think it would be better to celebrate your final season— whenever that may be—with someone you love supporting you through it?"

I swallow the lump forming in my throat. I'm *really* regretting driving Zach to the airport now.

"Wow, I don't think I've ever heard you say so many words at once," I mutter under my breath.

Carter snorts behind me.

"We worry about you, man. Just think about it, yeah? You're getting ol—"

"If you finish that sentence, I'm gonna pull over and kick you out right here on the highway, and you can walk to the fucking airport," I warn with a glare.

Zach snickers, and I can't help huffing out a laugh.

I love the guy, I really do, but I hate that he's right. I *am* deflecting. I'm fucking scared out of my mind that if I let someone in, especially while I'm still playing, something will go wrong.

Then my mind would be focused on that, and my last chance at winning the Cup again would be gone in a puff of smoke.

My stomach twists and tightens, and there's acid burning up my esophagus as I pace the living room. I've just buzzed Jacob up, and every inch of me is on edge. I'm due to leave for England in four days, and even though I would never admit this out loud, I'm hoping with every fiber of my being that he will be coming with me.

And it's not because I went ahead and purchased two plane tickets, including one that may or may not be in his name.

Call it wishful thinking.

I never knew how much I wanted to just be with him until Blaine planted that stupid idea in my head.

*It's not stupid; it's brilliant.*

Whatever.

When there's a knock at the door, I rush across the hardwood and then come to a stop. Hand frozen mid-air.

Fuck. I need to get out of my head.

I don't want him to feel pressured. I don't want him to think he needs to come with me due to some weird sense of obligation, but in the state I'm in right now, he'll feel the desperation pouring off me in waves.

Shaking my hands out by my sides, I take a deep breath through my nose before opening the door, putting on what I hope is a welcoming smile.

"Hey, Jacob. Come in." I step aside to let him through.

"Hi." He smiles.

When he steps by, I notice he's holding a glass baking dish covered in aluminum foil. I close the door behind me and motion him to the kitchen, where he places it down on the counter.

"I made you a baked ziti," he says, his words coming out in a rush as his fingers fuss with the edge of the foil. "I didn't know if you'd eaten, and…well, I bake when I get nervous, but I ran out of baking supplies at home, which is ironic considering I bake for a living, so the next best thing was pasta, so I made—" He stops abruptly and rolls those gorgeous eyes. "I'm nervous rambling, sorry."

My lips twitch. "Thank you. I haven't eaten yet, so it's appreciated."

Jacob gives a small nod, looking everywhere except at me.

"Can I get you a drink? Water? Coffee? Wine?"

"Oh, I'd love a glass of wine, please."

I pour him one and lead him into the living room, taking a seat next to him on the couch. He's sitting on the edge, his back stiff as a rod. The wine glass is clasped between both hands like he's worried I'll take it from him.

"You can make yourself comfortable. You don't have to sit like you're in a library."

He hesitates for a beat, then toes off his shoes and curls his feet beneath his ass.

A rush of warmth fills my chest at how comfortable he looks in my space. It's not the first time he's been in my apartment, but this is the first time he's been here where *I've* been nervous, too.

Jacob takes a sip of his wine before resting the glass on his knee. There's this contented-but-awkward silence between us, and I can practically hear the wheels turning in his head about how to address the elephant in the room.

I'm about to open my mouth to speak, but he beats me to it.

"So, I've been thinking about your proposition, and I've decided I'll come to England with you, but there are some things I'd like to talk about first."

My heart flips in my chest. I want to wrap him in my arms and thank him for doing this for me, but I try to play it cool instead. The last thing I want to do is spook him, so I simply nod and let him continue. "Fire away."

"Firstly, nothing changes with our agreement. My business is my priority, and I can't let Alex down again."

I want to argue that he didn't let Alex down, but that's a conversation for another time.

"Of course. Everything will remain the same. You have my word."

He gives a small smile. His hunched shoulders drop slightly.

"Secondly, I would like to know why it's so important for you to have me play your boyfriend. Are you hiding from something? Or someone?"

Sighing, I run my fingers through my hair, then rest my arm on the back of the couch, picking at the seam of the cushion.

I haven't opened up about Ian in a long time. I knew Jacob would ask, and even if he hadn't, I would've told him eventually. I wouldn't have allowed him to be blindsided.

"I'm not a big fan of weddings in general, but my ex-fiancé is the best man in this one."

Jacob blinks, clearly surprised. I watch as he opens and closes his mouth a couple of times before finally asking, "You were engaged? When was this? I had no idea."

"Nobody knows, not really." I lean back, closing my eyes briefly, as I dig into the part of my past that I've buried deep. "We met when I'd just turned seventeen. I had a short break in the summer, so Mom and I went over to England for a week to visit her family. There was this pub she loved to go to, and every Friday they would host a quiz night. I didn't really want to go, but it made her happy, so I went, and as soon as we walked in, I saw him." I glance out the window, focusing on the still water of the lake. Hoping the calmness will ease the thundering of my heart against my ribs.

"I was drawn to him. I found out he was friends with my cousin, Samantha—she's the one who's getting married—and we started hanging out every day. By the time I had to leave, we weren't ready to be done. It didn't feel right to simply put the connection we had down to a summer fling and be done with it, so we did the long-distance thing. He visited me in Toronto, and when I was drafted, he came to visit me in Chicago. He was at university at the time, so once he graduated, he moved out here."

"You were drafted at eighteen, right?"

I raise a brow, the corner of my lips kicking up. "Have you been researching me, Jacob?"

He shrugs. "Yeah, I have. I don't really know you aside from you playing hockey with Blaine, so I needed to know the little things before I meet your family. You know, your star sign, where you grew up, and a bit about who you are. A boyfriend would know."

I chuckle. He really thought this through.

"What's my star sign?" I ask.

"You're a Cancer, which is good because it means we're a good match as I'm a Pisces."

"I have no idea what that means."

"Don't worry about it; I've got it covered." He waves me off and takes another sip of his wine. "So, what happened after he moved to Chicago?"

"When I look back, it was when he moved here that the cracks started to show. We'd get into arguments over little things, and whenever I had team obligations, such as charity functions or dinner with the guys and their partners, he would get angry at me, even though he was invited, too."

"Angry about what?"

A burning sensation travels through my veins. I'm angry at the memories I've kept suppressed for so long. "He would complain that I never had time for him, and it was unfair that I had to do all those things when I'd been on the road for so long."

Jacob's nose scrunches up. "But that's part of your job! You have sponsors to keep happy, charities that need your name to help bring in donations. If he was invited, why didn't he just go with you?"

I shrug.

I wish I had an answer for that, but he wouldn't tell me. His go-to answer was that I wouldn't understand. But how could I even begin to understand if he wouldn't tell me what I needed to fix?

With a sigh, I confess, "I thought if I proposed it would show him I was serious about us, and it did get better for a while. We were going to get married in Mexico, and it was his idea to arrive at the airport separately. He said something about it being similar to spending the night apart before the ceremony, only he never showed up."

My throat tightens, a dull throb forming at the base. This is the first time in a decade that I'm allowing myself to remember how I really felt that day.

The shock. The confusion. The humiliation.

The way my heart cracked in two. Left in a million pieces on the pristine O'Hare floor.

"I waited for hours by the check-in desk. I called and texted. Nothing. I stood there, listening to the final call for our flight. Security kept coming over to question me as I was pacing and getting distressed, until he finally texted me, saying he couldn't do it anymore. That he was done pretending to love me, and it was all over. It was like my world imploded. I didn't know what I did wrong or what happened for him to leave without saying goodbye. It was like being seven again, coming out of hockey practice and realizing my dad wasn't coming to pick me up. That he was never coming home."

*Fuck!*

Why did I blurt that out? As if it wasn't bad enough that I'd opened up my wounds to Jacob, I had to bring up the person I hated the most.

Unable to sit still any longer, I get up and walk to the sliding doors that lead onto the balcony. My muscles quiver with the anger flowing through my bloodstream. I flex my fingers before balling them into a fist and shoving them into the pockets of my sweatpants.

I'm too on edge to hear Jacob approaching. His soft breath against the bare skin of my arm startles me.

"I'm so sorry." His voice cracks, thick with emotion.

"It is what it is," I mumble between clenched teeth.

"Well, it shouldn't be. Nobody should have to go through something like that, on both counts."

Shaking my head, I squeeze my eyes closed. I don't want to see the look of pity in Jacob's eyes. This is why I don't tell people about Ian or my dad. They give me the same pitiful look, and it makes me so fucking angry.

"Ian is a dickhead for not having the courage to speak up and give you the opportunity to work on whatever he deemed was broken, but mainly for not appreciating the incredible man you are." He runs his hand smoothly up my bicep, gently motioning for me to turn and face him. The sunlight sparkles in those blue eyes, and just the sight alone makes me want to cave.

Jacob barely reaches my chin, but he stretches up to cup

my jaw. I close my eyes for a moment, trying to resist leaning into his touch.

"But most of all, I'm sorry that the man who is supposed to love you unconditionally left you when you were too young to understand. Being a father is a gift. It's a title you need to earn, and I'm sorry that he didn't stick around to get to know the wonderful son he was given."

Biting down on the inside of my cheek, I allow myself to get lost in the feel of his thumb caressing the stubble lining my jaw.

"Thank you," he whispers.

I open my eyes to see him smiling. "For what?"

"For telling me. I can sense that you struggle trusting people, and rightly so, given what you've been through, so thank you for telling me." His eyes gleam as he pokes a finger into my chest. "Now, I'm going to be the best damn fake boyfriend ever. Little ol' England won't know what hit it."

I snort, thankful he's lightening the mood. For being the sunshine I need to help me escape the dark gray clouds. "Oh, yeah?"

"Yep," he answers firmly, popping the P.

He drops his hand and although it was only a finger against my chest, I miss the contact instantly.

"And as for you, your first boyfriendly duty will be taking me for afternoon tea. I want the quintessential British experience. This needs to be the most unforgettable vacation."

I'm sure I can make that happen.

# Chapter Six

Elliot: Ethan, I miss you already.

Ethan: I'm still in Chicago.

Elliot: But STILL! I miss you.

Ethan: …

Blaine: All set for your vacay?

Ethan: Yeah. Picking Jacob up in thirty minutes.

Blaine: Cool.

Elliot: Cool.

Ethan: …

Ethan: What are you two up to?

Peyton: Ohh! The twins are up to no good again.

Mitch: Don't be suspicious.

Mitch: Don't, don't be suspicious!

Peyton: I'm surprised you're old enough to know of Parks and Rec, rookie!

Mitch: Fuck off! I'm not that young.

Zach: Mitch, re: P&R, weren't you like five when that came out?

Ethan: Oh my god. I'm so fucking old.

Peyton: *cries into my oatmeal*

Mitch: I dunno, dude. I watched it on Netflix last year.

Zach: Sometimes I wonder if we should kick you out of the chat because you really do have a way of making us feel old.

Peyton: Says the guy still in his twenties.

Kendrick: I'm always late to the party.

Peyton: You're always late to everything.

Ethan: Seriously. Olsen x2, what are you up to?

Elliot: Nothing! *angel emoji*

Blaine: We just want you to have a really good time.

Elliot: With Jacob.

Blaine: Yeah, we want you to have a good time with Jacob.

Ethan: I'm sure I will.

Ethan: Behave yourselves while I'm gone. I don't want to hear you've had the fire department out because you locked yourself in the bathroom.

Elliot: THAT WAS ONE TIME!

Elliot: Can't fault a guy for trying. They're hot.

Blaine: We will behave. Have fun, captain!

Peyton: Drink all the tea!

Kendrick: Make sure to pack lube.

Zach: Have fun old man.

Ethan: *middle finger emoji*

# Chapter Seven

*Jacob*

"I don't know if I like this, Ethan." I grip the arm rest as the plane accelerates down the runway, my knuckles turning white from how hard I'm squeezing.

The second the seat belt sign went on and the doors closed for takeoff, my nerves skyrocketed.

At first, I was too in awe of the first-class lounge. I was already living my best fake-boyfriend-of-a-famous-athlete life when we boarded the plane, and that was before I realized our seats could turn into beds. We were given pajamas that were so soft that I had to stop myself from rubbing against them like a cat, all while sipping on a glass of champagne and getting giddy over an amenity kit.

Yep, I was rendered speechless as I sat there, taking in the luxury. My mouth gaping like a goldfish to the point where Ethan ended up leaning over to close it with his finger.

However, now my knees are bouncing at a nervous rhythm. My nails dig into the soft leather of the armrest, and the distinct taste of copper hits my tongue as my teeth bite the inside of my cheek.

Alex and Blaine returned from California yesterday, and I'm pretty sure I drove Daniel crazy with how panic-stricken I was, making sure everything was set so they wouldn't need anything. He even tried to send me home a few times just so he could work without me stressing out every five seconds.

But there's no going back now.

I'm going to be over four thousand miles away, and the voice in my head keeps asking if I can really do this.

"What if Alex needs me, or the bakery? What if everything falls apart while I'm thousands of miles away? What if there's a fire? Or a power outage?" My words come out in a rush.

Ethan places his hand on my knee, halting the bouncing. His other hand lands on my chin, turning me to face him. Those dark brown eyes bore into mine as he gives me a soft smile.

"It'll be fine," he affirms. "Alex will be fine; he has Blaine, Daniel, and Aria, Elliot, too. And if he needs any more help, the Kendricks are in town. Jonathan Peyton will also be back from his vacation in a few days."

He drops his hand from my chin, and my breath comes out in a whoosh. I instantly miss his touch.

"If there's a fire, they'll call 911, and if there's a power outage, they'll work through it. The bakery is in safe hands. You deserve this break, Jacob. You need to refuel your soul so you can continue thriving."

I try to focus on the heat of his palm seeping through

the fabric of my pants. The curve of his lips and the stubble that surrounds them.

"Well, when you put it like that," I huff out a laugh, trying to quell my anxious thoughts. I glance out of the window at the blue sky passing by us. "Don't you get scared?"

"Of flying?"

I nod.

"No, I wouldn't say so." He scoots as close as he can with the divider separating us. "I've taken thousands of flights, and I've never been scared. Sure, there's been times where turbulence has made me feel a little uneasy. Everyone's different, though, eh." He pauses for a beat. "But I'm here, okay? You don't need to be afraid because I won't let anything happen to you."

I drag my teeth across my bottom lip. His brows are furrowed slightly, like he desperately wants me to believe he'll protect me, so I give him a shaky nod.

Then the plane bumps with turbulence, and my heart shoots up into my throat as my hands grip the leather armrests again.

"J," Ethan calls me calmly. When I look over at him again, he's holding his hand out over the divider. "I've got you."

I shakily slip my hand into his, and he gives it a gentle squeeze, his thumb coasting over my knuckles in a soothing caress.

"Keep your eyes on me. Remember to breathe through your nose and out slowly through your mouth."

Taking a deep breath in, I slowly exhale, watching as his

face morphs into a smile. I keep my eyes locked on those chocolate orbs as I focus on my breathing.

"I've got you, J," he whispers so quietly that I barely hear him over the noise of the aircraft. "I always will."

Ugh! Why does he have to go and say things like that? Why does he have to be helping me breathe through the anxiety and nerves with kind words and gentle sweeps of his thumb against my skin?

It should scare me to realize how relaxed I am around him. He encompasses everything I've stayed away from most of my life, but there's just something about him that puts me at ease.

He makes me feel safe. Like he would be there to catch me if I fell.

And that, in itself, should terrify me.

But then I think back to the other day when I watched the strong armor he wears slowly disintegrated, showing me the emotional wounds that have been left by ghosts of his past. He's been hurt, not just once, but twice, in such monumental ways.

I've been through the heartbreak of losing both of my parents and grandparents, but it's a different kind of heartbreak.

The people in my life didn't choose to leave, but his did.

And those wounds have to be the hardest to heal.

"Jacob, we're here."

I rouse at the rumble of Ethan's voice, slowly blinking my eyes open. My neck aches from falling asleep at an awkward angle against the car window, and I let out a groan as the sun hits me in the eyes.

I don't remember a single thing since we got off the plane and collected our suitcases. Jet lag is hitting me like a freight train, leaving me a little delirious. I'm not sure I can remember my own name right now.

After we had some food on the flight, the cabin crew made up our beds, and the anxiety must've wiped me out because I slept the entire flight—holding on to Ethan's hand. He must've been so uncomfortable, but he didn't say a word about it when I woke up. He just gave me one of his small smiles and carried on reading his book.

Oh, and another thing that has added fuel to my very inconvenient crush?

Ethan wears glasses.

Yep. He was in full-on Clark Kent mode: dark eyes, dark hair, dark-framed glasses, and a broody expression. It was a good thing I had a blanket covering me because there was no way my pants alone would be able to conceal the semi I was sporting from the visual.

I apparently revert to my teenage years whenever I'm close to him.

Ethan opens the door to the rental car and gets out, the sound of the door closing behind him snapping me out of my daydream. I shield my eyes and open my own door and see the stunning house for the first time.

Vivid wisteria climbs up one side, a pop of color against the centuries-old sandstone. Stone mullion windows give it that typical British country home vibe you see in magazines, along with the immaculately landscaped grounds.

It's picturesque. Postcard-worthy.

"Is this your house?"

"Yeah. Do you like it?" I note the slight hesitation in his voice.

I turn around to face him, shocked. How could anyone dislike this?

"Ethan, it's beautiful."

He smiles coyly, like my words mean a lot to him.

I remember Blaine telling me they haven't met his mom, which must mean none of them have been here to visit. Blaine has also mentioned before that they all travel during the off-season, either going back to their hometowns or on vacation.

So aside from his mom, does Ethan spend every summer on his own?

The thought makes me sad.

"Can I help?" I ask as he begins to unload our suitcases from the trunk.

He hands over the keys. "Wanna open up?"

"How long have you had this place?" I ask while unlocking the door.

"About five years," he begins, following me into the hall. "My mom had been begging me to find something permanent instead of renting or staying in hotels whenever I visited, so when this house came on the market, I knew I had to get it."

"What made you choose it? I mean, aside from the fact that it's absolutely gorgeous."

"There are no neighbors for a mile or so, and it's still within an hour's drive from London. It's peaceful and fairly isolated, but close enough if I need anything. I love it."

I look up at the exposed wood beams, taking in the plain

jasmine-white walls, oak finishes, and neutral-colored carpets. It has a modern touch while keeping a lot of the original features. I don't see any photos or the kind of finishing touches that make a house a *home*. It's so…sparse, and a part of my heart breaks at that.

My home is the house my grandparents handed down to me when I turned twenty-one. The same home they brought me and Alex up in after our parents passed away. It's still full of memories: photos, vinyl records, ornaments, and trinkets. Each piece tells the story of something I experienced or learned from my grandparents. But Ethan's apartment back in Chicago—and apparently his British home too—feels empty. Almost temporary. Like he doesn't know if adding a personal touch is worth it.

"Just wait until you see the backyard. It's the best part," he says before winking, and I damn near trip over my own feet as he catches me off guard.

"That sounds amazing." I can't help but grin. "But can I take a nap first? I'm so tired, I think I could fall asleep standing right here." Right on cue, I cover another yawn with my hand.

"Of course."

Ethan leads me up the stairs, carrying both my bags with ease. I follow closely behind, admiring how his strong arms carry the suitcases with ease.

And his ass?

Holy. Shit.

It fills out his jeans to an inch of their life. I have to stop myself from reaching out to pinch it to see how firm it is.

Needing to distract my brain from giving into the urge, I ask. "Will I get to meet your mom today?"

"Yeah, she'll be over a little later." Ethan pushes a door open and walks inside, placing my bags at the end of a king-size bed. "This is your room."

I toe off my sneakers and fall face down into the plush white bedding.

"Omigod, it's like a cloud," I mumble into the sheets.

He chuckles under his breath. "Go ahead and get some rest. I'll get you some water." He pauses in the doorframe. "Her name's Jennifer."

I look over to him, confused.

"My mom. Her name's Jennifer."

I nod into the bedding.

Jennifer. Such a pretty name.

I think I say it out loud, but I can't be sure. My eyes suddenly feel so heavy, tiredness taking over me in a rush. I manage to strip down to my briefs and slip under the covers, unable to keep my eyes open any longer. I'm floating on the edge of unconsciousness when there's a clink from what I think is Ethan placing a glass on the nightstand.

"Thank you for being here," I hear him whisper, and I'm not sure if the gentle press of his lips to my forehead is real or if I've already drifted off into a blissful dream.

# Chapter Eight

*Ethan*

Fuck. I don't know why I did that.

No, that's a lie—I know exactly why I did it.

I gave in to the urge that's been bubbling inside me since I saw the fear in his eyes on the plane.

It made me feel like a prized asshole because I forgot what it was like to fly for the first time—the nerves, the anxiety at every strange sound—and when you add that first turbulence experience, it's no wonder he was nervous.

Flying is so common in my life, with traveling for away games and visiting Mom, that it didn't occur to me how Jacob would take it.

I haven't been able to stop thinking about how his hand felt in mine, holding on tight, even while he was asleep. Like I was his anchor in a storm, and he was afraid to let go.

So, seeing him lying there, so peacefully, so relaxed, did

something crazy to the stupid organ in my chest. But kissing him was a foolish move on my part.

Rubbing my face with my hands, I head to my room and distract myself by unpacking my suitcase before taking a quick shower to get rid of the plane stench. Knowing my mom, she'll be here any minute. She normally gives me an hour to sort myself out before she rushes over, and thankfully, she's stocked up the fridge and pantry, so I put a record on and start preparing lunch.

No more than five minutes later, I hear the telltale sound of the front door opening and closing and my mom's voice filtering down the hall.

"There he is!" She practically skips across the kitchen, reaching up on tiptoes to wrap her arms around my neck in a tight hug. "I've missed you so much."

"I've missed you too, Mom." I return her hug, pressing a kiss to her temple. "I've got something to tell you."

Her face lights up. "You've got a boyfriend?"

I roll my eyes, snorting a laugh. "Well, not exactly."

She gasps. Her hands fly to her face, and her eyes fill with joy.

"Before you get any ideas, he's not my boyfriend. He's a good friend of mine who agreed to play the part of my boyfriend for the wedding."

She frowns, dropping her hands to her sides. "What do you mean, *play the part?*"

I don't answer her right away. I busy myself by making her a cup of coffee and carrying it over to where she's taken a seat at the kitchen island. I can feel her glare burning the back of my head the entire time.

"I met Jacob at the start of the year. His brother, Alex, is dating Blaine. You'll see for yourself when you meet him, but there's something about Jacob that just…draws me in. He's fun and charismatic, but when we first met, it was like his light was dimmed by debt."

A look of understanding and sympathy washes over her.

"He owns a bakery. It's quite successful now—it was the one where we filmed with the team earlier this year—but you know how it is with start-up businesses. He was barely keeping his head above water, so I offered to help."

I don't need to say any more, because Mom knows. She leans over, patting my hand, an appreciative smile on her lips.

"You've always been a caregiver, Ethan. Look at the times you took on any job you could, even with school and hockey, just to help me out. I don't want you to ever change, but…are you being careful about this?"

I don't know how I managed it when I was a teen, but I found a way because I hated seeing Mom work all the time. Being the paper boy or mowing the neighbors' lawn was the least I could do.

"We have a contract," I clarify. "He was adamant that we did it officially, so we're both protected. All his debt has been paid off, and he pays me a certain amount each month —not that I need it back, but just seeing him smile has been…" I trail off, shaking my head.

"Oh, Ethan. That's such a lovely thing to do."

I glance out the window, trying to ignore the swelling in my chest under my mom's praise.

"So, how did the fake boyfriend thing come about?" she asks, taking a sip of her coffee.

A groan escapes me. "A few of the boys turned up at my

apartment because I kinda went into hiding after the season ended. They demanded to come inside—you know what they're like—and I ended up mentioning how I didn't really want to come to the wedding."

"It was Blaine's idea, wasn't it?" She grins.

She never met the guys. I don't really know why I've kept my two worlds separate, and it hits me that she only knows about them from what I've told her. She's been the only constant in my life since I was a kid. The only one who hasn't given up on me, who supported me through every up and down. It's like I don't want to share her with anyone else in case she's taken away from me too.

But for some reason, I didn't get that feeling in my gut with Jacob.

The need for him to be here with me was so much greater than my fears, and that's terrifying in and of itself.

"You bet it was." I laugh. "He thought it would be good for both of us, but more so for Jacob, because he deserves a break. Up until Christmas, he was often working sixteen-hour days, seven days a week. As soon as I found out, I wanted to—"

"Do everything you can to help." Mom smiles, but it's hinted with sadness. She barely made ends meet up until I was drafted, when I gave her everything I got from signing with the Thunder. She can relate to Jacob's struggles more than anyone.

I nod.

Mom takes another sip of her coffee, eyeing me over the top of her cup, her curious eyes never leaving me. "I've gotta say, I think this is the most spontaneous thing you've ever done."

"What's that supposed to mean?" I frown.

"You don't exactly trust easily, darling. You keep everyone at arm's length because, that way, you're the one in control. They're close enough to feel like they're part of your life, but never close enough to hurt you. So, Jacob must be quite special for you to bring him over. You haven't even brought your own teammates to visit before."

Needing to avoid my mom's quizzical gaze, I get up and continue dicing the vegetables I was preparing before she got here.

I don't really know what to say.

My teammates are the closest thing I have to family aside from my mom, and it's not like I don't want them here. Maybe I'm afraid of bringing them to the only place that's truly been just mine, letting them see this side of my life, and facing their rejection.

Jacob is the first guest I've had, and I want to take care of him. I want him to want for nothing.

I turn toward the door at the sound of soft footsteps on the stairs. Jacob appears looking fresh-faced. His dark blond hair is damp and slicked back from his face, and my gaze travels over his body. His gray t-shirt hugs his slim torso while baby-blue pajama shorts showcase his smooth, hairless legs, and my eyes land on the ruby-red painted toenails that pop against his fair skin.

He's so fucking beautiful, it hurts.

Immediately retrieving another cup from the cupboard, I set it under the coffee machine for him. "Hey. How did you sleep?"

"Amazingly, thank you! That bed is incredible. I think I fell asleep the second my head hit the pillow." He beams, but his eyes go wide when he spots my mom. "Oh, hello! I'm sorry, I didn't see you there." He walks over to my mom and holds out his hand. "I'm Jacob; you must be Jennifer."

My mom's eyes light up, a wide smile taking over her face. She takes his hand, a bright smile on her lips. "Indeed, I am. Welcome, Jacob; I'm delighted to meet you."

I slide Jacob's cup of coffee across the island, where he sits next to my mom, talking animatedly about his first flight experience, while Mom keeps sneaking glances at me.

Leaning back against the counter, I listen to them talk and laugh. The sight of them getting along so well causes a pang in my heart. Is this what it could be like if I lower my defenses? Spending the off-season with my mom and a boyfriend?

Except when I think of the word *boyfriend*, all I see is Jacob.

Fuck.

I can't think like this. I can't let my heart distract me from what I need to focus on.

As if sensing my thoughts, Mom gives me a knowing wink.

A couple of hours later, after we've finished lunch, I wave goodbye to Mom with the promise to see her tomorrow and head back into the kitchen to finish loading the dishwasher. Everything stops, though, when I find Jacob bent over, loading the plates into the tray. His pajama shorts have risen up, exposing the soft curve of his ass. My cock twitches at the sight of those two perky globes on display, and when I catch a glimpse of thin lace straps framing the bottom of his cheeks, I swallow a groan.

"Jacob, it's okay, I can do that." I manage to find my words, but my voice comes out like gravel.

He stands upright, an easygoing smile on his lips. "It's no bother; you cooked lunch. It's the least I can do."

I open my mouth to argue, but he crouches down again, and those damn shorts go up his crease. Would it be irrational of me to ban shorts in this house? Or better yet, to demand he keep them off at all times so I can take a look without the fabric obstructing my view?

I need to distract myself before I do something stupid, like bend him over the counter and rip off those shorts.

"I'm gonna head to the gym," I grumble and leave without waiting for an answer.

I change into a pair of gym shorts and forgo a t-shirt. British summers tend to be humid, and I need to sweat out the primal desire to claim Jacob like I'm some wild animal, so it's best I wear as little as possible.

Sliding open the patio doors to let in some air, I put on a playlist and begin my warm-up routine. When it comes to the off-season, I don't go as hard as I normally would, but it's still important I keep up my level of fitness.

When I'm finished with my warm-up, I move to the pull-up bar, watching my form in the floor-to-ceiling mirror that spans the length of the wall. It's only then that I allow my mind to drift.

I often wonder what it would be like to just *be*. To act on my wants without fear of rejection. To knock down my walls and live in the moment. To act on the attraction that has been burning up inside me for months on end. The rational part of my brain knows it's ridiculous and I'm wasting time allowing the past to impact my here and now.

But the past…still hurts.

"Fuck," I grunt, baring my teeth as my muscles cry from fatigue. My feet hit the floor after the final pull-up, and I quickly grab the towel to wipe my face.

When I look in the mirror, I see Jacob standing at the door, eyes wide. He doesn't realize I can see him as he takes me in, his teeth trailing over his bottom lip.

Taking advantage of the moment, I allow myself to gaze at his body again. When my eyes land on his shorts, the evidence of his arousal is clear as day. Sure enough, my own cock swells despite my exhaustion, leaving me slightly light-headed as all my blood rushes south.

I run the towel across my bare chest in a slow, teasing move, wiping away the beads of sweat caught in the dark hairs, enjoying as he follows my movements and watching him stare at the bulge in my own shorts.

"Like what you see, Jacob?" I growl.

Jacob's eyes lock with mine, and when he realizes he's been caught, the apples of his cheeks flush a deep pink. I don't miss the hitch in his breath. His mouth opens, then closes again. His throat works as he swallows, his tongue swiping over his bottom lip.

"I…uh…I…" he stammers.

I take a step forward, but before I can get close enough to touch him, he turns around and quickly disappears, and all I can do is watch his retreating ass in those fucking shorts.

I don't know how I'm going to be able to control myself or my attraction for him—protective walls be damned.

## Chapter Nine

*Jacob*

Curling my toes into the soft grass, I tip my head back and close my eyes behind my sunglasses.

It's so peaceful here. There's no traffic noise or people talking. I've been able to lose myself in a book or watch as a little robin runs around looking for food in the grass. The sense of tranquility makes me want to lay back and fall asleep right here to the sound of birds singing.

But I need to fight it, because even with my two-hour nap yesterday, jet lag is kicking my ass.

Last night, I swallowed my mortification over being caught staring at Ethan and how much I enjoyed him growling at me. We talked about other stuff while he cooked dinner for us, but he didn't bring it up, so neither did I—not even when I fell asleep on the couch, only to wake up to find I was using Ethan's broad shoulder as a pillow.

So, here I am, trying my best not to sleep during the day to get into some kind of routine.

I don't know when I'll get to experience England again, if ever, so I need to make the most of my time here.

I keep thinking about how much Grandma would have loved this backyard. She would be in her element. Looking at every single flower, stroking the petals between her fingers, and reciting facts about every bird she spotted in the sky.

*You let her flowers die.*

My chest tightens. It's true. Over the years since she passed, all her flowers have wilted. I didn't know how to care for them—I didn't have time to learn how or to even think about them.

Now every time I go outside, I feel this immense guilt that I've let her down. That she's watching me from wherever she is, cursing me for allowing her garden to die.

It's my plan to learn to garden and replant them in her memory.

My phone vibrates on the blanket beside me. I take a few slow, gentle breaths to try to ease the ache in my chest. Shielding the screen with my hand, I see Alex's name flashing, and I quickly swipe my finger across to answer his Face-Time call.

"Hey!" He says, cheerfully. I see he's in the bakery kitchen, his phone propped up on the counter in front of him while he decorates some donuts. "Are you outside?"

"Hey! Yeah, I am. We're having a lazy day today before going into London tomorrow, so I thought I'd come outside and read for a little while. It's so beautiful! Look at the back yard!" I turn the camera around, showing the colorful flowers, expansive lawn, and clear blue sky before turning it back to me. "Ethan's working out in the gym."

After yesterday, I needed to make sure I was out of the house so I wouldn't be tempted to go and sneak a peek at him again.

Not that anyone could blame me for it.

I don't understand how one person can be so damn hot. Seriously. His rippling muscles, sweat-soaked skin, and the way his hands gripped that metal bar?

Holy shit.

I didn't know I had such a thing for big hands, but all I could think about was how desperately I wanted to know what his would look like wrapped around my throat as he drove inside me.

*Whoa!* Where the hell did that come from?

"Jake?" Alex prompts, pulling me out of my wayward thoughts.

"Sorry, what was that?"

"Where did you go just now?" He smirks, waving his finger in a circle in front of his face. "You got a dreamy look on your face."

I'm glad it's warm because my sun-kissed skin hides my blush. "I may have been caught watching Ethan work out last night, and I haven't been able to think about anything else since."

Alex barks a laugh, the noise bouncing off the kitchen walls. He leans closer to the phone, his blue eyes swimming in glee as he lowers his voice. "Tell me everything. I can only imagine he's incredible to watch. I like watching Blaine when he works out, but there's something about Ethan that's so…" He snaps his fingers. "What's the word?"

"Potent? Sexy? Commanding?"

Alex nods. "Yeah, all of that! What did he do when he caught you?"

I shiver at the memory of the carnal look in his eyes and how his shorts tightened over his groin. There was no hiding my erection either. My lacy jockstrap did nothing to disguise the swelling, and the material of my pajama shorts was so thin that I might as well have been wearing nothing.

Did I put them on in hopes he might notice them? Maybe.

I can't deny it crossed my mind, knowing the straps beneath my ass cheeks would be visible if I bent over slightly.

I got the reaction I was hoping for, too.

"He asked if I liked what I saw. I couldn't reply, though; I just stuttered like a fumbling mess and ran away." I lay back on the blanket, holding the phone above me. "I don't know how to be around him, Alex. My natural instinct is to flirt and tease and see where it leads us, but what if I do and it messes everything up? We've finally got the bakery in a good place, and I feel like I can finally breathe...I don't want to mess it up by acting on a crush."

"It won't mess it up, Jake. You're both adults. You have a conversation, and if he's on the same page, you set boundaries. For example, if you want it to be some summer fling, then you draw a line in the sand when you come home. There's no need to make it more complicated than it needs to be." He shrugs.

I sigh. "I know, but let's be real here—he's not interested in me. He was probably just teasing because he caught me looking. I need to get over this thing I have for him and just focus on why I'm here, which is to help him."

"No, you're there to pretend you're his *boyfriend*, and in order to make that convincing, you need to have chemistry. What better way to build up chemistry than to flirt? Explore this underlying connection you have, and if you end up getting a little hot and sweaty in the process, then bonus!"

"I hate how logical you can be sometimes." Although he can't see, I roll my eyes behind my sunglasses.

"Hear me out," Alex pleads, his voice taking on a more sincere tone. "Ethan is serious most of the time, but I'll bet he has a hidden side to him. You're supposed to be in the honeymoon phase of the relationship. The time when there's plenty of sexual energy, so use it. Tease him. Flirt with him. If you decide to pursue it, that's when you set your ground rules. You've got nothing to lose."

*Except for the contract*, I want to argue.

But I know Ethan's better than that.

If we did what Alex is suggesting, explored this connection we have, and things went south, he wouldn't pull the deal out from under my feet because it's not in his nature. He's already given me his word.

But his friendship is also important to me, and we all know that sex can blur the lines of friendship.

"I don't know how I feel about getting sex advice from my baby brother," I admit, scrunching up my nose.

"Be lucky it's not Blaine giving you the advice."

We both burst out laughing.

"Why don't you treat tomorrow like a real date?" he suggests.

"I'll think about it. Now stop talking about me and tell me about the shop."

I listen as he goes into detail about how things are going, the orders we've received, and how well Daniel and Aria have been doing. It fills my chest with joy that I'm finally in a position where I can entrust the business to the capable hands of someone else.

Out of the corner of my eye, I see Ethan walking toward me. He's wearing nothing but a pair of tight black compression shorts that do nothing to disguise every ridge and groove of muscle or the impressive package between his legs. His arms flex as he runs a hand over his naked chest, and the closer he gets, the more my jaw drops open.

Am I drooling? I'm pretty sure I'm drooling.

The sweat coating his skin glistens under the sun, and when he rakes his fingers through his hair, I can't control the small noise that escapes me.

"Jake?" Alex's voice filters through the phone. "Are you okay?"

I manage a shaky nod, tearing my eyes away from the sexiest man I've ever laid eyes on, and quickly sit up. "I've gotta go. Can I call you later?"

Clearly confused, Alex nods but, thankfully, doesn't question me. We say our goodbyes, and I drop my phone next to my book just as Ethan comes to a stop, his sneakers touching the edge of the blanket.

"You look like you're enjoying yourself," Ethan says as he smiles, shielding his eyes from the sun with his hand.

I wet my lips and swallow, trying to clear my throat before I speak. "Y-yeah. I thought I would enjoy the sunshine. Alex just called, too."

"Yeah? Is he all right?" He toes off his sneakers and sits down beside me. His large body takes up most of the blanket, his wide-set shoulders brushing against mine as he leans back on his elbows.

My eyes follow a bead of sweat as it travels down the side of his neck, between his incredibly sculpted pecs that are dusted with dark hair. It glides down over the plains of his abs before disappearing under the waistband of his workout shorts.

My tongue unconsciously darts out to lick my bottom lip again.

What would it be like to follow all that muscle with my tongue? Would those flat, brown nipples be sensitive if I sucked on them?

By the time my eyes meet his again, he's smirking. A brow arched in question. I've been caught red-handed yet again, ogling the guy who bailed me out of one of the hardest times of my life.

"He…umm…" I shake my head, clearing the filthy fantasies from my mind. "He's good. They're managing well, which means I can stop worrying now."

"Good. I knew they would be fine." He smiles, then tilts his head back and closes his eyes.

I take the moment to really take him in. Sure, I've checked him out about a million times whenever he's visited the bakery or anytime he's been over at Alex and Blaine's apartment, but I've never been able to see all of him.

His dark hair has a slight wave to it, and there's a few strands of gray at his temples, which only adds to his distinguished look, along with the fine lines at the corners of his eyes. Long, dark lashes shadow the top of his cheeks, and day-old stubble lines a razor-sharp jawline. A crooked nose, no doubt from playing hockey, and frown lines crease his forehead and between his brows, but when I look closely, I can see a small crease in his cheek beneath the stubble. The kind of crease that comes with…

"You have dimples," I blurt out, then slap my hand over my mouth.

*Did I really just say that?*

Ethan opens one eye, those full lips tipping in a grin, making said dimples pop. "Are you checking me out again, Jacob? Should I be worried about you objectifying me whenever I'm not wearing a shirt?"

I fucking love how he says my name in that deep, growly voice.

"No! Yes. Ugh!" I cover my face with my hands, groaning. "I mean, how can I not when you look like that?" I wave my hand at his bare chest. "You've just come out of the gym looking like some kind of superhero, all sweaty and ready to rip apart a tree stump with your bare hands." I flop back against the blanket and cross my arms over my face, mumbling under my breath before I have the chance to stop myself, "I wish I was a tree stump."

"A tree stump, eh?" Ethan snickers, and I hear him move just as I feel a shadow cast over me. I open my eyes, peering behind the safety of my sunglasses.

He's leaning on one arm, his big body partially covering mine as he comes closer. His chocolate brown eyes slowly roam my body, leaving a path of fire in their wake.

"And you think you're not a tease, Jacob?" His voice takes on a deep, husky tone. "The only thing I want to be ripping apart right now are those fucking indecent shorts you wore yesterday. Did you think that coming downstairs yesterday and bending over the way you did wasn't a tease? Did you think I wouldn't notice that lacy little jockstrap you were wearing and be left wondering whether you'd let me tear it off you with my hands? Or my teeth?"

I gulp. *Please do all of that* on the tip of my tongue.

"You're playing with fire, J. I'm just here, ready to stoke the flame." He winks, then gets up and heads back into the house.

# Chapter Ten

*Ethan*

The wedding is tomorrow, and anxiety is beginning to fester in the pit of my stomach. It also doesn't help that I'm finding it increasingly difficult to stop myself from pretty much throwing myself at Jacob.

Every time I catch him checking me out, I want to just say fuck it and take his mouth with mine because surely an off-season hook-up wouldn't hurt, right?

*Or it could be catastrophic.*

Well. Yeah. That too.

And while I don't think Jacob has a bad bone in his body, it's that damn fear that I can't quite break past.

Heartbreak can do weird things to you in the long run.

After that interesting *conversation* in the backyard, where I may have said too much—or maybe not enough—my mom came over for dinner. She made us a roast dinner and the three of us lost track of time talking about ourselves and our lives back in Chicago. My mom had a lot of questions for Jacob about himself, the bakery, and Alex, and he answered all of them without hesitation.

It's clear to see that he loves his job and that he fits right in.

In this house.

With my mom.

With me?

*I can't be thinking like that.*

She raised her brows at me a few times when she caught me staring at him, and all I could do was shrug.

Because what the *fuck* am I doing?

Taking a sip of the coffee I made for the drive, I wait at the bottom of the stairs for Jacob. We're heading into London for the day to hit up a few of the tourist hot spots and one of the bookstores Jacob wants to visit.

Except our agreed departure time is long gone.

I glance at my watch, then back up the stairs. "J? You gonna be much longer?"

"Two minutes!" he replies.

Sighing, I take another sip and wait, and just as I'm about to call up again to see if he's okay or needs help, he appears wearing ripped jeans and a worn Fleetwood Mac t-shirt, his sunglasses perched on his head. When he reaches the bottom step, he grins and looks at me expectantly.

"Ready?"

"I've been ready for the last twenty minutes," I grumble, but he ignores me and takes the coffee from my hand.

I should turn away and head to the door so we can get on the road, but I don't. I decide torture is the better option. I stare as his lips purse around the lid of the travel cup, where my own mouth was only seconds ago. His lips are glossy, almost fuller, like he's wearing some kind of balm, accentuating his bow-shaped lips, all pouty and pillowy.

And that deviant part of my mind wonders how good they would look wrapped around my cock.

*Fuck.* Said cock twitches in my jeans at the idea. It likes that thought a lot.

I internally groan, willing my half-hard dick to go down.

"Let's go," I say through gritted teeth.

Five minutes later, we're driving toward Central London. Jacob fiddles with the radio, humming along to whatever song is playing. He's been taking photos out of the window and tapping away on his phone. He's practically bouncing with energy, and it's the only excuse I can think of for why I keep sneaking glances at him.

"I've been thinking," he announces.

I cast a quick glance and arch a brow at him. "Sounds dangerous."

He rolls his eyes and snorts, lightly slapping my bicep with his fingers. "So, for your family to believe we're a real couple, we need to be convincing, right?"

"Right," I say, focusing back on the road.

"I think we need to use our chemistry to our advantage. I mean, I already think there's something simmering between us, so what if we just…" He pauses, pulling his top lip between his teeth, before continuing. "I think we should treat today like we're going on a date."

I almost slam on the brakes. I wasn't expecting him to say that. I clear my throat, trying to sound nonchalant.

"Uh, sure. We can do that."

"I'll be quite a touchy boyfriend, holding hands,

touching your arm or chest, that kinda thing, so you can't be stiff or look uncomfortable around me."

Small chance of that happening, considering there's part of me that's often *stiff* around Jacob, and it's definitely not because I'm uncomfortable.

✕

I hate being a tourist.

It's not that I don't like London; I do. It's a great city. I just don't like people, and there are hundreds of them outside Buckingham Palace. Tourists don't seem to understand the concept of personal space, and I'm about two seconds away from telling the next person who pushes into me to fuck off.

Jacob, though?

Jacob is on cloud fucking nine.

He's taken what must be nearly a million photos of the palace, the fountains, the horse guards—even one of a pigeon.

"London pigeons are different from Chicago pigeons, and I think Elliot will appreciate it," was his reasoning.

Our goalie does get amused by the weirdest shit, so I can't fault him for his thought process.

"Isn't this fun?" Jacob gleams.

"Yes, I'm having a great time," I deadpan.

"Aw, come on!" He stands on his tiptoes and wraps his arms around my neck. "Look at all this history around you. It's kinda magical."

I place my hands on his hips, pulling him closer to me and out of the way as a group of people walk by.

"If you say so."

Jacob ignores my quip and gets out his phone again. "Let's get a photo with the Palace in the background."

That's another thing.

He's taken his decision to treat today like a date very seriously, and I've had to pose for more photos in the last twenty minutes than I did for my job last season.

Seeing how good we look together should alarm me, but I guess it'll make it all the more believable.

He holds the phone up, leaning into my side, and I wrap an arm around his shoulders, but he doesn't take the photo.

"You could at least try to look like you're enjoying yourself."

I groan and give a tight-lipped smile. He takes the photo and inspects it.

"We need to work on your grumpiness, because this," he says, holding up the phone with the photo displayed on the screen, "does not say we are in a very steamy and loving relationship, Mr. Parkes."

"Just put an emoji over my face or something, or we'll take another one when there aren't seventy thousand people around."

He rolls his eyes.

I sigh, placing a hand on his neck and angling his head to face me. "It's not that I'm not enjoying my time with you, J; I just hate all of this." I motion toward the crowd with my other hand.

His eyes softens slightly.

"Come on, let's take a walk through the park. Maybe it'll be quieter there," Jacob suggests, slipping his hand into mine and lacing our fingers together. He leads us through the throngs of people and toward St. James Park.

"Oh, what is this?" he asks, then gasps excitedly. "An ice cream truck! We've got to get an ice cream."

I watch as his eyes roam the menu printed on the van window, practically bouncing on the balls of his feet. He orders a soft serve ice cream in a waffle cone, topped off with a flaky chocolate stick poking out of the side. I politely decline ordering anything, but when Jacob goes to pay, I quickly tap my phone against the card reader.

"Ethan," he protests.

I raise a brow. "Jacob."

"I could've paid."

"Yes, you could have, but I wanted to get it." I lean in and whisper in his ear, "Boyfriend privileges."

He tries his best to look annoyed, but the smile playing on his lips makes me the winner.

Guiding him away from the truck with my hand on the base of his spine, we find an empty wooden bench facing the lake and sit down.

My eyes zero in on Jacob's tongue curling around the ice cream, his own eyes closing as he swallows and lets out an indecent moan.

"Omigod," he whimpers before taking another seductive lick. He takes a bite out of the crumbly chocolate stick, and another sultry moan rumbles in his throat. "This is so good."

With every sensual sound that he makes and each tantalizing sweep of his tongue, my dick thickens behind my zipper. I clench my teeth and ball my hands into fists in my lap as I try to control myself.

Is he trying to kill me? I can't act on this in the middle of a busy park.

"Wanna try some, E?" He holds the cone out to me, his tongue peeking out to lick over his swollen lips.

Or can I act on it? Because if he wants to play a teasing game, then I'll up the stakes.

Keeping my eyes fixed on his, I grab his wrist and bring his hand to my mouth. Taking a long, slow lick of the smooth ice cream, I imagine I'm running my tongue up his hard length.

His breath hitches. Twin pink circles color the apples of his cheeks, and his eyes dart between my mouth and where my hand is wrapped around his wrist, his cornflower-blue orbs darkening with each second that passes.

"Mm-hmm," I hum, slowly sweeping my tongue over my bottom lip. "Delicious."

I let go of his wrist, but it remains poised mid-air. It's only when a bit of ice cream drips down the side of the cone onto his fingers that he moves.

He's flustered, and I can't help but grin. He eats his ice cream with small, tentative licks now, his eyes fixed on mine.

I lower my voice. "What have I said about teasing me, Jacob?"

He swallows, wide eyes blinking up at me.

I lean over, taking another bite of the soft serve as I ghost my lips over his. "It's a dangerous game you're play-ing. You're too good for me. Don't waste your wishes on someone who isn't worthy of you."

"Don't you think that's up to me to decide?"

His voice is strong for someone who was just blushing hard. His hair falls forward in the light breeze, and I reach up, pushing it off his face. I allow my fingers to linger, taking in the softness of it and the way the gesture makes his breath hitch. There's something in those kind eyes that I can't decipher.

I'm not able to answer him. Of course it's up to him to decide who is worthy of him, but it isn't me. He deserves things I'm not able to give him.

Doing what I do best, I let go of his hair and change the subject. Quickly looking at my watch, I stand up. "Shall we head over to the book shop?"

A line appears between Jacob's brows. The muscle in his jaw twitches, and I prepare myself for him to call me out on my bullshit, but it doesn't happen. He silently finishes the ice cream and wipes his hands on a napkin, then stands. There's this uncomfortable silence between us and I fucking hate that I put it there.

He begins to head toward the nearest underground station, and I can't take it anymore.

I slip my hand into his, giving it a small squeeze. Letting him know without words I'm sorry for fucking up the moment.

We walk into the bookstore ten minutes later, and he stops abruptly, causing me to bump into him. I step to his side, watching as Jacob's eyes widen in awe as he takes in the high ceilings, marbled floors, endless shelves, and round tables filled with books. I follow closely as he takes off toward the elevators and scans the sign listing the seven different floors and each of the genres.

"What are we looking for?" I ask, pressing the call button.

"Romance." Jacob looks up at me, his eyes beaming.

Fuck, I love seeing that twinkle in his eyes. I want to be the one to put that look on his face all the damn time.

The elevator doors open, and my hand gravitates to the small of his back as I follow him inside. He presses the button, then bounces on his toes as it ascends. His excitement is palpable, and I want to bottle it up so I can experience it again and again.

Once the elevator arrives on the fifth floor, he heads straight to the section labeled "Romance." Shoving my hands in my pockets, I watch him from a distance as he picks up a book and flips it over to read the back, the tip of his tongue peeking out in concentration.

He closes his eyes and takes a deep inhale, a bright smile on his face. "The smell of books is up there with cake fresh out of the oven and peonies."

"I don't know what peonies smell like."

His mouth drops open. "Don't you smell the flowers in your backyard?"

I shake my head. "No. They were there when I purchased the house, and I pay a landscaper to handle the yard for me, or Mom does it."

He looks at me like I'm insane, then shakes his head, tsking under his breath. I make a mental note to smell every flower in my backyard when we get home before asking him which ones are his favorites, so I can buy some for him when we're back home.

It's normal for friends to buy each other flowers, right?

Propping my shoulder against the edge of a bookcase, my eyes follow him with avid curiosity as he moves around the section. He treats each book he picks up with such care and attention, placing it gently back on the shelf before picking up another, and when he has two in his hand, I hold my hand out, offering to hold them while he continues looking.

Jacob gives my outstretched hand a quizzical look, then tilts his head. "What?"

"I'll hold them for you."

He looks stunned, his eyes searching mine. For what? I don't know.

But when he places the two books in my hand, his bright smile hits me square in the chest.

"Thank you."

"A boyfriend would hold his boyfriend's books, no?"

"Uh…I don't know. I've never had one."

"Well, I would. I would also buy all the books my boyfriend wanted, so pick whatever you want."

"Ethan…" he sighs affectionately.

I press my finger to his lips. "Don't argue with me. You wanted today to be like a date, so this is my rule. You want a book? I'll buy you the book. You want a hundred books? I'll buy you every damn one."

His pupils dilate, darkening under my heated stare. I feel my blood burning as I stamp down the need to take his lips here and now. Quickly dropping my hand, I take a step back to create a safe distance between us.

"So, why romance novels?" I ask, clearing my throat.

He shakes his head, like he's trying to clear it.

"I just love love." He shrugs. "I've never been in love, and while I desperately want to experience it for myself, I don't know when or if it'll happen. Reading romance novels means I'm able to experience thousands of different love stories. I've had my heart broken and put together again in so many beautiful ways through words on a page. They've given me the chance to learn so much about myself and to escape to another world when reality becomes too much. I know I'm always guaranteed a happily ever after with these books, so they help keep loneliness at bay."

His words wash over me like a bucket of ice water.

"You're lonely?"

He laughs, but it lacks any humor. "Ethan, I'm a dreamer. I want the fairytale and a man who will whisk me off my feet, but life decided to put me on a different path. I haven't had anything to offer anyone recently. I was barely holding my head above water, so I didn't want to drag someone else down with me."

"J, what are you talking about? You have a lot to offer."

He shakes his head and turns away from me.

"I'm serious." I grab his elbow, turning him to face me again. "You're kind. Caring. You're incredibly creative and ambitious, and don't get me started on how fucking gorgeous you are."

His teeth dig into his bottom lip as he drops his chin to his chest as he looks at the floor. I press my finger under his chin and lift his head, and that's when I see it—a glimpse of the loneliness he keeps hidden away.

How often does he do this? Wears his feelings behind a mask and pretend everything is okay.

"It wouldn't have been fair to bring someone into my life when I was barely surviving. Nobody deserves to be dragged under the dark cloud that was covering me. Until you saved me."

"And is that why you're here?" I voice the fear in my head. "Do you feel obligated to do this for me?"

"No, not at all." He takes a step closer, smoothing his palms up my chest, stopping on the side of my neck. "I'm here because I want to be here, E. You could ask me to go to the other side of the world with you, and I would find a way. Don't you see it? You can ask me anything, and I'll say yes. You just have to stop being afraid to ask."

# Chapter Eleven

*Ethan*

"I have an idea," Jacob announces as he walks into my room.

I turn my head to face him without a word and continue fixing my cufflinks. Today is the day of the wedding, and it's safe to say my mood is grim.

Yesterday was amazing, I didn't want it to end. Roaming around the city, watching Jacob's expression as he experiences London for the first time. I enjoyed it more than I would like to admit.

There was a flick of hope in my chest that maybe it wouldn't be the last time.

But Jacob has been walking on eggshells around me all morning, but I guess he's finally had enough of my glum mood.

He stops in front of me and places his hands on his hips. The navy fitted dress pants sit perfectly on his slim frame, and his white shirt is open at the collar, exposing the smooth skin of his chest.

His gaze roams over my chest, then back to my face as I take him in myself.

"Your family is going to expect us to be super in love. We're in the honeymoon phase. So, I think we should kiss now, before we leave, so we don't have our first kiss in a room full of your family."

My hands freeze mid-air, my heart lodging itself firmly in my throat.

Did he just say what I think he just said?

"What?"

"If we kiss now, any awkwardness will be gone, and it won't be obvious that we're faking it. I think it would be kinda weird if we didn't kiss at what is a romantic event where the love in the air is supposed to be stifling."

I blink at him, stunned into silence, but he makes a very valid point.

They don't know me that well, but my family would see right through us. We're already playing a risky game by pretending, but it would more than likely blow our cover if we didn't indulge in some form of public display of affection.

Also, throw in the fact that Jacob is the first guy I've brought to a "family" event since Ian, and all eyes will be on us when they're not on the bride and groom. Any slight hiccup and this fake dating ruse will be for nothing.

"If we're to make this believable, we need to kiss now to make sure we're not, you know, rusty."

Despite the way my mouth waters at the thought of tasting him, I quirk a brow and smirk. "Rusty?"

"Yeah…Well…" He waves his hand between us. "I don't want us to be banging our teeth together or using too much tongue because we're… uh… not used to each other. We've only recently started dating. We're supposed to be unable to keep our hands and mouths off each other, so we'd be incredibly familiar with each other's mouths and tongues at this point."

Damn, I've been dying to be familiar with his taste.

Without needing any further convincing, I close the distance between us in a heartbeat. He opens his mouth to say something else, probably to give me another reason why we should do this, but there's no need.

I cut him off, wrapping my hand around the back of his neck, and slam my mouth against his in a blistering kiss. A small noise escapes him, clearly unprepared for me to take action right there and then.

But I don't need time to think about it.

I've been wanting to get my hands—and mouth—on him any way I can since the very first day I met him.

His body relaxes into me. His hands smooth up the front of my shirt, no doubt feeling the erratic drumming of my heart beneath his palm as I lick a path over his bottom lip. My other hand moves to hold his hip, and when he parts his lips for me, a low growl mews in the depths of my chest. He welcomes my invading tongue with a soft moan that goes straight to my cock.

He tastes so fucking sweet that I could feast on him for hours.

I know this is supposed to be an experiment. A way to dust away any potential cobwebs, but we don't need to fake chemistry that's always been there.

His hands trail up around my head before his fingers rake through the hair on the nape of my neck. He gives it a gentle tug, and I groan, my dress pants tightening as my cock hardens. He feels so good in my arms, pressed up so close against me that there's not an inch between us. I kiss him until he's gasping for breath, and when his eyes flutter open, a wash of crimson coats his cheeks.

"Yeah, that was…I…Mmm...Yeah…Wow…Um…Oh, that was…Mmm," he fumbles over his words. Taking a controlled breath, he pats my chest, smoothing his palms over the fabric of my suspenders. "Great. That was…Top job."

"Jacob." I smirk.

"Mmm?" He looks up, his eyes hooded and dark with arousal, and I'm tempted to skip the fucking wedding so we can stay home and practice some more.

Preferably without our clothes in the way, so I can learn the sounds he makes when our dicks brush together.

"We don't need to worry about looking rusty, but I appreciate having the opportunity to steal your breath in privacy first."

I didn't think it was possible, but his face flushes a deeper shade of red, and a shy smile appears on his lips as he looks down at his shoes. I place my finger under his chin, making him look at me.

"And Jacob? That cherry lip gloss?" I lick my lips, savoring the taste of him on my tongue. "You better wear that more often because you taste fucking delicious."

"Wow, this is so beautiful," Jacob says in awe, gazing up at the gothic architecture. "It's like something out of a fairytale."

It is. The wedding is being held in an early eighteenth-century mansion. History oozed from every inch of the grounds, from the ancient trees lining the gravel driveway to the acres of green land and the decorative crenellations lining the top of the walls. The winding white roses surrounding the entryway only add to the romantasy vibe.

Placing a protective hand on Jacob's lower back while he takes what I assume is another hundred photos with his phone, I eye the guests arriving, all dressed to the nines. None I recognize, but it doesn't stop my pulse from rico-cheting.

Is it too late to leave?

"Can we take a photo to send to Alex?" Jacob's voice pulls me out of my head.

"Sure." I move to stand behind him, keeping up appear-ances by snaking my hand around his waist to rest against his stomach. He angles the phone up and smiles brightly, but his smile quickly turns into a frown.

"Ethan, what did I tell you yesterday?"

"I *am* smiling."

"No, you're not; you're scowling. How are we supposed to sell this relationship if you look like I've pissed in your pasta?"

I snort at his analogy.

"Now, smile." He leans back into me, and I wrap my arm a little tighter around him. He grins, and I do the same.

This time, it isn't forced or constrained. The vision of us on the phone screen makes the stupid organ in my chest swell. His natural, ethereal beauty is a beacon. A sharp contrast to my rugged, crooked features.

He's the beauty, I'm the beast, and he's everything I've told myself I couldn't keep.

He makes me want to let go of my tightly held reins and just *be.*

To give in to temptation, lean into the *want,* and pretend I'm not broken as fuck inside.

"Ethan!" My head snaps up at the sound of Mom's voice. I let go of Jacob just as she wraps her arms around me in a bone-crushing hug. "I'm so glad you could make it, sweetie."

"Well, it's not like you gave me much choice," I grumble.

She laughs. "True, but still, you look so handsome, and Jacob! You look amazing!" She hugs Jacob and smooths her hands down the sleeves of his shirt. "This is so soft!"

"Oh, thank you, Jennifer. You look absolutely beautiful. This dress is such a good color on you."

"You're a darling; thank you. Shall we head inside?" Mom links her arm with mine, and I automatically reach for Jacob's hand. He laces our fingers together, giving me a gentle squeeze.

*It'll be okay,* he silently communicates with a soft smile.

Inside, the seats face a grand staircase. More white roses line the banisters, along with twinkling lights that cast the perfect sparkle in Jacob's blue eyes as he roams the extravagant hall, brimming with wonderment.

"Wow," he whispers.

"They've done a fantastic job," Mom beams.

"Mmm," I offer.

She leads us to our seats, and as I'm about to sit down,

my skin prickles. The feeling of someone watching me sends chills through my body all the way to my toes. I glance up, and that's when I see him.

Ian.

He's staring at me.

No. Not me.

Jacob.

His lips are curled up in disgust. My hand balls into a fist because how fucking dare he even look in Jacob's direction?

"E, sit down." Jacob squeezes my thigh.

Once I'm seated, Jacob places his hand on my stubbled cheek, angling my face toward him. He presses the sweetest kiss on my lips, and the tension evaporates within an instant.

"He's not worth it," he murmurs for my ears only.

He isn't, but it doesn't stop the anger I've been harboring for a decade from threatening to blow up like a volcano.

Thankfully, the ceremony goes seamlessly. Both Jacob and Mom tear up, causing me to roll my eyes. We're led into another room for a champagne reception before dinner. Mom pulls us to extended family members I barely know, but I exchange pleasantries, introducing Jacob as my partner and ensuring my hands are on him at all times.

When Jacob slips off to use the bathroom, Mom pulls me toward the makeshift bar set up on one side of the room.

"I like him."

I sneak a look at her out of the corner of my eye, waiting for her to continue.

"He's good for you."

I chuckle under my breath with a shake of my head. "And what makes you say that?"

"Well, for starters, I haven't seen you smile wide enough that your dimples pop since you lifted the Stanley Cup." She taps my cheek with her finger. "And secondly, don't think I haven't noticed the way you're looking at him. You haven't looked at anyone that way since he-who-shall-not-be-named, and even then, it didn't quite hold the same flame."

My eyes find Jacob weaving his way through the crowd toward us with such grace. He smiles at everyone who stops him. His energy is so magnetizing that even strangers are drawn to his light.

"He's too good for me," I say, quietly enough that only Mom can hear.

"That's bullshit, Ethan, and you know it," she hisses. "Isn't it lonely shutting people out all the time?"

I grunt, unable to deny it.

Because it's true. It *is* lonely, but it's also safer.

"He likes you, too."

Jacob's face lights up when he catches me watching him, wiggling his fingers in a wave as he gets closer.

"I think you should give this a chance. You and Jacob. I think it'll be good for you. For both of you."

Thankfully, she doesn't say anything else when Jacob steps up beside us, linking his arm with mine.

"Those bathrooms are absolutely divine," he coos. "I could've spent hours in there just looking at the decor."

"It's magical, isn't it?" Mom loops her arm through Jacob's other side.

While they talk animatedly about the rooms, I order us drinks and find us an empty space by one of the windows overlooking the gardens.

"I'll leave you two; I'm going to mingle for a bit," Mom gives me a subtle wink, then disappears into the crowd.

Motioning for Jacob to step in front of me, I wrap an arm around his waist.

"It's so beautiful here," he whispers, resting his head back against my chest.

I look down at him. The subtle tip of his lips, the radiance of his skin. The way his eyelashes frame the most exquisite eyes I've ever seen.

He's the most beautiful thing I've ever seen. Nothing could hold a candle to his beauty.

"Yes, it is," I reply, keeping my eyes locked on him.

"Well, isn't this cozy?"

The sound of the familiar voice halts this moment between us. I slowly turn around and am greeted with a face I haven't seen in a decade. His smarmy smile makes me want to punch him in the face.

"Hello, Ethan. It's good to see you." Those eyes I used to love losing myself in trail down my body, but now all they do is make me feel sick. "You're looking really well."

I resist rolling my eyes. I jut my chin and grunt.

"This is my husband, David," he says, introducing the man behind him, who steps forward and holds out his hand.

I glance down at the outstretched hand. Does Ian think he can act as if we're long-lost friends? Doesn't he recall leaving me at the airport without a single reason? Torpedoing our relationship into pieces without a simple goodbye?

And I'm not jealous of this guy. Hell, no. But I'm pissed that Ian thinks I'm just going to act like we're old buddies.

Giving David's hand a quick shake, because it's not his

fault he's married to an asshole, I try to stamp down my annoyance as I will not let him ruin Samantha's wedding.

"This is my partner, Jacob." I wrap my arm protectively around Jacob's shoulders, bringing him close to me. He rests a hand on my chest, his fingers toying with the strap of my suspenders.

Ian's eyes widen slightly as they trail over Jacob, before he manages to control his features. "It's lovely to meet you, Jacob."

"Thanks, although I wish I could say the same about you," Jacob says coolly, forcing a tight-lipped smile.

I smother a laugh with my hand.

Ian's mouth drops open. He looks at me, probably wondering how much Jacob knows and questioning whether I'm going to say something, which I won't. Jacob can sass him as much as he likes.

"Could I..." Ian's eyes bounce between Jacob and me. "Could we have a moment somewhere private? To talk?"

I tilt my head. "Whatever you have to say, you can say in front of Jacob."

Ian looks over his shoulder to his husband, who simply kisses his cheek and walks away.

"It's okay, I'll go get us a drink." Jacob leans up and kisses the corner of my mouth. "Macallan?"

I nod. "Thank you, baby."

*Whoa.* Wait a second. *Baby?*

The word just slipped out of my mouth without a second thought.

The small smile that plays on his lips hits me square in the chest, and my eyes remain locked on his retreating form as he heads toward the bar.

"He's not who I thought you'd end up with."

My head snaps to Ian. That pleasant feeling quickly turns into anger as I wonder who the fuck he thinks he is. "Excuse me?"

He shrugs. "I assumed you would go for someone more…athletic. One of your locker room buddies since you used to spend so much time with them."

*The fuck?*

I take a deep breath and mentally repeat to myself, *Do not punch him in the face.*

Do not. Punch him. In the face.

"You don't know him—or me, for that matter. You gave up that right when you walked out of the life we had."

He goes to roll his eyes, but manages to catch himself and lets out a sigh. "I suppose I should explain that."

A choked laugh escapes me. "You think?" I spit.

He finally has the decency to look ashamed. "I'm sorry about the way I handled things. I should have talked to you, told you how I was feeling." He glances around, avoiding eye contact. "You were never home, and I didn't want to live in a country where I didn't know anyone. I was so fucking lonely! I wanted to be your priority above everything and everyone else, and I knew you wouldn't be able to give me that. I couldn't compete with hockey, and I knew hockey was your first love, so I…" He casts his gaze over to David, and everything begins to fall into place.

"And he was able to make you his priority." The words are faint even to my own ears.

My heart pounds in my chest, hands balling into fists by my sides. I should be happy I finally have closure, but I'm fucking furious.

"No, it wasn't like that. We met after I moved back to England, but it just solidified the fact that you and I were never going to work."

"You should have told me instead of making me believe you were in love with me."

"I know, I know!" He holds his hands out. "I'm sorry, alright?"

Sweat beads down the back of my neck; my muscles are rigid. "No, it's not alright. You knew what you were getting into when we met. Hockey wasn't a new thing. Fuck, I thought you were fucking supportive of me."

"I was!" he raises his voice, his arms out at his sides. "But Christ, Ethan. Do you know how fucking hard it was to date someone like you? I get you have to be selfish in your profession, but *everything* was about you. We had to plan our vacations around your schedule. We had to plan meals around your diet. Nobody wanted to be friends with me because all they cared about was you. You were so hard to love, and I didn't want my life to be all about you."

*You were so hard to love.*

The chatter in the room becomes distant. Like I've been plunged underwater. The pressure of being submerged steals my breath, pushing against my lungs like my chest is caving in.

All of my fears are being vocalized.

I was too hard to love, so he left.

Just like my dad.

"Is everything okay?" Jacob's voice pulls me out of it.

Accepting the glass of Macallan from him, I drink it in one swift gulp, grimacing from the burn but welcoming it as it travels down my throat. "Everything's fine. Ian was just leaving."

"Ethan—" Ian pleads.

"Don't," I snap, dismissing him. "Just go. You've said your piece—now go."

Jacob steps in closer, placing a protective hand on my stomach as he addresses Ian in a tone I've never heard from Jacob before. "I think it's best if you leave, before I make sure you do."

Ian looks from Jacob to me, frowning. He opens his mouth to say something, but he must think better of it as he flattens his lips and gives a curt nod before walking off.

Jacob immediately steps in front of me. His eyes search mine, concern creasing his brow. "Are you okay?"

I give a small nod, taking a deep breath to try and steady my raging heartbeat. He hands me his glass of wine, and I down it in one, placing the glass on a nearby table. His hands move up my arms, soothing me, before resting on my pecs.

This time, the roles are reversed.

He is my anchor. My calming force in a raging storm.

And despite how pissed off I am, I'm glad I'm finally able to close the door on that part of my past. I'm no longer left wondering what happened or how it ended up going wrong. It sucks that it's taken so fucking long to get here, but I guess it's better late than never.

Because now I can focus on this incredible man in front of me, looking up at me with bright, kind eyes. His palms run over the material covering my chest, his teeth bury into the pillowy flesh on his bottom lip with worry as he waits for my answer.

"I think I finally am."

Resting my hands on Jacob's hips, I lean down and press a gentle kiss to the top of his head.

"Thank you," I begin, closing my eyes for a moment before opening them again.

"For what?"

"For being here," I whisper.

"You're welcome." Jacob smiles before adding, "I heard what he said. You're not hard to love, Ethan. In fact, you're quite the opposite."

# Chapter Twelve



*Jacob*

"Ethan, can you try and look like you're at least enjoying yourself a little bit?" Jennifer chuckles.

He grunts, scowling at her from beneath his dark, furrowed brows. He definitely has that stoic, stern expression down to a T. "I wish people would stop telling me to cheer the fuck up."

"Language."

He rolls his eyes. "I don't understand the point of all of this. It's so pompous, and what the hell is up with the tiny portions? We're eating meals so small and pointless it wouldn't even satisfy a mouse."

I snort a laugh into my wine glass.

He has been grumbling since the cup of soup landed in front of him. He turned to me and asked if he was supposed to take it like a shot of tequila. I'll admit—it's incredibly over the top and pretentious, but from what Jennifer has been telling me, the groom's family are quite wealthy, and this is the norm for them.

"I eat over six thousand calories a day. I'm so fucking hungry right now that I could eat this tablecloth, so no, I won't pretend I'm enjoying myself. I'm hungry, and I want to go home," Ethan grumbles, rubbing his hand over his stomach.

Jennifer rolls her lips, suppressing a laugh. "You're as stubborn as a mule."

"Could eat one of them, too," he grunts.

I've kept a close eye on Ethan throughout the night. Ian was lucky I didn't throw my wine in his face for the awful words he said, and while I'm not a violent person, I was wishing he'd refuse to go so I could make him.

But the wine is too good to waste on an asshole like him.

Still, I caught every word, and although Ethan was trying to hide it, I could see the pain Ian caused.

It made all the Ethan-sized puzzle pieces fall into place. He's had his heart broken by two significant people in his life—his father and ex-fiancé—so he doesn't let anyone get close. He only allows himself to care from a distance, so when they ultimately leave, he won't get hurt.

Whereas I'm the opposite. I love and care fiercely and openly because I'm scared that one day I'll wake up and they'll be gone, taking away my chance to tell them I love them.

Luckily, Ian stayed away for the rest of the evening, but I still kept my hand on Ethan's thigh over his black dress pants, massaging my thumb into the firm muscle. Loving that my touch eased the tension slowly from his shoulders.

I turn my head to face him, watching as he frowns as he

looks around the room. When his eyes land on me, that frown is replaced with a relaxed smile.

Ethan props his arm on the back of my chair, his fingers toying with the short hair at the nape of my neck. "Want to get some fresh air?"

"I think we'd better. You're getting a little hangry."

He smiles briefly at that, and I place my napkin on the table before taking his hand and following him outside. Ethan leads me down a pebbled path, coming to a stop in front of a pond. We take a seat on a bench. It's silent, apart from the faint beat coming from the music playing inside.

The entire property is exquisite. It looks like it could be the set of a regency drama. It could have been the home of royalty or an insanely wealthy family where they wore buttoned waistcoats, tightly fitted pants, and top hats.

I can see it in my head. The Lord and the stable hand spending their summers here in the garden, stealing forbidden moments together. It's very romantic.

Chewing on the inside of my cheek, I want to bring up Ian and what he said, but there's no need as Ethan beats me to it.

"I had a feeling it was about my job," he begins, his gaze locked on something in the distance. "He was so supportive of me in the beginning. Excited when I was drafted, and whenever I had games while he was in England, he would stay up late to watch."

I angle my body toward him, resting my arm on the back of the bench and propping my head up with my fist, giving him my undivided attention. "You mentioned before that it started to feel strained once he moved out to Chicago."

He nods, his fingers absently toying with the scruff on his chin. "Yeah. He would get angry all the time, but I never saw the signs that he was lonely."

"But that's not on you, Ethan. He's a grown-ass adult. Yeah, making friends when you're an adult can be hard, but it was his choice to move out and live with you. He knew who you were and what you did, right?"

"Yeah."

"So he knew what he was signing up for. He can't put all the blame on your shoulders because he could've gotten more involved. People invited him, and he didn't go—how is that your fault? Hell, I've been welcomed into the fold because of Alex. I had my concerns, but everyone is great. It feels like a family."

There's a beat of silence before I let out a sigh and carry on.

"I'm sorry he couldn't see what an incredible person you are, Ethan." I place my palm against his cheek, gently turning his face toward me. "I'm sorry he didn't value your love, but please don't believe you're in the wrong here for chasing your dream. Someone who really loved you would be by your side while you did."

Dark eyes stare into mine. Neither of us moves or says a word. Blood rushes through my ears, muffling out any sound. His gaze drops to my mouth, and like instinct, my tongue darts out and runs across my top lip.

Butterflies swarm my stomach as Ethan's eyes meet mine again, silently asking permission. Nothing could stop me from nodding. A meteor could hit, and I'd still want to feel him again.

He leans in and presses his lips to mine. It's softer than

the kiss we shared in his bedroom earlier. The gentle sweep of his tongue sends tingles down to my toes.

My hand runs down his neck to his chest, my fingers toying with the fabric of his suspenders. When I saw him wearing them earlier, I nearly dropped to my knees and begged him to do wicked things to me while keeping them on.

His warm hand cups the back of my neck, and I whimper into his mouth as his fingers gently tug on my hair and I lose myself in the exploratory glides of his tongue.

The next thing I know, he's pulling me onto his lap, and I'm straddling him. My moan echoes around the quiet pond as he trails his lips down the column of my throat.

"Shh," he murmurs against my skin, his tongue flicking over my Adam's apple.

Ethan's hands grab the globes of my ass and kneads. I roll my hips instinctively, seeking some form of friction as my cock swells impossibly hard. When our mouths meet again, it's desperate.

Needy.

Frantic.

This kiss isn't pretend. It isn't for show. It's giving in to the mountain of want that's been bubbling beneath the surface for so long—the one we can't fight any longer.

I want this man more than I've wanted anything in my life. And knowing that this may be all I'll ever have of him makes me want to bury all my doubts.

To take a risk and jump.

"I want you," I confess.

"I want you, too," he mumbles against my mouth. His hands halt my grinding hips. "But if we do this, you need to know that I can't offer you anything more than the off-season." He leans his head back, raising his hand and running his thumb over my lips. "And we need to set some rules, like not telling anyone back home. They'll only interfere."

I frown. "Why is our friends knowing a bad thing?"

"Because if we tell people we're hooking up, they'll jump to conclusions. They'll be expecting more, and I can't offer you more, J."

I want more, but I don't push. I can compartmentalize my feelings and take what I can have.

Temporary bliss.

Maybe once I've had my taste of him, the crush will diminish.

*Liar.*

Okay, well, I can try.

"When we get back to Chicago, I've gotta focus on my career. I don't know how long I've got left. I have one season left on my contract, then I'm an unrestricted free agent. I don't know whether the Thunder will want to sign a thirty-nine-year-old. I need to start thinking about who I am outside of hockey."

I want to tell him that he doesn't give himself enough credit. Of course the Thunder will be jumping at the chance to sign him again. I might be oblivious about the sport, but even I can see he's a valuable asset to the team.

But I swallow down my opinion.

This isn't the time or the place, and determination is written across his face. There's no changing his mind.

It's the off-season or nothing, and maybe I'm a glutton

for punishment, but I would rather have this summer than nothing at all. I wouldn't be able to live with the what-ifs.

Giving a shaky nod, I run my fingers over the scruff on his face. "Okay."

"Okay?" His dark eyes hold mine.

"Yeah, it can be our British summer secret."

Ethan grins. I skim my fingers along the indentation of his dimples. The sheer beauty of him is breathtaking.

"I know we've joked about it a lot, but you really should smile more often."

"Why?"

"Because you're beautiful, Ethan."

He shakes his head in my hands. "Nah, you're the gorgeous one."

I snort. "Just shut up and take the compliment, you big caveman."

He grips both of my wrists and tugs me closer until our noses touch. Desire swims in those sparkling, dark orbs.

"Caveman, eh?" His gravelly voice goes straight to my cock.

"Mmm."

He quickly stands with me in his arms and shifts to throw me over his shoulder. Laughter bubbles out of me as he begins to walk back up the walkway toward the party.

"Ethan! Put me down!" I protest with a laugh.

"Nope. You're mine now. Call me a caveman, and a caveman is what you'll get."

My breath whooshes out of me as he puts me back on my feet. He takes my face in a heated kiss, then rests his forehead against mine.

"Would you like to dance?"

"Mmm," is all I can manage as he captures my mouth in another kiss.

I don't know how long we stand here, wrapped up in each other's arms, kissing until we have to come back up for air.

But we never make it onto the dance floor.

We may have opened our very own Pandora's box and the timer is ticking down on our time together.

I don't know about Ethan, but if I'm getting the chance to act on my crush, then I don't want to waste a single second.

"Take me home."

# Chapter Thirteen

*Ethan*

Jacob places his hands on my chest and pushes me onto the large armchair in the corner of my bedroom. I sit down, pulling him onto my lap, and thrust my hips up, my throbbing cock seeking pressure.

He moans into my mouth, his fingers combing through my hair as he rolls his hips against mine.

Once we managed to peel ourselves away from each other on the venue grounds, we headed back inside to say goodbye to my mom and Samantha. The thirty-minute drive was fucking torture. Thirty minutes of subtle touches in the backseat, heated glances, and my pants becoming tighter by the second.

We got home less than ten minutes ago and I'm ready to combust.

But the day went better than I expected, and it was all

because of Jacob and his ability to read me like nobody else, without me saying a single word.

I can't lie and say the flash of disappointment in his eyes didn't hurt when I said we could only have the off-season, but it's more for his sake than mine.

He deserves better than me, but for now, I'm going to be selfish and take as much of him as I can while I have him.

"I need a few minutes to freshen up." Jacob presses a kiss to my lips and gets to his feet. "Wait here."

"Like I would go anywhere."

Jacob grins, and I watch as he walks to the bathroom, his hips sashaying. He throws a wink my way over his shoulder before disappearing behind the door.

"Fuuuck," I groan under my breath, palming my aching cock through my pants, eyes fixed on the door. The sound of running water and my fast-beating heart is all I can hear.

The door opens again after what feels like an agonizingly long time, and Jacob stands there in nothing but a black jockstrap. His palms slide up the door frame, elongating his heavenly body.

"Fuck, baby, look at you." I squeeze my dick and crook my finger at him. "Come here."

He saunters toward me, his eyes trailing down my body like I'm the best thing he's ever seen.

I widen my legs, letting him stand between my thighs. He leans down, resting his hands on the arms of the chair, as his minty, fresh breath coasts over my mouth.

"Can I undress you?" he asks.

"Mmm," is all I can manage. I'd agree to anything he wants right now.

I keep my arms on the chair as he makes work of the

buttons on my shirt, spreading it open and running his hands up my chest. His thumb ghosts over my nipples, and I let out a hiss.

His smile turns wicked. "I wondered if they'd be sensitive."

"Does that mean you've been thinking about me, Jacob?"

"Mmm," he hums, trailing his hands back down my chest and over my stomach. "I've been thinking about you a lot. About the noises you'd make when I played with your nipples, or when I played with *this.*" His hand stops at my belt buckle. His fingers flirt with it, the heel of his palm purposely massaging my hard cock through my pants. I ball my hands into fists as I fight the urge to take control.

"Jacob," I warn, jaw clenched.

"So impatient," he whispers.

I let out a relieved groan when he unzips my pants and pulls my dick free, tucking my boxers beneath my balls.

A small gasp escapes him as he tests the weight of me in his soft palm, gliding it up and down my length. His hand looks so small wrapped around me. His thumb grazes the underside of the head, over the tip, collecting the bead of precome there before bringing his thumb to his mouth and sucking it clean.

*Goddamn tease.*

Jacob drops to his knees and dips his head, taking one of my balls into his mouth. I moan, combing my fingers through his hair to brush it from his face. Big blue eyes look up at me as he licks and sucks my balls, then runs a hot, wet stripe up my cock with the flat of his tongue before wrapping those luscious lips around the swollen head.

"Fuck, Jacob," I groan.

He hollows his cheeks as he takes me deeper and deeper until I'm hitting the back of his throat, his fist pumping me in time with his mouth as his tongue swirls and massages the tip. He releases me with a pop, tears prickling in his eyes from gagging on my cock.

I cup his jaw with my hand, tracing my thumb across his lips as he takes me back into his mouth. "You look so beautiful with your mouth full of me, baby."

The vibrations of his moan cause my toes to curl into the carpet and my restraint to shatter. I grab the back of his neck and haul him onto my lap, our lips crashing together, teeth colliding as desperation sinks in. He straddles me, hands cupping my face, as we fall into the hottest kiss of my life.

With one hand on his neck, I reach around and smooth my hand over the base of his spine before my fingers travel down the cleft of his ass. I tap my middle finger against his fluttering hole, and he whimpers into my mouth. I do it again and again, then pull back and bring my fingers to his mouth.

"Suck," I demand.

Jacob doesn't hesitate. He sucks two of my fingers into his warm mouth. His tongue rolls and curls around my fingers, just like it did with my cock. His hand continues to pump my shaft, his thumb teasing the slit.

"Please, Ethan," he whimpers.

"Please what?"

"I need to feel you inside me. Get me ready to take this big, beautiful cock of yours," he begs, eyes dark with hunger.

My dick throbs in his hand as he gives it a squeeze, and I take his mouth again in a scorching kiss, reaching my hand back around to his raised ass. I circle his rim with the tip of one finger before applying pressure, slowly pushing inside.

Jacob moans into my mouth as he pushes back on me, taking me in to the first knuckle, my name a delicious cry on his lips.

It's my new favorite fucking sound.

"Fuck, baby, that's it," I praise, slowly working my finger inside him, breaching the tight ring of muscle. "Good boy."

His entire body trembles at my words.

Once I'm all the way inside, I brush his prostate, and he moans. "More," he pleads. "Give me more."

I pump my finger a few more times, then pull out. Circling his rim with two fingers this time, I gently ease my way back inside, and the carnal noise that escapes him causes my balls to tighten. I'm not going to last if he keeps making these sounds, but skipping on prep is non-negotiable. Even more so because I'm a big guy.

By the time I'm three fingers deep, he's riding my hand while jerking my cock. Precome pools in my foreskin, smearing down my shaft with every stroke of his fist. Shifting to the edge of the seat, I slip my fingers from him, standing up as I wrap one arm around Jacob's lower back and the other around his ass cheek. His legs and arms wrap around me, and I carry him over to the bed with our lips still locked.

I gently place him on the bed, and he swiftly moves onto his knees. He begins to remove my clothes, sliding the straps of my suspenders off my shoulders and then pulling off my shirt. I remove my dress pants and boxers, kicking them out of the way and quickly tossing my socks aside. I take Jacob's face in my hands again and kiss him.

I kiss him like he's my only lifeline.

"Lay back," I murmur against his mouth.

He crawls backward up on the bed. His heavy-lidded eyes remain focused on my hand, which slowly pumps my cock.

"Take them off," I order, jerking my chin toward his jockstrap, and when he lifts his legs and bends his knees to pull them off, I growl at the sight of his slick, relaxed hole.

"You're fucking breathtaking, Jacob."

A flush travels up Jacob's neck at my compliment. I press a knee into the mattress and crawl up to him between his open legs, watching his hard cock rest against his creamy skin.

When I reach his knees, I stop and sit back on my haunches. Lifting one of his legs, I press a kiss to the inside of his knee before pressing featherlight kisses up the inside of his thigh.

"Ethan." His breath hitches.

I nuzzle my face into the juncture of his thigh, his tight sac only a breath away from my lips. His body is trembling, and I haven't even started worshiping him the way I want to.

I suck his balls into my mouth. His moans and whimpers are quickly becoming my favorite soundtrack.

Hands grip my hair, fingers pulling tightly on the strands. Wrapping my fingers around the base of his shaft, I close my lips around it and swallow him down to the base.

His back bows as his moans fill the room. The fingers in

my hair tug to the point of pain, but I don't care. He tastes fucking sensational.

"Ethan, please," he pants.

I tongue his wet slit, watching his chest rise and fall with his labored breathing.

"Do you want me, Jacob?"

He nods eagerly. "Y-yes!"

Resting my hands on either side of his head, I run my nose along his jaw, stopping by his ear, and whisper, "Do you want to feel me inside you? Stretching you so good?"

His hands graze down my ribs to my ass. He squeezes my cheeks, urging me to move, so I rut against him, our slick cocks brushing together.

"Yesss! Please, Ethan."

"I've always wanted to know what it would feel like to have your tight hole wrapped around my cock." I nip his chin. "Can I find out?"

"Yes. Please. I want that too."

I capture his lips in a kiss, then reach over to the nightstand to retrieve a condom and a bottle of lube. I sheath myself and lube myself up. Jacob wraps his hands under his knees, pulling his legs up to his chest, and I line the head of my cock against his hole.

Slowly rolling my hips in shallow thrusts, I press light-weight kisses over Jacob's neck and under his jaw. Tremors rake through his body as I ease my way inside him.

"You're so fucking tight," I growl.

"You're so fucking big." Jacob responds with a breathy moan.

I remain still for a moment once I'm fully inside him, my heavy balls pressing up against his skin. I'm so close to blowing my load from how good he feels; I need to think about something else for a second, or it'll be over too soon.

Jacob winds his arms around my neck and wraps his legs around my waist. The heels of his feet dig into my ass cheeks. "Move, please."

My resolve slips, and I can't hold back any longer. I rock my hips. The sound of our flesh slapping together fills the room.

Shifting, I sit up and pull his body closer, angling my hips so the head of my cock brushes against his prostate on every thrust.

"Oh, God! Ethan!" He grips the bedsheets.

With one hand on his hips, I take his hard, leaking cock in my hand and give it a long, delicious stroke before rolling his balls in my hand. The soft, desperate whimpers escaping his lips only add fuel to my burning fire. Trailing my fingers further down, I circle his rim, watching as my cock goes in.

"Look at how well you're taking me. Such a good boy."

His eyes are completely blown out with arousal, his breath coming out in erratic pants. I cover his body with mine and swallow the soft mewls with my lips.

My thrusts begin to falter as I can't keep my release at bay any longer. Fire runs down my spine as my balls tighten. Warmth seeps between our bodies as Jacob comes and his muscles ripple around my shaft, tipping me over the edge.

The roar that rumbles out of me is animalistic as I fill the condom. I collapse on top of him, lightheaded from the most incredible orgasm of my life. I must zone out, as the next thing I know, Jacob's running his fingers gently through my damp hair, pushing it from my face.

He presses a soft kiss to my sweat-soaked forehead.

Wordlessly, I slowly ease my softening dick out of him and dispose of the condom. I return with a washcloth, cleaning up his stomach and wiping between his cheeks, and when I slip back between the sheets, I pull him close to me.

I'm unable to speak. Too pent-up on an emotion that I've shied away from for years.

I know I said we have a deadline, but now I've had a taste of him. Now I know what he sounds like, tastes like, *feels* like, and I don't think ten days is going to be enough.

I don't want to give him up, but I know I'll have to.

# Chapter Fourteen

*Jacob*

Rolling over onto my side, I stretch my arm out across the mattress, expecting to find Ethan's warm body, but my hand meets the cold, empty sheet instead.

I can't believe how amazing last night was. Well, I can. Mainly because my body has that delicious ache to it. A pleasant reminder of being fucked so spectacularly.

So thoroughly.

*Twice.*

I slip out from under the covers and head to his closet to pull out a pair of pajama pants. They're huge on me. The sight makes me chuckle. I tighten the drawstrings, then head downstairs where I'm greeted by the smell of fresh coffee and cooking. The mellow sound of John Mayer filters through the house from the speakers, and I find Ethan at the stove cooking breakfast.

He's refused to let me cook once since we arrived,

claiming he wants me to fully relax and not worry about a single thing. It's just another thing to add to the never-ending list of reasons why he is a truly magnificent man.

I lean against the door and watch him. He's wearing nothing but a pair of basketball shorts and his glasses, the muscles in his broad back rippling as he moves so effortlessly around the kitchen. The reminder of how he picked me up as if I weighed nothing last night plays like an endless reel in my mind.

His hips sway slightly to the somber tune, and there's something so attractive about a man who goes barefoot in his home.

His chocolate brown eyes light up when he spots me, his lips morphing into a wide smile. I know he doesn't smile often, but it seems to be a common occurrence around me.

My romantic heart can't help but think I'm the reason.

It's a dangerous thought.

I move toward him, but he meets me halfway, scooping me up in his big, strong arms and pressing his mouth to mine in a scorching kiss.

"Good morning."

"Good morning," I reply, wrapping my arms around his neck. "You're cooking me breakfast?"

"Always." He kisses me again before letting me go, and pulls out a stool at the island for me to sit down on before moving to grab a cup and placing it under the coffee maker. "I like taking care of you."

Butterflies flutter in my stomach at his earnest expression. It's been so long since someone took care of me. Or, more like it's been so long since I've *allowed* someone to take care of me. Alex did when I had the flu last year. I was so sick, I couldn't even get out of bed. I didn't really have a choice.

"How are you feeling?" he asks, sliding the steaming cup of coffee across the counter.

"Good." I smile, wrapping my hands around the cup. "I haven't slept that well in a very long time."

"I figured. You were out cold when I got up." He smiles back. "You're not sore, though?"

Leaning over, I squeeze his hand and shake my head once, smiling. "No, I'm okay, thank you."

Seeming content with my answer, he nods once, then goes back to the stove. He cracks some eggs into a bowl and whisks, adding a small dash of milk and tossing them into a pan. I take a sip of my coffee, just watching him move.

"What are you making?"

"Breakfast burritos," he says while shredding some cheese. "Sausage, scrambled eggs, tomato, avocado, and cheese."

My stomach chooses that moment to growl loudly. Ethan looks over his shoulder with a grin. "Won't be too long, don't want you to get hangry on me now."

I scoff and stick out my tongue. "I won't, I'm not you."

A few minutes later, he browns the tortillas and plates them up, sprinkling some chopped chives on top of the eggs, and I'm moaning around mouthfuls. "This is so good."

"Yeah?"

I nod. "I could eat this every day."

Ethan opens his mouth, then must think better of it and closes it again. He presses his lips together and smiles before taking another bite.

"Who taught you to cook?"

"My mom." He says between mouthfuls. "I wanted to be able to cook so she didn't need to worry about it when she got home from work."

There's an ache in my chest at his admission. I don't know what to say. I don't think there's anything I *could* say that would tell Ethan just how much my heart breaks for younger him.

"I borrowed some recipe books from the library, and the days when she worked until late, I would make sure she had something ready."

I bite down on my bottom lip, willing the back of my eyes to stop burning. "I—"

"It's fine, J," he says gruffly. "It's in the past now, but I guess I like to take care of people, and what better way to care for them than through food."

I smile, but the twitch in his jaw tells me he's done with this conversation.

"Do we have anything planned today?" I ask, changing the subject.

He shakes his head. "No. I need to review some game tape. I…" He hesitates before continuing. "I need to start thinking about my future after I'm done playing, so I was wondering if you wanted to brainstorm with me."

My eyes widen slightly. I know that's been weighing on his mind. I don't know what I can offer considering I don't know anything about hockey, but my heart squeezes that he's opening up slightly. "I would love to."

After we both shower, we retreat to the living room. Ethan makes notes in his notebook as he watches his game footage while I'm trying to read one of the books he bought me in London. The second I sat down on the couch, he pulled my feet into his lap, and the whole thing feels very…domestic.

He has one hand on my foot, his thumb absently massaging the arch in a way that has me trying to stop myself from groaning. With his eyes fixed on the TV, he scribbles notes on his pad, then sometimes pauses the game to draw something on his pad before pressing play again.

It's absolutely fascinating. The way his brows furrow in concentration. His lips slightly pursed. By the time he's filled several pages of his notebook, the game has ended, and another one is about to begin, but he stops it.

"What made you get into baking?"

I glance up from my book to see Ethan looking at me. The TV is paused, his notebook balancing on the arm of the couch.

"My mom," I answer, slipping my bookmark into the page. "My earliest memories are of baking with her. We'd always make those box mix cupcakes or brownies for my dad, and when Alex was old enough, he would help out too. Although he didn't really help—he would just try and eat the mixture out of the bowl." I let out a small laugh, but there's a heaviness in my heart.

I don't really talk about them. I usually only look back when I'm on my own, and there's no one to see the pain that still consumes me all these years later.

"Every Sunday we baked something my mom found in a magazine or a recipe book we borrowed from the library. It became like our thing, so when she passed away, I wanted to keep baking as a way to stay close to her. My grandma actually picked it up with me, knowing how important it was to me. We would do some baking while Alex and my grandpa watched hockey, and when I was old enough to understand the way the world worked, I knew I wanted to make a business out of it. I knew I wanted to carry that tradition into my everyday life somehow."

"I know you were a child, but how old were you when they passed? If you don't mind me asking."

"I don't mind you asking at all. I was ten, Alex was seven."

Ethan's face drops, sadness whirling in his eyes. "Fuck, Jacob. I'm so sorry."

I shake my head slightly, giving his hand a gentle squeeze to silently say thank you.

Glancing down at the book on my lap, I take a deep breath and recall one of the darkest days of my life.

"Me and Alex were staying at my grandparents' house as my parents had gone away for the weekend to celebrate their twelve-year wedding anniversary. My mom was so excited. She picked out this lakefront cabin that had a hot tub out on the deck, and I helped her make an anniversary cake that she was going to surprise my dad with. It was his favorite, red velvet. But on their way home, they were hit by a drunk driver." My voice cracks, tears welling in my eyes. "I remember the day the police came to the door like it was yesterday. My grandma told us to go to our rooms and not come out until she came to get us. Alex was too young to understand what was going on. He started doing this puzzle on my bedroom floor while I peered out the window."

Ethan leans over, taking my hand in his. He gently caresses the inside of my wrist with his thumb, his other hand resting on my knee.

I wipe my eyes with the heel of my palm and sniff.

"When I came out of that room, it felt like time stood still but like I had aged a few years at the same time. I knew something bad had happened because I'd never seen my grandparents cry before. They explained that my parents had been in an accident, and they wouldn't be coming home." A choked sob escapes. I quickly hide my face in my free hand as tears begin to fall down my cheeks.

"Alex asked if they'd gone to heaven, and it was that moment I knew I had to be strong for him. I had to put my own grief aside because he needed me more than ever."

Just like last night, Ethan scoops me up into his lap like I'm as light as a feather. He wraps his arms around me, holding me tight as I let my emotions run free.

Society tells you that after a certain time, you're supposed to "get over it" and move on, even though you're still numb inside.

But grief is a tangible thing. It ebbs and flows like an active current. At different speeds at different times. Sometimes the wave is small and shallow, a gentle reminder it's there, but then it grows and becomes huge. It'll pull you under, leaving you struggling to breathe because the pain is so intense. Making you feel like your heart is being pulled from your chest.

Grief never goes away. It has no expiration date. No timeline. It's always there, and you learn how to disguise it with time. To hide it behind a mask. But sometimes the mask slips, even over something inconsequential, and the pain washes over you again.

Raw and excruciating.

"I'm so sorry," he murmurs into my hair and presses a kiss to my head. "No child should ever have to go through that. I'm glad you had each other and your grandparents, but you're allowed to grieve, J. You could have grieved and still been there for Alex."

"I think it was my way of coping. If I squashed my emotions, I could pretend it wasn't real. If I didn't let myself feel, then it wasn't happening." I raise my head to look at him. "My grandparents were amazing, though, as I was in denial for quite some time. They let us handle things in our own way, but also made sure we always felt loved and supported. They never pushed us to do anything we didn't want to do or weren't ready for. They were our pillars of strength for most of our lives. But Alex..." I hiccup. "He's all I have."

I often find myself questioning if I could have done more. Could I have taken my grandma to the hospital sooner? Could I have showered my grandpa with more love so his heart didn't shatter the second she took her last breath? Could I have stopped my parents from going away on their trip? Did they know how much I loved them?

Sometimes the questions float in my head like a never-ending tornado I'll never be able to break away from.

"Did you have any other family?"

"No," I answer, shaking my head. "Both my parents were only children, so we had no aunts or uncles or cousins, and my mom's parents were already gone."

Ethan's hand comes up to cup my face, his thumb wiping under my eye. Dark eyes gaze into mine, unwavering. "You have me, J. You'll always have me."

I give him a wobbly smile. My body trembles from the pain, from the emotion of saying all this out loud. I suck in a shaky breath and dip my chin to my chest, my fingers playing with the hem of his t-shirt. "I'm sorry."

He frowns. "For what?"

"I'm usually much better at keeping myself together."

Ethan shifts slightly underneath me. He places his finger beneath my chin and lifts my head, his face serious.

"Jacob, don't *ever* apologize for being upset. You can be yourself with me. Whether you want to laugh or cry, sit in silence, or talk about it, I'm here. Grieving isn't something to be ashamed of. Grieving is a sign of love that has nowhere to go, and that is such a powerful thing. It's a *brave* thing because you get up every morning even though your heart is broken. Healing doesn't have a timer, J." He wipes under my eyes again, catching the tears that continue to fall.

"I'm sure there were days where you were close to crumbling, and you didn't give up. You went after your dreams, knowing the two people who were supposed to be there cheering for you were taken away far too soon. You were strong, not only for yourself but also for your brother. You've put everyone before yourself since you were a child, and Jacob? You're the most incredible person I've ever had the honor of knowing."

I feel my chest swelling, but this time it isn't from pain. It's from the kindness in his eyes. The gentle caress of his fingers against my cheek as he wipes away my tears.

"Does Alex know how you feel?"

I shake my head. "I didn't want him to think I wasn't his strong big brother."

He gives me a sad smile. "J, he wouldn't think any less of you. Your strength is admirable. To still see the glass half-full after experiencing so much heartbreak..." He shakes his head, a small smile on his lips. "I wish I had an ounce of your strength."

"I wasn't always strong. I had to learn. I knew that if I was strong for him, he'd be able to get through it, and when we lost our grandparents, he was months away from graduating. I couldn't let him fall behind when he'd come so far."

The death of our grandparents really hit Alex hard. We lost our grandma to leukemia within weeks of her being diagnosed, then only seven days later, our grandpa passed suddenly. The doctors couldn't pinpoint what his cause of death was, just put it down to a broken heart after losing the love of his life. It happened so fast. Before I could fully process what was happening, I was planning my grandpa's funeral too.

Alex was four months away from graduating college. He wanted to drop out to help me with the business and settle my grandparents' affairs, but I wouldn't let him.

I often wonder if it was cruel to make him stay at college, where he couldn't properly grieve, but I couldn't bear to see all his hard work go to waste when he only had a few months left to go.

"One thing that keeps me from spiraling is knowing my parents wouldn't have wanted me to be sad. They would have wanted me to enjoy life, to be happy, to do spontaneous things that bring me joy. Like dancing in the rain or baking cookies at two in the morning. Losing four of the most important people in my life taught me that life is precious. It can be taken from you like that." I click my fingers. "You only get one chance."

Some days, I can breathe a little easier. I don't feel so lost. But then everything comes crashing down, my heart breaks all over again, and I struggle to breathe because I remember they're never coming home.

I'm never going to hear the sound of their voice or their laughter, feel the way they smelled, or the warmth of their hug again. It hits me a little more often since Alex moved out. I'm completely alone for the first time in my life, and my mind has space to wonder.

There are so many moments they would have loved to experience—like seeing Alex be so disgustingly in love with someone who worships the ground he walks on.

"One of the things that haunts me and hurts the most is knowing my father—and my grandfather—won't be with me when I walk down the aisle. They won't get the chance to give me away, threaten my future husband to take care of me, or dance with me at my wedding."

There are so many moments in my life they should be here for, but they're gone because of someone's reckless actions.

The muscle in Ethan's jaw ticks. The fine lines around his gorgeous eyes crease a little as he looks at me, listening intently.

"I'd do anything to have them back, even just for a day. I always try to do something to keep their memory alive, like opening my bakery for my mom, listening to my grandpa's records on a Sunday, lying under the blanket my grandma knitted me, or wearing my father's Northwestern sweater that's hanging on by a thread." I smile, wiping my cheeks with my fingers. "I like to think they're with me every single day, as wild as that sounds, and that is what keeps me positive. That they're rooting for me, wherever they are, and I want to make them proud."

Ethan presses his mouth to mine so tenderly, like I'm made of glass, and rests his forehead on mine.

"They would be so fucking proud of you, J."

"Do you think so?"

"Yes." He nods slowly. "Because to have gone through loss like you have, and still have such a big heart?" He places his palm on my chest over my heart. I'm sure he can feel it beating wildly like a drum. "It takes an immense amount of strength and courage, and whoever gets to receive an iota of your love…I hope they treasure it and know exactly how precious it is."

*Will you treasure it?* I want to ask, but the thought gets stuck in the back of my throat.

He presses me against him and whispers, "I'm fucking proud of you, too."

# Chapter Fifteen



*Ethan*

I run my fingers through Jacob's soft hair, listening to his quiet breaths as he sleeps, his head resting on my chest. After his heartbreaking confession, we laid down on the couch, where I just held him while he quietly sobbed into my neck.

And I've never felt so helpless.

My heart shattered at the whole heap of emotions swirling in those beautiful eyes. The pain, the heartache Jacob harbors are so visceral, it feels like a heavy weight on my chest.

He's been carrying the weight of the world on his shoulders for nearly two decades. Putting everyone else first and not allowing himself time to grieve properly.

Just burying his head in the sandbox of denial and hiding his pain behind a sunny exterior, hoping the dark cloud won't show until he's alone, so he can drown in private.

I can't begin to imagine how he felt when he was burdened with debt, too. That alone would be enough to break some people, let alone with a mountain of grief on top.

I want to be a safe haven for him. A landing pad for when the grief becomes too strong to hide. I want to be his life raft. I want to be the one to show him he doesn't have to wade through the treacherous storm on his own. I'll hold him until he finds a man worthy of his all-encompassing love…and then I'll silently hate the fact that it's not me.

He deserves so much more than what I can give him, and I'm not selfish enough to ask him to wait for me.

*You were hard to love.*

Even after what Jacob said, Ian's words keep coming back to haunt me. They shouldn't phase me, not now that I finally have closure, but it still cuts deep, bringing back the fear I've hidden since I was a kid—that I'm unlovable, and that's why my dad left.

My phone begins to ping in quick succession where it's resting on the arm of the couch. I grimace, putting it on silent, and look down at Jacob. Thankfully, he doesn't stir. All the emotions pouring out must've really drained him.

The screen begins to fill with text bubbles from the group chat I'm in with some of the guys, and my stomach twists with guilt. These guys have tried so hard over the years to be a more prominent part of my life. They've shown me nothing but love and support, and the way I've repaid them is by keeping them at arm's length.

Fuck. How they haven't given up on me yet is a mystery.

Opening the group chat, I roll my lips to suppress my laughter.

Elliot: Who do you think would win in a fight? Han Solo or Indiana Jones?

Blaine: What kind of question is this?

Elliot: A valid one. *eye roll emoji*

Peyton: How can they fight when they are played by the same person?

Elliot: I'm asking hypothetically. I don't mean REALLY fight because it just wouldn't happen. Duh, Jonathan!

Zach: Han Solo would win, hands down.

Elliot: But why, Zachary?

Zach: How could he not? He's the best.

Peyton: But Indiana Jones has the strength. Han would try to charm his way out of the fight after a while. He'd probably shoot first, because that's what he does, but Indy would find some cover and wait until Han got all cocky thinking he'd won, then Indy would pull out the whip or throw a punch.

Zach: Nope. Not having it.

Zach: Han is a scoundrel, man. He would win the fight easily.

Peyton: I don't know, dude. I think he'd give up. Plus, I'm pretty sure Indy has been in more fights than Han.

Mitch: I have no idea who you're talking about.

Blaine: ... WTF?

Zach: You don't know who Han Solo and Indiana Jones are?

Mitch: No? Should I?

Peyton: Holy shit. Kick the rookie off the team. Now!

Zach: How can you not know who they are?

Mitch: Because I'm not old?

Peyton: GASP! What the actual fuck dude? Have you been living under a rock?

Blaine: Want me to put shaving cream in the rookie's gloves and skates? Pickles in his pants?

Elliot: Yeah! *high fives twinny*

Zach: How can you not know the coolest dude in the galaxy?

Mitch: Like Rocket Raccoon?

Zach: This conversation physically hurts me.

Elliot: Mitchell Henry, go away because you're distracting everyone from my joke.

Peyton: I thought it was a genuine question?

Blaine: I don't think El even knows what it is.

Elliot: The answer is...They could just fight...Solo.

Elliot: :D

Elliot: That was good, no?

Blaine: That was fucking terrible, twinny.

Peyton: *facepalm emoji*

Zach: ... Sometimes I question why I'm friends with you.

Mitch: I'm still confused.

I snort a laugh, then wince as Jacob shifts.

Shit.

I don't move an inch as he stirs before nuzzling his face back into my chest and going back to sleep, his hand curling around my ribs.

These guys, man. I don't know where I'd be without them. I know I need to be better, and after listening to Jacob, I need to apply the same logic to my life.

Because what if something happened to one of the guys and they didn't know how much I care for them? How much I genuinely love them? It would wreck me. I know it's going to take some time to rewire my brain away from self-preservation mode, but I need to.

Jacob's right.

You can't take things for granted. What if tomorrow never comes?

I chew on my bottom lip; it's time to start knocking down the proverbial barriers.

Ethan: I miss you guys.

Ethan: PS: Indiana Jones would win.

Elliot: Who is this Ethan imposter?

Blaine: Whoa! Hold my beer! (I'm drinking coffee but same thing) did I read that right?

Zach: … Am I dreaming?

Peyton: Is this another one of Elliot's lame jokes?

Elliot: My jokes are not LAME. You're lame. You big lanky lame-o.

Elliot: ETHAN! Have you been abducted by those British guards in the big furry hats?

Elliot: Send a Christmas tree emoji if you need help.

Elliot: It'll take me approximately twelve hours to get to you by the time I've packed and navigated the airports, but I'll be there!

Guilt washes through me like a wave. My chest tightens. Shit. It shouldn't come as a surprise to them that I care, but I know this is all my fault. That's what I led them to believe.

I'm going to change this. I have to.

Ethan: No, I don't need help, and no, I haven't been abducted by the King's Guards, but thank you for the offer, El. I realized I don't tell you guys enough how much you mean to me. I love you guys a lot. I hope you know that.

Peyton: Love you dude.

Blaine: Love you!

Zach: We love you too.

Mitch: ^^^ what they said.

Elliot: Aw grumpy pants, I'm getting a little misty eyed! I love you too. Here, have a photo of me as a superhero.

A second later, a photo comes through of Elliot in Jacob's bakery. He's twisted the apron around his neck like a cape. With one hand on his hip, the other punching the air, and his legs in a lunge, he looks like he's about to take off and fight some outer space enemies.

I smother my laughter with my hand and reply.

Ethan: Thanks, that's my new lock screen.

Elliot: You're welcome.

Elliot: PS: please bring back gifts *heart emoji*

"What's got you smiling like that?" Jacob's sleepy voice startles me. I didn't even feel him wake up.

I look down at him. His blue eyes are a little glassy from his tears and sleep. A soft smile on his face. I click on the photo and hand my phone over to Jacob.

He bursts into laughter, eyes sparkling with glee. "He's such a great guy."

I nod, grinning. "He is. He's got a heart of gold. All the guys are protective of him because he's just one of the good ones, you know? He would help anyone with anything, and I love that he doesn't give a shit about what anyone thinks."

Jacob hands me my phone back and gives me a sad smile. "You could learn something from him."

"What do you mean?" I frown.

He places his hand on my chest and rests his chin on top, looking up at me. "He is the epitome of living life to the fullest. He seems to just enjoy every day. He lets people in and wears his heart on his sleeve. I'm not saying the way you cope with things is wrong, but these guys?" He points at my phone. "They love you, so much. You're important to them, but you have this, like, barrier separating them from you. Life is too short to keep people who genuinely love you on the outside, because before you know it, it'll be too late, and you won't get that time back."

"I was just thinking about that." I stretch out and put my phone on the coffee table. "I've been playing in the NHL for nearly twenty years now, and I haven't let anyone get close to me. Peyton and Kendrick are probably the closest, but even then, not that much. I couldn't stop thinking about what you said—that life is precious, so I told them I missed them, and they thought I was joking around."

He gives a sorrowful smile. "How did that make you feel?"

"It made me feel like shit," I confess. The ache in my chest returns. "I couldn't help but think, *What if something happens to them and they don't know I care?* I would fucking hate that. I know I've gotta change. I don't want to be this guarded asshole who's afraid of showing his emotions."

"I think they know you care. People have different love languages, and love languages aren't just exclusive to romantic relationships—they filter into platonic relation- ships, too. Some people will know you care because you do something for them or because you give them your undi- vided attention, but some need to hear the words. They thrive on words of affirmation, so they need to hear you say it to believe it."

"That makes sense." I lick my lips. "What is yours?"

"Mine?" He chuckles. "Physical touch. I'm a sucker for hand-holding, kissing, or a subtle caress. I'm a cuddler, if you hadn't guessed." He squeezes my torso with one arm, then rests his chin on my chest, looking back up at me, a sweet smile on his lips. "It's okay to show them you care. It won't take away their love for you—if anything, it'll only make it grow stronger."

"What's it like? Playing hockey?" Jacob asks.

We've just finished eating dinner outside because it's such a beautiful night. It's still warm enough to sit in shorts and a t-shirt. The sky is soft pink with orange hues as the sun sets, casting Jacob in the most gorgeous glow.

"It's incredible, but it can also be pretty tough at times. You experience the highest of highs, and the lowest of lows. You're being paid to play the sport you love, which is awesome, but with that comes a lot of stipulations. It takes a lot of dedication and sacrifice. I didn't really have a normal childhood growing up. My dad had me skating before I could actually walk, then I started learning how to play hockey at four, and I would skate most mornings before school and then again after school."

Jacob takes a sip of his wine, eyeing me over the glass. "Will you tell me about your dad?"

I take a few gulps of my beer and sigh. "We didn't have the best relationship, but I couldn't see that when I was younger. It was very one-sided. I used to look up to him. I thought he was the best person in the world, but now that I'm older—and wiser, I guess—I can see that he put a lot of pressure on me. His expectations were too high, especially for a kid still learning."

Jacob frowns. "What did he do?"

"If I had a shit practice or lost a game, he would give me the silent treatment. Wouldn't speak to me for days. He used to give me this look like he was ashamed of me. Like I was a disappointment."

"I… I don't know what to say. I'm so sorry you went through that."

I shrug. "In a way, I'm glad he's not in my life anymore. He wasn't always a nice guy to my mom, either, but I still think about the day he left. I waited for over an hour for him to pick me up. My coach came out and found me sitting on the curb with my bag, so he called my mom, but she couldn't leave work, so he took me home. He stayed with me until she arrived and made me this giant bowl of pasta." I hold my hands out to mimic the size of it. "It was fucking huge, bigger than my dad ever let me have, but then I saw the pity in his eyes and clammed up. I couldn't eat it because I hated that look in his eye."

Jacob doesn't say anything. He just reaches for my hand and holds it. But I can't help but notice that he's not giving me *that* look.

He doesn't pity me.

He gets me.

To some of us, the ice is our safe haven, and it became that for me. It was the only time I could switch off my brain and feel like I was good at something. The second my skate touched that ice, the noise in my head stopped. It was silent. Peaceful.

Touching Jacob feels the same way. We're stepping into dangerous territory doing what we're doing. And that's why I can't let my feelings go any further.

# Chapter Sixteen

*Jacob*

"Soooo?" Alex drawls. "How's it going? Any exciting developments I should know about?"

I roll my eyes and laugh. "You're relentless sometimes."

"Come on. You've had this glow on your cheeks every time I've spoken to you since the wedding, and I know what that glow means, Jake, because it happens to me every time Blaine fu—"

"La la la!" I sing, covering my ears with my hands. "Fine, fine! I'll tell you."

He grins wickedly, doing a "give it to me" gesture with his hands.

I get up from where I've been lying on the bed and close the bedroom door. I took advantage of Ethan's jacuzzi bathtub while he's in the gym, secretly wishing he was here enjoying it with me, and I was about to relax with a book when Alex called on FaceTime. He's currently got his phone propped up on the counter in the bakery while getting today's selection started. It's six in the morning there, so luckily, he's on his own and we can talk without anyone overhearing.

"Well, I'm not supposed to tell you, so please don't share it with Blaine, but we're having a…fling," I announce, but the word tastes bitter on my tongue. It doesn't feel right.

I mean, the sex is incredible, and I'm learning things about myself.. Ethan has this…dominant energy about him, and I wouldn't have expected to enjoy it the way I have.

But it feels like more than *just sex* because there's emotion behind it. Or maybe my brain is romanticizing it because we're essentially having a time-restricted friends-with-benefits arrangement.

Except I have feelings.

Feelings that are growing every day we're together.

Alex's jaw drops. His eyes widen comically before his face lights up with a giant grin. "Stop, really?"

I nod, sitting back down on the bed and leaning back against the pillows. "It's only while we're here, then it ends when we go back to Chicago."

His brows knit in concern. "And you're okay with that?"

"Yeah, I am. I mean, would I like to see where things go when we get home? Of course I would, but he's got things he needs to focus on, and call me crazy, but even having this…whatever it is, has been one of the most exhilarating experiences of my life."

It's the most exciting my life has been in a very long time. I used to be a social butterfly before my grandparents passed away, but I've been too busy with the bakery.

Plus, no one from that time cared enough to stick around anyway.

"As long as you're sure. I don't want to see you get hurt."

"I won't. I wouldn't have agreed to this if I wasn't sure."

Alex hums, clearly not believing me, but thankfully he doesn't call me out on it.

"Can I ask you something?" I ask.

"Anything, always."

Since I bared my soul the other day to Ethan, his words have been playing through my mind. I've been trying to be strong for Alex all these years, when maybe I didn't need to.

"Do you ever think about mom and dad?"

Alex freezes. His mouth opens and closes twice before he swallows hard.

"All the time," he says, his voice sad. "I sometimes feel like shit because my memories are patchy, and then I get mad at myself for not being able to remember them as clearly as I should."

"You were so young, Alex; it's normal not to remember everything. Please don't be mad at yourself for that."

"I know, but I should remember. They were our parents, you know? I wish I had memories other than the stories I've been told or the photographs."

My heart breaks because I remember a lot. Like the type of cake I'd bake with my mom or my dad getting frustrated with my math teacher because she was giving me complex homework I couldn't understand. Vacations at the beach and day trips to the zoo. And little details like the exact pizza place my dad would order from every Saturday night or the time he let me beep the horn in his truck and I thought it was the funniest thing in the world. Thinking back to when they were here helps me through the harder days.

But Alex was only seven when they passed, and he doesn't have that.

"I wish there was something I could do."

He shakes his head and smiles, but it's a sad smile.

"I told Ethan about them and how some days are harder than others."

"Jake, why didn't you ever tell me that?"

I look down at my lap, fiddling with the hem of my shorts. Chewing on the inside of my bottom lip, I take a deep inhale. "I've always wanted to be strong for you, and I thought it wouldn't be fair to share my grief with you. I didn't want to be a burden when I was supposed to be your support."

"You will never be a burden to me, Jake. You can share anything with me—literally *anything*. I wouldn't be the person I am today without you, and I could've helped you through it. We could've done it together and shared the weight of it together."

Wiping my eyes with the heel of my palm, I give him a shaky smile. "I'm sorry. I'll try to be better."

"You're everything to me, Jake." His voice cracks, his own emotions bubbling. "I'd be lost without you, and I'm always here for you. Whatever you tell me, I'll never think differently of you. Well, unless you tell me you killed a dog or something, but I love you so much." He wipes his eyes. "I'm sorry if I've ever made you feel like you can't come to me."

My eyes sting. "I love you too, and you haven't made me feel that way at all. It's all in my head."

"I think we've been so focused on trying to stay strong for each other that we've ended up hurting ourselves in the process."

Shit. He's right.

Between the spiraling debt and trying to run a business, we've been in survival mode. I've suppressed my feelings to keep going, but disregarding them is not healthy. It's just been building up inside, like a boiling pot threatening to spill over.

Weirdly, sharing my vulnerable side with Ethan helped. I feel lighter in some ways simply for acknowledging that I struggle sometimes.

I guess we're similar in some ways. He doesn't like to show emotion because of his previous trauma, and I don't like to share my grief because I don't want my brother to see me as anything but strong.

When he's actually a lot stronger than I give him credit for.

"J?" Ethan calls out from the kitchen. "Jacob?"

I look up from where I've been curled up on the couch, completely engrossed in the book I started this morning. I don't know what time it is or how long I've been reading for, but when Ethan appears in the doorway, there's a playful grin on his lips.

"It's raining."

Stretching, I glance over my shoulder to the window. The rain is coming down so heavily I can barely see the rosebush outside the window. I've been so lost in my fictional world that I didn't notice it turn cloudy and gloomy.

I turn back to Ethan, puzzled. "But it's summer?"

He shrugs. "It's England, J. It rains ninety percent of the time, regardless of what time of year it is. Come." He holds his hand out.

Placing my book down, I slowly stand up. Slipping my hand in his, I ask, "What are we doing?"

"You mentioned the other day that you like to do things that bring you joy, and one of the things you mentioned was dancing in the rain." He grins, leading me through the kitchen to the patio doors. He picks up the remote to his sound system, presses a button, and Fleetwood Mac's "Rumours" begins to filter through the speakers. "So, we're going to do just that."

My stomach flips. He remembered that? Wow. This man. Ian was a fucking idiot for thinking this man was hard to love.

And how did he know this was my favorite album?

Ethan is nothing but perfect to me.

I slip my feet into my shoes and follow him outside.

"Ohmigod!" I shriek, my hands instinctively coming up to shield my eyes.

The rain is coming down in sheets, and I'm soaked within seconds, but the temperature is still surprisingly warm.

Ethan wraps his arms around my waist, pulling me close. My arms wind around his neck, and our bodies sway to the music coming through the doors, mixed with the sound of the raindrops hitting the patio and thunder crackling in the distance. I grin up at him as he smiles down at me. Those cute-as-fuck dimples pop on his cheek. The dark hair peeking out from beneath his backward baseball cap sticks to his face.

He's so devastatingly handsome, it hurts.

I press my lips to his in a tender kiss before closing my eyes and tilting my head up to the sky.

I feel so carefree. I don't give a shit that every inch of me is soaking wet. It's like the rain is washing away all the burdens that have been weighing me down, cleansing me and my soul.

Ethan takes my hand, and with the other on the base of my spine, he leads me around the patio in a waltz. He hums along to "Dreams", spinning and dipping me in an extravagant way. I'm so freaking happy at this moment that my cheeks are aching from smiling.

When he pulls me back to his chest, he dips his head and captures my lips with his. I lose myself in the warmth of his mouth.

In the soft but guided strokes of his tongue against mine.

My hands snake up around his neck, finding purpose as I lean into his solid body.

His kisses captivate me. Own me in ways I've only ever read about in books. I didn't think it was possible for someone to make my toes curl in my shoes with a single kiss, but he does.

The hold Ethan has on my jaw is possessive, powerful. His kiss is tender but sexual and demanding at the same time.

It feels like he's claiming me.

The next thing I know, he has his hands beneath my ass, and he's picking me up. I wrap my legs around his waist, feeling his hard length through his shorts, and cradle his face in my hands. His dark chocolate eyes are completely black. Shining like obsidian.

I trace my finger over his swollen lips, then tap his nose. Once.

Raindrops roll down his face, some getting caught in his eyelashes, and the smile he gives me knocks the breath from my lungs.

I kiss him again and again. Our tongues tangle in gentle but needy caresses, causing goosebumps to erupt across my skin that have nothing to do with the British weather.

Ethan carries me inside, holding me up with one arm while he opens the door and kicks off his shoes before carrying me up the stairs. The entire time, our mouths remain locked. Fused together with nothing but pure heat and want. The only time we separate is when he sits me on the edge of the bathroom counter in his en suite.

I take in the gorgeous man in front of me. His chest rises and falls in quick succession. His clothes are dripping, his white shirt now see-through. Every ridge of his muscles is visible, his nipples poke through the fabric, and his shorts do nothing to conceal his erection.

He's mouth-watering.

Ethan reaches behind the glass screen and turns on the shower, then strips out of his clothes, leaving them in a wet heap on the floor. I move to take off my shirt, but he raises his hand to stop me.

"Let me," he says.

He takes my hand, guiding me back onto my feet, and starts to slowly remove my t-shirt, pressing soft butterfly kisses over my shoulder and collarbone and up my neck.

My t-shirt joins the pile of wet clothes on the floor as he kneels in front of me. Slipping my shoes off, he places them to one side before unbuttoning my shorts. He curves his fingers into the waistband and pulls them down my legs carefully, taking the time to kiss the inside of both knees as he goes.

When I'm down to just my black briefs, he sits back on his haunches and takes me in. His thick cock juts out hard and heavy, precome beading at the tip. I feel the searing heat of his stare as they travel from my feet all the way up my body, taking me in, inch by inch, until our eyes lock.

With any other man, I might have felt self-conscious standing here, completely exposed. But with Ethan? Ethan has this ability to make me feel like I'm the most beautiful man to walk the earth. He boosts my confidence in a way I've only ever dreamed of.

"You're so fucking sexy, J." His tongue licks over his bottom lip, eyeing me like I'm a decadent dessert.

My dick twitches in my briefs, and he smirks.

"I've got you." He leans forward to remove my under- wear, gently lifting my leg with a hand on my ankle.

Ethan's hands roam up my legs, ghosting over my calves and curving around the backs of my thighs, stopping just beneath my cheeks. His warm breath ghosts over the head of my cock, and I shiver.

"Let's get you warmed up," he says as he looks up at me, smirking.

Standing up, he wraps an arm around me and lifts me off my feet. He carries me into the shower and carefully puts me down. I sigh as the warm water hits my wet skin.

"Oh, that feels so good!" As I turn to put my face under

the water, Ethan's hands glide around to my stomach, and his cock rests against my crease.

"Mmm, it does." He rolls his hips, sliding his cock between my cheeks.

He nuzzles his face into the crook of my neck as I lean back against him, pressing kisses over my pulse before grazing his teeth and sucking on the skin where my neck meets my shoulders.

"Ethan," I breathe.

He grabs the bottle of shower gel and squeezes some into his hand before gliding it over me, across my arms and chest, and between my legs, giving my hard cock a teasing stroke before moving around to wash between my crease.

Ethan peppers kisses all over my skin as he washes the soap away, and once I'm rinsed clean, he takes my chin in his hand and angles my head toward him. The fire in his gaze sends desire down my spine like a wildfire.

"Can I taste you?" he whispers.

I nod wordlessly.

With a fierce kiss to my mouth, he lets my chin go and drops to his knees.

"Hands on the wall," he demands.

Shaking, I place my hands on the tiled wall and glance over my shoulder. The sight of him on his knees is one I will never forget. He pulls my cheeks apart, and I catch him as he slides his tongue over his lips before he leans in and flicks the tip over my hole.

My eyes roll to the back of my head, my moan echoing off the bathroom walls. He licks and sucks and eats me like I'm his last meal. His tongue spears in and out of me, moaning and slurping, and I lose my goddamn mind from the rough scrape of his stubble against my heated flesh.

"Ethan! Fuck," I moan, curling my fingers into the tiles.

His hand connects with my ass cheek in a firm slap as he pulls back, and I whimper at the loss of his mouth and the pleasant sting from his hand.

He steps out of the shower and grabs a condom and some lube from a drawer, returning seconds later with his thick cock sheathed and covered in lube.

"You taste so fucking good, Jacob," he growls as he moves my head to the side so he can claim my lips again.

"I could eat you every day," he states before our tongues entwine as his lubed fingers coat my hole.

He lines himself, and I tense slightly as he breaches the ring of muscle, letting out a shaky breath. His hands are on my hips, pulling my cheeks apart, but he's letting me take control. I ease back more, feeling him break past that initial burn, and he groans.

"You look so beautiful. Your hole wrapped around my cock, taking me like such a good boy."

I moan as he traces my hole with his thumb.

"You're so fucking hot. You love my cock, don't you? You love how it fills you up so good. How deep I can fuck you."

"Yesss!" I nod desperately. "Yes, I love how good your cock makes me feel."

His thumb continues to trace my stretched hole, and my breath comes out in a shudder. Once he's bottomed out and my ass is pressed up against his hips, he leans in and nips my ear. "I'm gonna let you do the work, baby. Fuck me. Use me like I'm one of your toys. I wanna see how desperate you are for me."

Holy shit. I think I may combust from his words alone. I begin to slowly rock my hips, easing off him a few inches before rolling back and taking him in deep. His hands are resting loosely on my hips, keeping me steady while his words make me go wild.

"Fuck, baby, that's it, back up on me. Take all of my cock. Good boy, you take me so well."

I moan, arching my back. The angle causes him to hit my prostate with every glide of my hips. I drop one of my hands from the wall to stroke myself, then freeze as Ethan's hand smooths over the curve of my spine and wraps around the front of my throat.

Those things I didn't know I would enjoy before Ethan? Add hand necklaces to the list, because there's nothing I enjoy more than Ethan's hand around my throat while his cock is buried so deep inside me.

"Don't touch yourself. I'll tell you when you can come. Your come is mine, and I'll be the one to decide when I want it."

His tone is commanding, and I'm barely holding on. My eyes roll as I bounce back on his cock in fast and shallow thrusts, moaning his name. His labored breaths in my ears send shivers down my spine.

I'm so close.

"That's it, baby. Fuck yeah. Ride me, just like that. Milk my cock and make me see heaven, Jacob."

I can't take it anymore.

"Shit, I'm gonna come," I gasp.

He nips my ear with his teeth, his hand reaching around to fist my cock as he growls, "Come for me, baby."

My toes curl into the shower floor as my release hits. My body shudders, convulsing as ropes of come hit the tiles, and within seconds, Ethan roars as I feel the searing heat of his orgasm through the condom.

Tingles rush through my veins, my legs turning into jell-o from coming that hard. I slump against Ethan, and he hugs me close to him, holding me up.

I'm aware of him washing away the lube from between my cheeks and turning off the shower. I'm aware of how he carries me out of the shower and wraps me in a towel.

I'm also aware of how hard my heart is pounding for this man and how much it's going to hurt when this is over.

# Chapter Seventeen

*Ethan*

"I find all of this so fascinating," Jacob states, gazing up at the marble statue in front of us. The information sign says it's Apollo, sculpted in 1577. "I wonder if the people who made these ever thought that they would be displayed proudly in a museum centuries later."

"Probably not," I reply, turning to face him. "But I've always wondered why all these sculptures have small cocks."

"Ethan!" Jacob snorts under his breath, slapping my arm playfully with the back of his hand. "I think I read somewhere that having a small penis was a sign of virtue, and having a big cock was a sign of barbarism, little self-control, and a gluttonous appetite."

He gives me a knowing look. "Which, we know, isn't the case now, as you are far from a barbarian."

I roll my lips, suppressing a smile. "Are you saying that I

wouldn't have a marble statue of me in the nude in the future? Maybe in the Hockey Hall of Fame?"

"No, I'm not saying that, but if they did, I would be the first in line for the unveiling," he says, winking.

We've come to London to do some more exploring, including a visit to the Victoria and Albert Museum, which was on Jacob's bucket list. I booked us a night at Claridge's and also booked a table tomorrow for afternoon tea.

Our time here is coming to an end. In a few days, we'll be heading back to Chicago, and I'm not sure how I feel about it. When I suggested giving into desire while we're here, I didn't expect to find myself so…at ease with Jacob.

It feels very natural. Seamless.

It makes me question whether we could continue this when we get back, but then the negative side of my brain questions if it's this good because there are no expectations. If it's easy because we're just giving in to the chemistry, no strings attached.

"Do you think you'll end up being in the Hockey Hall of Fame?" Jacob asks after a beat, pulling me out of my head.

I shrug. "No idea."

There are rumors I'll be nominated once I'm eligible. You have to be fully retired for a minimum of three years before you can be considered, so it's not something I like to think about.

"I think you will. I can understand your fears, Ethan, of not knowing who you are outside of hockey, but you can have this." He motions around us. "In the world of hockey, your name would be here. Your legacy will be so magnificent, so awed by many, for generations to come. You won't be forgotten the second you hang up your skates. Like, your name is engraved on the Stanley Cup how many times?"

My lips twitch. "Five."

"Five, Ethan, *five*. I know nothing about hockey, but I know for sure that that is an incredible achievement. Plus, you've won Gold for Canada in the Olympics twice, along with a number of other gold medals and awards."

Unsure how to handle his high praise, I turn and walk to the next statue, gazing up at the magnificent sculpture.

Hockey has been my life for as long as I can remember, and it's a bittersweet pill to swallow knowing that my time playing professionally is coming to an end.

Jacob steps in front of me, reaching up to cup my face with one hand. "Don't run away from me. I don't think you truly see how special you are—which is amazing. You're incredibly humble for someone in your position, with your talent, but I think you underestimate the power your name has. Just because you hang up your skates in the professional sense doesn't mean your involvement in hockey is over."

I furrow my brows in a frown. "What do you mean?"

"What if you started something like a foundation for underprivileged kids to play hockey? Kids just like you were. Think about how many kids are out there who have so much potential, but whose parents or caregivers can't afford it."

There's a pang in my chest at the thought. I was fortunate that my mom never gave up. She saw something special in me. Saw the passion and dedication I had and did whatever she possibly could to ensure I had the means to keep playing, but not all kids get that opportunity.

And it's not for a lack of trying. Some parents can't physically do what my mom did, working three jobs and pouring every cent that wasn't for rent or food into my hockey future.

I'm so fucking lucky to have my mom.

"There were a lot of kids like me growing up. It's an expensive sport, and kids grow out of their equipment so quickly." I chew on the corner of my lip. "I'm not very… personable, though."

I'm not good with people, despite having been chosen as Captain. But that's different. When it comes to hockey, I'm in my element, talking to guys already on the same wavelength.

I struggle with everything else.

"I don't know how it would work. You'd probably need some legal advice, but you could hire someone to do the people-ing, and you could be as much or as little involved as you wanted."

"Maybe I could speak with some of my sponsors, see if they would want to donate too." My mind begins to run wild at all the possibilities. "I could provide equipment and help pay for ice time, and it would be completely inclusive, since so many girls don't get the same opportunities boys do." I slip my phone out of the pocket of my jeans and start to type in my notes app as the ideas rush to the surface. "I could do like an age bracket. Five to seventeen or something, because if you're picked up by a top NCAA college, you'll usually get your equipment for free."

"There you go." He squeezes my bicep, tipping his head up to face me, and flashes me a dazzling smile. "I have no idea what you just said, but the passion in your eyes speaks volumes. Just because you're not on the ice yourself doesn't mean your impact on the sport has to end there. Help pave the way for the next generation of superstars in honor of that little boy who never gave up."

Fuck. The stupid organ in my chest swells at his earnest expression. I lean down, pressing my lips to his in a sweet kiss. "You're wonderful, you know that?"

"Well," he drawls with a teasing grin. "I have my moments, but I'm not opposed to hearing it coming from you."

I wrap my arms around his waist, reaching around as I slip my tongue into his mouth and swallow his soft moan as I squeeze the delicious globes of his ass.

"Ethan," Jacob says in a hushed tone against my mouth. I raise my head slightly, trailing kisses down the column of his throat. "You're being a barbarian in front of Jason."

I chuckle quietly into his neck. I glance up at the marble statue and give a small nod. "I do apologize, Sir." I turn back to Jacob. "Maybe the big cock myth is right because I do have a gluttonous appetite when it comes to you—and very little self-control."

Jacob bites down on his bottom lip, smoothing his hand up my chest. "You're insatiable, and I love it."

I tug his lip between my teeth. "How soon can we get out of here, then?"

Jacob props his head on his fist, the index finger of his other hand tracing the lines of the tattoos on my arm. His cheeks are flushed pink from his recent orgasm. Dark blond hair damp with sweat.

We should probably take a shower, but I'm too worn out to move.

When we left the museum, we visited Harrods before working our way through various bakeries in Soho and Covent Garden. By the time we returned to the hotel, I was on such a sugar rush that I needed a nap, but it was worth every second.

Watching Jacob get so inspired by the different delicacies we tried, I knew I would break my diet every day to watch the way his face lit up the way it did.

After we napped together, we ordered room service, then devoured each other for dessert. Since that night of the wedding, I've become ravenous for him.

Starved.

And no matter how many times I taste him or fuck him, I don't think I'll ever get enough of Jacob. I wasn't kidding in the museum earlier when I said I have a gluttonous appetite when it comes to him.

"Have you ever lost any of your teeth?"

I turn my head on the pillow to look at him, confused. "Don't they do pillow talk in those sexy books you read, J?"

His mouth gapes. "You've been reading my books?"

"I haven't read them, no." I give him a wry grin. "But I may have flicked through some pages. I've gotta admit, no wonder you're a little firecracker."

He left one of his books on the kitchen counter the other day, and curiosity got the better of me. It was safe to say I was hard within a few pages, my mind replacing the two guys on the page with Jacob and myself. It had me slapping the book closed and hunting him down so I could make it real.

He ghosts his hand down my chest to where my soft cock rests against my thigh. He cups his hand around me and gives my junk a gentle squeeze.

I hiss between clenched teeth. "You need to give me time to recover. I'm ten years older than you, remember?"

"Mmm," he lazily agrees, leaning in to nip my chin. "And aged like a fine wine."

I choke out a laugh. "Okay, enough of that." I roll over onto my side and slip my arm around his waist, pinching his ass. "I've lost my three front teeth," I admit, baring my teeth and pointing to the ones in question.

His brows shoot up. "How did that happen?"

"I took a puck to the face."

"Oh my god," he gasps, his hand cupping my jaw. "Aren't you scared they'll come out again?"

"I have a flipper, so they just pop out. I lost the first one in the juniors. Then in my second year with the Thunder, I took a slap shot to the face and lost another two. I figured there was no point in getting them fixed until I retire in case it happened again."

"How come I've never noticed this?"

"Because I don't take it out around you." I huff a laugh. "It's not the most attractive thing, J."

Jacob's eyes sparkle with mischief. "Let me see."

I raise my brows. "You want to see me without my teeth?"

He nods, more excited than I thought he would be at

seeing me that way. Ian hated seeing me without my teeth in.

"Come on. I lived with my grandparents, both who had dentures. I'm used to seeing a gummy smile."

I snort, shaking my head. I quickly pop them out, giving him a wide, toothy—or rather, tooth*less*—smile before putting them back in.

He grins, pressing a kiss to my lips. "I still think you're the most handsome man I've ever seen."

"Such a charmer." I shake my head slightly, feeling my face heat under his compliment.

He runs his fingers through the hair on my chest, grazing his nails against my skin. "Just being honest. Plus, is it weird I kinda want to know what it would feel like to get a blow job from you without your teeth in?"

I burst into laughter.

He grins. "What?"

Shaking my head, I trail my lips up his neck and nip his lobe.

"Do you ever go to the games with Alex?"

He shakes his head. "No, I haven't been to any. This sounds a little crazy, considering I'm laying in bed, naked, with you, but I haven't had the best experience with guys who play sports."

My body goes rigid. "What do you mean?"

"When I was in high school, I was bullied by some of the guys on the football team and a couple from the hockey team. I've always been smaller and quiet, and I was kind of a loner because nobody wanted to be friends with the kid whose parents died. They saw me as weird, and they used to say some pretty awful things to me."

I rise up on my elbow, keeping my eyes locked on him. My jaw clenches as I try to squash the anger bubbling away inside me as he continues.

"They would push me around, or steal my lunch, or do things like knock my books out of my arms while I was walking down the stairs…" He sighs, "Basically, they were just assholes, but their size scared me. I knew they could really hurt me, and I wouldn't have been able to protect myself, and that terrified me. I didn't fight back or report them because I was too afraid of what they would do."

"I'm so sorry that happened to you." I cradle his jaw with my hand, smoothing my thumb over the curve of his lips. "If I'd been there, I would have broken their fucking legs if they laid a finger on you."

He kisses the pad of my thumb and smiles. "You were busy being a hockey superstar when I was in high school. They idolized you. They had photos of you in their lockers and everything," he admits, laughing quietly. "Alex and Blaine have invited me a few times, but I haven't taken them up on it. It took me a while to teach my brain that you guys weren't going to hurt me, but every time I meet someone new, it's like a wave of panic, even after all this time."

I noticed how his shoulders tensed up the first time when we filmed in the bakery. The subtle way Alex would comfort him. It pains me that he went through that, and that the aftermath of those kids' actions still impacts him to this day.

I chew on the inside of my cheek, debating whether to ask the question that's been playing on my mind. Taking a deep breath, I bite the bullet and ask, "Were you afraid of me when we first met?"

Jacob's silence tells me everything, and my heart sinks

into the pit of my stomach. He gives me a small smile, but it's filled with sadness.

"Yes, but I think part of that fear was because I found you so damn attractive. You were a danger to me in a very different sense than those idiots in school. You were a danger to my heart."

## Chapter Eighteen

*Ethan*

The featherlight feel of fingers tracing my abdomen stirs me awake. Blinking open my eyes, I'm greeted by sunshine, but it's not the one in the sky. The morning sun creates a glowing halo around Jacob's smiling face.

"Good morning, birthday boy," he sings, leaning down to press a smacking kiss against my lips.

Before he can pull away, I curve my hand around the back of his head and deepen the kiss. I want to hit the pause button and stay here in our bubble, but I know reality won't wait for a daydream.

"Good morning." My voice comes out like gravel. "I have to say, this is a great way to wake up."

He grins at me. "Good. I don't want you to think about anything today except relaxing and enjoying yourself." I open my mouth to argue but he silences me, pressing a finger to my lips. "Nope. That means no cooking or even making a cup of coffee. You're doing absolutely nothing all day. Although, maybe I'll let you work out if you want to, but I think we should try another form of cardio." Mischief sparkles in his gorgeous blue eyes.

Lacing my fingers through the strands of his dark blond hair, I pull him forward until our lips are a breath apart.

"Is that right?" I mumble.

"Mmm," he hums.

Our lips meet again. He tastes like minty toothpaste and smells like his passion fruit shower gel, and I'm mentally kicking myself for sleeping in.

For wasting time when I could've been with him.

I greedily swallow each of his low whimpers as we suck on each other's tongue with little finesse, and when I pull him on top of me, his lithe body lays between my legs. My cock is hard and heavy against my stomach, and there's no way he can't feel how hard I am beneath the sheets.

"Mmm, we don't have time right now as your birthday treat is in the oven. Save it for later, big boy." He props himself up on his elbows, but teasingly rolls his hips.

I tip my head back into the pillow and groan. "You're a fucking tease, do you know that?"

"Yep." He grins before adding, "But you'll thank me later."

With a final kiss to my lips, he climbs off me and heads back downstairs before I can argue.

When I'm showered and dressed, I head to the kitchen. The smell of vanilla makes my stomach grumble, and as soon as I walk in, my mom throws her arms around me and squeezes the breath out of me.

"Happy birthday, my favorite child."

"I'm your only child," I grumble.

"Exactly. I didn't want any more because you're my favorite." She grins, patting my cheek. "Come, open your cards and presents. Jacob tells me you haven't got any plans today so I'm taking you both for lunch. There's a cute little pub that does the most amazing Sunday roast."

"You don't have to do that."

She places her fists on her hips and glares at me. "Ethan, you're my son and it's your birthday. It's part of my motherly privilege to take you out to celebrate so just be quiet and open your cards."

I fight a smile and do as I'm told, taking a seat at the island where they've placed a few cards and presents. There's a balloon on the counter too which reads, *Practically Prehistoric*.

Jacob chuckles, placing a cup of coffee in front of me. He presses a kiss to my cheek, and I catch my mom's eyes light up.

I know how much she wants me to find someone. While she's never settled with someone since my dad left, she's always championed love. Always encouraged me to get out there and find my guy.

I hope one day she does meet someone who is worthy of her because she's such a fucking amazing person, and anyone would be lucky to have her in their life.

It's early in the evening when Jacob grabs my hand and leads me into the living room. After having lunch with my mom, we got back to my house where Jacob banished me from going anywhere near the kitchen. So I stayed in the gym until he came to get me.

For the first time in years, I've really enjoyed my birthday, and it's all because of this guy.

With a hand on my chest, he pushes me back onto the couch, then points his finger at me.

"Now wait here. I'll be right back." He starts to walk backward, keeping his eyes fixed on me. "Don't move."

Once he's out of sight, I shift to get comfortable, but the sound of his shout from the kitchen causes me to freeze.

"I said don't move!"

I grin and settle back down on the couch.

A few minutes later, Jacob walks into the living room, holding a delicately decorated cupcake. It has a lone lit candle, shielded by his palm. He drops his hand to his side when he's standing between my knees and begins to sing "Happy Birthday". I can't contain my bashful grin. I'm pretty sure my cheeks are heating with embarrassment.

When the song comes to an end, he holds the cake out in front of me. "Make a wish."

I close my eyes and make my wish.

*Can I keep you when we get home?*

I blow out the candle and smile at Jacob. "Is this what you were doing this afternoon?"

He nods. "I baked them this morning and just finished decorating them."

"Thank you."

"You're welcome. Now sit back." He pushes my chest so I'm back against the couch before carefully removing the candle and placing it on the coffee table. Then he drops to his knees between my spread thighs. "It's time for your birthday gift."

"You're very bossy today," I tease.

Placing the cupcake on the floor beside him, he smooths his hands up my thighs to my groin, his teeth digging into his plush bottom lip. My cock takes notice instantly, thickening inside my boxers.

"J…" I say in warning.

His fingers curl into the elastic waistband of my shorts and tug them down my legs, along with my boxers. My hard dick slaps my abdomen. Precome beads at the tip, smearing against my stomach, and it takes everything in me not to take over.

"Shit," I gasp, gripping the couch cushions to stop myself from grabbing his head. "You're killing me here."

"Your thighs," he says, desire laced in his voice. He runs his hands up the sides of my quads. I shiver as he drags his nails against my skin on the way down. "They're so thick and solid. I love them."

My dick twitches, wanting Jacob to love that part of my body rather than my thighs.

His lips quirk. "Impatient, I see."

Leaning up on his knees, his delicate fingers wrap around the base of my cock. He pumps his hand up and down my shaft, rolling my foreskin down to expose the swollen mushroom head. His tongue peeks out to swipe the bead of precome while his eyes remain fixed on mine. Those blue hues blaze with heat and a mischievous glint.

"Jacob," I moan when his tongue teases the sensitive glans with another tormenting lick.

He wraps his plush lips around me and sucks on the tip,

his tongue teasing the sensitive glans. My head hits the back of the couch, and I actually let out a whine when he releases me.

He snickers, but as I'm about to tell him to keep going, he picks up the cupcake. He scoops up some of the frosting with two fingers, then wraps his other hand around the base of my cock to steady my shaft.

"Fuckkkk!" I grunt as he smears the frosting down the length of my cock.

The muscles in my thighs tremble as he slowly licks the frosting away from root to tip in tantalizing strokes of his tongue.

My body shudders as he takes me into the warm heat of his mouth. His lips stretch around my cock, taking me in deeper until I hit the back of his throat. Ecstasy burns through my veins, and my balls tighten. Jacob's fingers massage the heavy sac as his head bobs. There are tears swimming in his eyes from the way he deepthroats my dick like a dream, and he's the most beautiful man I've ever seen.

He pulls off with a pop and picks up more cupcake frosting to spread onto my balls before sucking each heavy nut like a starved man.

There's no way I'm going to last. Nails dig into the juncture of my thighs as he takes me in as far as he can, and I can't hold back any longer.

"J... I'm gonna come," I grit out behind clenched teeth in warning.

He hums around my length, sucking harder, and the vibrations trigger my release. He swallows every drop of come, sucking me dry until I'm shaking and disoriented. He releases me with a pop, and I sag into the couch like a deflated balloon.

Jacob stands up, wiping the remnants of my come from the corner of his mouth with his finger and sucking it clean.

"Happy Birthday," he sings, grinning.

My chest heaves as my lungs go into overtime, working hard to regain my breath. "I'm never gonna be able to look at a cupcake the same way."

His eyes twinkle in delight. He takes a bite of the cake and then holds it out to me. But it's not the cake I want.

Instead, I grab his hips and pull him onto my lap. Not caring that my dick is still exposed and sticky from a mix of come, saliva, and frosting.

Gripping his wrists, just like I did that day in London with the ice cream, I bring the remainder of the cake to my mouth and take a large bite, making sure to graze his fingertips with my teeth. His breath hitches, eliciting a groan from deep inside his chest.

"How many of these cakes did you make?" I ask once I finish chewing.

"Twelve."

I nuzzle my face in the crook of his neck, nibbling and sucking on the delicate skin at the base of his throat. His hand grips my shoulder for support, squeezing the muscle tight as he moans.

"Go get them, then go upstairs and get naked on my bed. I want to eat my cake and devour you as my gift." I lick his throat to his ear, tugging his lobe between my teeth. "Do you think you can do that for me?"

He nods shakily.

"Good boy," I growl. "I can't fucking wait to taste you."

# Chapter Nineteen

*Jacob*

Gazing up at the clear night sky, I bite back a smile at how freaking lucky I am right now. I don't think I've ever felt so content in my life.

I know it's all a pipe dream, relaxing with Ethan, stealing kisses and gentle touches, because in a few days it's going to be just a fond memory I'll get to visit when times get hard.

But the last few days have been incredible.

I had dreamed of visiting London. It has this romantic element to it with its history and the beautiful architecture, along with the cute parks and iconic landmarks such as Buckingham Palace. Plus, throw in the classic romance movies that were filmed there, and my little hopelessly romantic heart has been singing.

Exploring the capital with Ethan has only solidified

those thoughts, but it has come with a pang of regret—but not about coming here with him.

I will never regret that. I will cherish this trip for the rest of my life, but I regret allowing my heart to do exactly what I told it not to.

I'm falling for him.

That inconvenient crush I had on him has grown exponentially since we arrived, and I know that when we get back to Chicago and this comes to an end, I'm going to be crushed.

Ethan draws lazy circles on my arm with the tips of his fingers as I lay my head on his chest. He's just cooked us another incredible meal, and now we're relaxing on a blanket in the backyard, watching as the summer night sky turns to dusk.

Ethan's chest rumbles beneath my ear as he asks, "Will you tell me something nobody knows about you?"

I shift, leaning on my elbow, and grin down at him. "Are we exchanging secrets now?"

He nods, stretching his arms back so he can rest his head on his hands behind him. His biceps bulge, stretching the sleeves of his black t-shirt, and he looks at me when he probes, "What's your biggest fear in life?"

Well, shit.

I don't keep secrets from Alex, aside from the grief we've now discussed. We've always tried to be as open and honest as possible, but there is one thing that he doesn't know.

One thing that has been a deep-rooted fear of mine since I was a kid.

"I'm terrified of dying alone." My chest aches at the admission.

Unable to speak my truth while maintaining eye contact, I roll onto my back and stare up at the purple and pink hues of the sky.

"Even though I was young when they died, one of the things I always remember is how in love my parents were. My grandparents, too. I've been so blessed to be surrounded by so much love because I know not everyone gets that, so my biggest fear is never experiencing that for myself. Never being someone's favorite person. Never knowing I'm making their day better just by being there or by hearing my voice on the phone. Never knowing the best part of their day is when they are with me." I swallow down the lump in my throat as my eyes sting with unshed tears.

I sometimes wonder if the fear is a result of losing my parents. I try to find solace in the fact that they were together until the end, and watching my grandpa lose the will to live, literally, when my grandma passed… It wouldn't have been like that if he didn't love her with every ounce of his being. If he was able to carry on without her.

I know I'm only twenty-eight. I *know* I have time to find *the one*, but the more time I spend with Ethan, the more my heart calls for *him*, and the more it aches because my brain keeps reminding me that this is only temporary.

He hasn't given me any indication that this could be anything more, and I'm almost too afraid to bring it up.

Too afraid of the inevitable rejection.

"Jacob." Ethan's serious tone causes me to look over at him. "You really don't know how incredible you are, do you?"

He reaches over and cups my face with his warm hand, his thumb brushing away a tear that's fallen down my cheek. "You make my life better just by being in it. I don't think you realize the power your smile has, or your positive energy. You're so...vibrant. Just being around you brings color to my world. You won't die alone, I promise you. Any guy would be a lucky motherfucker to call you theirs."

*Even you?* I want to ask.

I want to shake him and ask him why he can't be that lucky guy, if he really means everything he's saying. But I don't want to push. I don't want to be like Ian, demanding things of him and ending up pushing him away.

"I try to stay positive because it's so easy for grief to make things dull. And...what if, on the day I wear my true emotions on my sleeve, my dream man walks in, thinks I'm a miserable grump, and walks away?"

"Even grumpy, you are still the most beautiful person I know."

Squeezing my eyes closed, I let out a shaky breath and voice my thoughts.

"And you? Why don't you allow yourself to try?"

"Try what?"

"To love and be loved again. To take a chance. Not everyone is going to be your father, or Ian."

He grunts. "My life is...complicated. Being with me is complicated because it would turn that person's life upside down. You heard what Ian said. Yeah, seeing him brought me closure, but there's still truth in what he said. It's still going to be tough on whoever I date because of my schedule. I have to stick to a strict regimen, at least until I retire and have more time. I travel a lot, and that adds too much weight to a relationship."

Turning onto my side, I prop my head on my fist and take in the deep furrow of his brows behind his glasses.

"You know, when I lost my parents, I didn't know how my life would turn out, but I kept strong for Alex. I could've easily allowed the grief and heartbreak to consume me, but I didn't, because I knew my parents wouldn't have wanted that for me." I sit up and cross my legs. "The thing about grief is that it isn't exclusive to the time of loss. You learn to live with it for the rest of your life, but it also teaches you to love with no limitations. And to love loudly, because you don't know if the person who walks out the door is ever coming back." I sigh, chewing on the inside of my cheek. "And heartbreak is kinda similar. Life is too short to allow people who aren't worthy of your love to stop you from finding someone who is. Don't allow the ghosts of your past to define your future."

Dark chocolate eyes stare back at me. I want to ask him to give *me* a chance. That I could be the one to love him the way he deserves to be loved, that I wouldn't give a shit about what he does for a living or his travels as long as he comes back home to me.

But he needs to be in a place to accept that love. And as long as he keeps those walls around him, I'm only going to be wasting my time.

"J—" he begins to protest, but I hold up my hand to stop him.

"Sometimes you just need that one person. Someone who can be your safety net, your sounding board. The one person who won't give up on you, no matter how hard things get. Someone who can hold you and tell you that they've got you through the good and tough times." I shake my head, a small smile playing on my lips. "But you and me? We're two wounded hearts, E. We both know what it's like to have loved and lost. Don't brush off the idea of being with someone, because not everyone is Ian."

*I'm not Ian!* I want to scream. I've bared my soul to him in so many ways. He must feel this between us. This connection. And while I haven't said the words out loud, he must know how I feel.

I wish he would let me in, but I can see he's retreating behind those invisible walls.

He stares at me, his mouth slightly agape. I don't know how much time passes as we silently stare at one another. Maybe I've pushed too hard. When he doesn't say anything, my heart fractures.

Maybe Alex was right. It was foolish of me to think anything would come of this. Maybe it is just a fling to Ethan, and the feelings I thought were there are only one-sided.

Maybe I've read him all wrong, but there's this part of me that is still hopeful.

Damn the Pisces dreamer trait.

Needing to change the subject before my emotions become even more obvious, I turn the tables on him.

"Will you tell me something about you that not many people know?" I ask quietly.

He remains silent. I know he's considering not answering me because the muscle in his cheek twitches as he clenches his jaw. I'm about to tell him he doesn't need to when he surprises me.

"I changed my last name to Parkes when I was eleven."

"Because of your father?"

He nods. "He'd been gone for four years, and I knew he wasn't coming back. It was around then that hockey started to become more serious. My name was being mentioned as 'one to watch', and I didn't want his name on the back of my jersey. I didn't want him to have anything to do with something that made me happy, especially if I ever made it to the pros, so for my eleventh birthday, I asked my mom if I could legally take her maiden name."

"Wow! How did she take it?"

"She cried," he chuckles, his mood lifting slightly.

A wide smile breaks out on my face. I can imagine Jennifer doing just that. She's such a wonderful mom. You can really tell that she would do anything for Ethan with how she loves him so unconditionally.

My mom would've gotten along so well with her. My grandma, too.

Getting to spend time with her has been really nice, but it has also made me realize how much I miss my mom and my grandma. I can't stop myself from imagining what it would be like if they were still alive, and this arrangement wasn't temporary. Would we have big family summer vacations here in England? Barbecues in the backyard. Laughter and wine late into the night.

My heart aches at all the things I'll never get to experience.

"But she understood why, and I told her I wanted her name on my back when I lifted the Stanley Cup, not my jackass father's, because she would be the reason I was there, not him. So, the morning of my birthday, we went down to City Hall, and I became Ethan Parkes."

"Has he tried to get in touch since you made the NHL?"

"No." He shakes his head. "I'm not on social media, and I made sure to change my number when I was drafted. The only way he could reach me would be through the team or my agent, and they know I never want to talk to him again."

"I'm glad they support you like that. I would hate for him to come into your life and mess with your head."

Ethan grunts and sits up. He runs a hand through his hair before taking a sip of his beer. His mouth twists slightly as he tucks his chin.

"As I got older, I knew I made the right choice because I didn't want my kids to have his name either."

My eyebrows raise in surprise. I wasn't expecting that. "You want children?"

"I don't know. Maybe?" He shrugs, lifting his head to look at me. "I don't know if I'd make a good dad. I didn't exactly have a great role model growing up, but I knew that if I did end up having kids at some point, I didn't want them to have any connection to him."

*Oh, you sweet man. What are you doing to me?*

"In a way, I think your childhood will make you an incredible dad because you know firsthand what not to do. You know the father you wanted to have, and you know all your mom did for you, so you'll do right by your child. You're not your father, Ethan."

He grunts, shaking his head as he stands up, effectively ending the conversation.

I can see the barriers slowly coming back up the closer we get to leaving. But I don't regret pushing. I want him to know I see him.

"I wish I could show you that you don't have to shut me out," I whisper to his back as he disappears inside.

# Chapter Twenty

*Jacob*

"I can't believe we leave in two days," I sigh, balancing my phone on the bathroom counter while I apply some body lotion.

I had just come out of the shower when Alex called to keep him company while he worked on today's baking—thankfully forgoing FaceTime this time.

"It's gone by really quick, but it also feels like forever, if that makes sense."

I laugh. "Weirdly, it does make sense."

"Can I pick you up from the airport?" he asks. "Daniel and Aria will mind the shop. I just…" He trails off, and I can hear the uncertainty in his voice. "I've just really missed you, and I kinda don't want to wait until Ethan drops you off to see you."

I close my eyes and swallow down my emotions. No matter how much I want to delay the inevitable, we're running out of time, and the thought of ending this, whatever *this* is, makes my chest ache.

While we've been here, I've seen Ethan's guard start to drop. He's allowed his vulnerability to show through, and it's made him even more beautiful to me.

But his guard is slowly going back up, and when we go back…I'm not sure how things will be.

I quietly clear my throat, hoping it helps me sound chipper when I speak. "Of course you can pick me up." I hang up my wet towel on the towel rail, then walk out into Ethan's bedroom, taking a seat on the armchair that he sat on the night of the wedding. I curl my legs up under me, resting my phone on the arm, and gaze out of the window. "How is everything back home?"

"It's going good," Alex replies. "Busy as ever. Blaine and Elliot have been helping out a lot. Well, Elliot's probably caused more chaos than anything else."

I snort. "Oh God, what's he been doing?"

"Just being Elliot," he answers with a laugh. "Daniel tried to teach him how to use the coffee machine, and he ended up burning his hand on the steamer. He almost dropped a tray of cookies on the floor too, but managed to catch himself before they slipped off."

I cover my mouth with my hand and laugh. "Oh wow. He's a wild one."

"He is, but he's been awesome. When Blaine's been helping out here, El's been looking after Ernie for us. He also found a really old Elvis vinyl and bought it for me the other day."

My heart squeezes in my chest.

Before they passed, our grandparents had a decades-long tradition of dancing to "Can't Help Falling in Love" by Elvis Presley every Sunday.

Since Alex told Blaine about it, they decided to carry on with that tradition. When Alex and I were still living together and Blaine didn't have a game, they would dance in the living room while I made myself scarce. I was so freaking happy for my brother, but that brought on a whole new wave of grief I didn't want him to witness.

"That was sweet of him."

"It was." I can hear the smile in Alex's voice. "Anyway, I better go open up. Daniel will be here any minute. Will you call me later?"

"Of course, I will."

"Cool! I miss you, Jake. I can't wait for you to come home."

That damn lump forms in my throat again, causing my voice to come out weak. "I miss you too, Alex. Have a good day."

We hang up, and I drop my head back onto the cushion, staring up at the ceiling.

There's a weird mix of emotions coursing through me. I want to stay here, wrapped up in this little bubble Ethan and I have, but I also miss home.

I miss seeing my brother, working at the bakery, and my own bed. I miss my routine and the constant reminders of my parents and grandparents around me.

I wish I could have it all.

Mentally shaking the gloomy cloud away, I get up and go downstairs, heading into the gym where Ethan is working out. He's sitting on the floor with a weighted ball, grimacing as he shifts it from side to side, and I take him in for a couple of minutes. I don't know if I'll ever be able to see him like this again.

The second he spots me, he places the ball on the floor and stands up. His inquisitive gaze roams over my face, a frown lining his forehead under the peak of his baseball cap.

"Is everything okay?" he asks, concerned.

I want to hate the fact he has the ability to read me so well after such a short period of time together, but I can't. I love how attentive he is, how he pays attention to the little details. I just can't let myself read too much into it.

"Yeah," I nod. "I was just on the phone with Alex and started to feel a little homesick."

His frown deepens, but I wave him off. "I'm fine, honestly."

Ethan's silent for a beat, just looking at me with those intense, dark eyes. "Need me to help take your mind off of it?"

I can pinpoint the moment his face changes—the glint in his eye, the way his lips tip up in a smirk, and the sight of those godforsaken dimples that make my knees weak every single time.

"Do you even have to ask?" I say, dropping my voice into a sultry tone.

He takes a step closer and leans down, his breath fanning the shell of my ear. His hands roam down my sides to the waistband of my shorts.

"You're going to be the death of me."

"Why?" I whisper.

"Your legs look fucking unreal in these shorts, Jacob." His hands slide around to squeeze my ass. "And they show off your phenomenal ass."

Tilting my head up, I graze my teeth over my lower lip, loving how his dark eyes flare with desire as they track the movement. I stick the tip of my tongue out of the corner of my mouth and smirk.

"Should I apologize?"

He grips my chin, his warm breath ghosting over my mouth. The way his lips slowly teases me by barely touching mine makes me whimper and groan as I become desperate for more.

"No."

"Why's that?"

"Because I fucking love it," he growls, and my body shivers from my head to my toes.

Ethan drops his hand from my chin and lifts the hem of my t-shirt, tossing it unceremoniously onto the floor before pushing down the shorts he was admiring only seconds ago. I lift my feet to step out of them, and he kicks them out of the way.

"And here I was, thinking you liked those shorts!"

"Stand there," he orders, ignoring my taunt and points to the full-length mirror that lines one wall of his gym. "And don't move."

Doing as instructed, I step around him and walk to the mirror. I can feel his gaze roaming my body from behind me, and heat prickles all over my skin. I subtly wipe my palms on the elastic waistband of my underwear, watching as he prowls toward me.

Determined.

Hungry.

I take in our reflection in the mirror as Ethan steps up behind me.

We're so different. Everything about him turns me on. He's a good five inches taller than me. His torso is as wide as my shoulders. The dark smattering of hair covering his hard, sculpted pecs. He's all strong arms and thick thighs and luscious calves.

I'm not built like that. Maybe I should be self-conscious about it and about him being fully clothed while I'm in a jockstrap. But I've come to realize that it doesn't matter.

Because we fit.

Because the way he takes me in makes me feel like…more.

Superior, in a way.

Like I can do anything. Like I'm the sexiest man alive, and I've never experienced that with previous guys.

My hands twist in front of me—I'm not sure what to do with them. I want to touch myself, but he told me not to move. My cock throbs. Pre-come seeps through the fabric of my jock, and when he tosses his t-shirt aside and drops his basketball shorts, an appreciative groan escapes me.

Does the whole not touching myself thing include jerking off?

The heat of his body warms my back as he presses his chest against me. Those dark orbs focus on me as he leans down and says, "Now, Jacob, I want you to keep your eyes open. I want you to watch every moment. If you shut them, I'll stop. Do you understand?"

I've lost my ability to speak, so I just nod.

"Good boy."

Fuck. Me.

Why does that make me lose my goddamn mind in the best possible way?

My eyes are glued to the mirror, watching as this man wraps a hand around my throat, while smoothing the other down my stomach to the juncture of my thighs. The tips of his fingers skim the fabric of my underwear, causing my entire body to vibrate with need.

His tongue peeks out to flick the lobe of my ear, then tugs it between his teeth. I'm fighting myself because I want to close my eyes and give in to the pleasure so bad. But also, I don't want him to stop.

"You're fucking breathtaking," Ethan whispers.

He trails his calloused fingertips up my stomach, ghosting over my belly button to the center of my chest.

A small gasp escapes me as he pinches my nipple. He's gentle, but every movement he makes is controlled and powerful, one hand still around my throat, fingers digging into the underside of my jaw just slightly.

My hands clench into fists at my sides. I'm desperate to touch myself. To touch him. For him to finally touch me the way I want him to. But I love letting Ethan take control. It's something I never expected to enjoy so much, given my history with "jocks," but Ethan is different.

Dominant but safe. I know he would stop the moment I told him to.

But right now, I'm aching for him. I need him to touch me more than I need my next breath.

"Ethan," I plead, curling my toes into the rubber mat beneath my feet. His hot, stiff cock nestles in my crease, and I'm unable to stop myself. I push back into him as he bends his knees, sliding his length between my cheeks.

"Do you want me to take you here, Jacob?" he growls.

"Do you want to watch as I fuck you, so you can see how fucking beautiful you are when I'm inside you?"

I lick my dry lips, my breath coming out in heavy pants.

"Jacob, use your words."

"Yes," I wheeze.

"Good boy, but remember—don't move."

I let out a choked whine when he lets go and walks away. My eyes remain locked on his retreating back as he quickly runs upstairs, returning a few moments later with a condom and a packet of lube.

Stepping behind me again, Ethan removes his boxers, then slides my underwear down my legs. He taps my ankles, giving me permission to move, and I step out of them.

I don't think I could be more turned on than I am right now, but then he proves me wrong.

He twists his baseball cap backward, drops to his knees, and spreads my cheeks apart before licking a hot, wet stripe over my hole.

I move my hands toward the mirror for some stability as my legs begin to quiver.

He's relentless. His fingers dig into my hips, keeping me still as his deft tongue opens me up. He slips one finger inside me, then a second, scissoring and sliding over my prostate in tantalizing strokes before adding a third. He alternates between pumping his fingers inside me and using his tongue. His teeth graze over my ass before he bites on the flesh and sucks.

A loud moan escapes me. He's going to leave a mark, and I want to tell him to mark me as his any way he wants to, but all I can manage is, "Please. Hurry," I beg.

He freezes. I catch his eyes when he tilts his head and

looks at me through the mirror. One dark brow raised, a devilish smirk on his lips.

"Ethan, I swear, if you don't get inside me in the next twenty seconds, I'm going to scream," I warn.

"Well, we wouldn't want that," he mumbles with a grin.

He stands to his full height and rolls the condom down his steely length, coating himself with copious amounts of lube and adding more to my hole. He widens his stance, bending his knees slightly to line himself up, then touches the center of my back, gently pushing me to lean forward slightly. The head of his cock brushes against my hole, and I open my mouth to tell him I can't take his brand of torture anymore.

But the words get lost on my tongue and I lose all coherent thought as he slowly eases inside.

I let out a long, satisfied groan. The burn from his cock stretching me causes my toes to curl into the rubber mat beneath my feet. Forcing my eyes to remain open, I watch his expression in the mirror. His eyes are locked on where we're joined, his brows furrowed in concentration beneath his cap. A hiss escapes him from behind clenched teeth as he pushes all the way in.

"Fuck!" he grunts, tilting his head back and exposing the thick column of his throat. "No one has ever felt this good, Jacob."

When Ethan finally starts to thrust in quick, shallow strokes, I lose my grip on the mirror and shift to find purpose as sweat coats my palms.

I glance down. My dick is leaking. Pre-come drips onto the mat with every thrust of Ethan's hips. I'm so fucking close that my legs are becoming weak, and I think they might give out the second I come. My entire body trembles with pleasure and sweat beads at my temples and at the nape of my neck before trickling down my spine.

"You need to touch yourself, baby?" he asks, his voice like gravel in my ear. "Well, too bad. Keep your hands on the mirror because that's my job."

He takes my aching cock in his hand, pumping me in time with each thrust of his hips, and wraps his other hand around my throat again. The sight makes my knees even weaker.

Who knew I would love hand necklaces?

All my words come out as incoherent moans. Grunts, moans, whimpers, and slapping flesh fill the air, and I know I can't hold back anymore.

"I'm going to come," I pant, praying he'll let me. Spots fill my vision, but when I go to close my eyes, the slight squeeze of Ethan's hand on my throat stops me.

"You can come, but Jacob…your eyes stay open."

My release hits me like a tsunami. Stars cloud my vision. I cry out his name as come spills over his fist, hitting the mat and the mirror in front of me.

My entire body shudders, and Ethan wraps a hand over my torso and shoulder, pulling me tight against his body to keep me upright. His thrusts turn frantic, like he can't control himself anymore.

"Jacob," he groans behind clenched teeth.

I can feel the heat of his come through the condom. He holds me close, his heart an erratic beat against my back. Our bodies are trembling with post-orgasmic bliss, but we just stand there—glued together, eyes locked in the mirror.

I don't want this connection to end.

There's a shift in Ethan's eyes. It looks a lot like hope, but it's tinted with fear. Like maybe Ethan wants me, but he's too afraid.

Afraid to let go and let himself feel. To open himself up to the concept of love. To *more*.

I desperately want to tell him I'll be patient. That I'll wait for him for as long as he needs.

I would tell him everything in a heartbeat if I knew it wouldn't scare him away.

Because his rejection would tear my heart in two, and I can't let myself go through that.

## Chapter Twenty-One

*Ethan*

I watch Jacob through the window as he fills the new bird feeders with seed and sprinkles nuts on the wooden table we purchased from a local garden center. He then stands in the center of the lawn, waiting for the birds to appear and feast on the freshly laid food.

He's been doing this almost every day—simply watching as the birds come and go or the squirrels as they run from tree to tree and stuff their little mouths with nuts.

In the city, I don't get to appreciate this. I guess he doesn't either. The tranquility of nature.

As much as I love my life in Chicago, I'm not ready to leave tomorrow. I want to stay here, with Jacob, in this tiny world we've created, but I know it's not possible. He has a life back home. He's itching to see Alex again and to get back to the bakery—he said as much—but I can't help but think he's itching to get away from me.

Covering up the late lunch I've prepared with a towel, I head into the backyard, making sure my movements are quiet and slow so I don't startle the visiting wildlife. When I reach Jacob, I wrap my arms around his waist and rest my chin on top of his head. He jumps slightly in my arms but soon settles when he realizes it's me.

"Give a guy a warning next time," he says quietly, leaning back into my chest.

"Sorry," I murmur, kissing his head. "What are you watching?"

"Some of these little birds that visit are so beautiful and colorful. I don't think I've ever seen them before." Jacob trails his fingers lazily up and down my forearm and over my hand wrapped around his middle, almost absently.

He seems a bit lost in thought, so I don't say anything and allow him to go on.

"I was reading this article, and it mentioned that in British folklore, the robin represents loved ones who are no longer with us. There's a phrase, 'When a robin appears, loved ones are near,' so people can take comfort in that whenever they see a robin, it's a loved one visiting to let them know they're at peace. It kind of stuck with me because it's heartwarming that you can try to find some form of solace in these little birds."

He's silent for a beat. I watch the bird in question peck at the lawn in search of worms. It's got a bright orange breast, a white belly, and a brown back.

"I've seen three of them every day since I've been here. Two always seem to be together, and sometimes they come so close, like they want to see me but they're too shy. I saw videos where people were able to feed them by hand." He tilts his head up to face me, blue eyes swimming with unshed tears. "I want to believe they're my parents or my grandparents, but then I wonder why there's no fourth robin."

I wrap my arms a little tighter as his body trembles with his next inhale. I know what he's about to say before he even speaks, and I'd fucking fight his pain away if I could.

"What if one of them isn't near? Or one of them isn't at peace?" His voice shakes as he struggles to find his breath. "What if one of them hasn't made it to wherever it is you go once you're gone?"

I hate the pain in his voice. His body shudders as he tries to keep a rein on his emotions, and it breaks my fucking heart. I want to make it better somehow, but I have no idea how.

So I just hold him tighter through his broken sobs and press a kiss to the top of his head, letting him know I'm here. When he turns around and hides his face in my chest, I wrap my arms around him.

"They're always with you, J. It doesn't matter if it's a robin or just in your memories and in your heart. They'll always be with you," I say quietly.

Since that afternoon in the living room, when he bared his wounded heart to me, I've seen it. The slight slip in his armor. I notice it from time to time, but he quickly recovers and puts on his positive face, but I see it.

I see everything about him.

Beneath his strength, there's someone who feels too much and has nowhere to channel any of it.

Someone who fights every day to keep going, to find the beauty and the good things in life, even when his own has been less than stellar.

Clouds may threaten to dampen his shine, but he chases them away with his sun.

*You could learn a thing or two from him.*

I internally slap myself because my conscience is right. I've been harboring so much resentment for my father leaving and for my failed relationship with Ian that I've kept myself locked under a dark cloud of my own. I've blamed and punished myself, ultimately missing out on building a connection with someone because of how people have treated me in the past.

I've let them win.

But this trip has shown me that Jacob already has my heart. He's chased away some of my clouds. All I need to do now is figure out how to bring down the barriers and let him in completely.

I have to.

"I've got you, baby," I murmur into his hair.

I want to be mad at these damn birds for making him feel this way, but part of me knows how much Jacob loves this backyard and being here.

I'm about to pick him up and carry him inside when a flash of orange catches my eye. I see one of the little robins running across the grass toward us, then another one following shortly behind.

"J, look," I whisper quietly into his ear, not wanting to startle the birds as they inch even closer.

He raises his head, and I hear the hitch in his breath when he spots them. They aren't close enough to touch, but they seem to be peering up at him. Tilting their little heads in curiosity. Maybe it's all in my head and I'm seeing what I need—what Jacob needs—to see, but when a fresh wave of tears stream down his cheeks, I know this time they are not from pain.

"They're always with you, Jacob," I repeat.

His teeth dig into his bottom lip as he hiccups. I wipe away the tears from his cheeks with my thumb, then wrap my arms around him again, bringing him to my chest.

"Why don't you talk to them?" I suggest. "If they're supposed to be loved ones who have passed, talk to them as if they're here. Lean into the folklore; it might bring you some comfort."

His brows furrow, looking at me like I'm out of my mind. When he remains silent, I start to speak to the two birds.

"Hello, Mr. and Mrs. Lowry," I say, eliciting a small, wet laugh from him. "I hope you're enjoying the bird seed, especially since it was the most expensive bag they had in the store."

Jacob wraps his arms around my waist and squeezes. The tears on his cheek seep through the fabric of my t-shirt.

"I just wanted to let you know that you would be so fucking proud of Jacob. I'm sorry for my language. I'm not sure whether you're the parents or the grandparents, but I suppose it's not good to swear in front of either." I grin at Jacob, who's looking at me with so much adoration in his eyes.

*Please be patient with me.*

*Please don't give up on me.*

"He makes the best damn cakes in Chicago and has the most beautiful laugh, but do you want to know what my favorite thing about him is?" I keep my eyes locked on his as I speak. "Well, I'm going to tell you anyway because you can't talk—being birds and all—but it's his heart. It's so fucking pure. So good. He's like sunshine. He's always so bright, so positive, so fucking warm that all I want to do is bask in his light every chance I get."

Another fat tear rolls down his cheek, and I quickly wipe it away with my thumb.

"You may not believe me, but you're so brave, Jacob. To have gone through so much heartbreak in your life and still be able to put that beautiful smile on your face…" I cup his face with one hand, tracing the curve of his lips with my thumb, before I lean down and press a tender kiss to his lips. "It's inspiring."

Jacob holds on to me, his palm resting over my heart, before he nervously drags his top lip between his teeth. Looking over his shoulder at the two little birds pecking at the ground, he squeezes his eyes closed and takes a deep, shaky breath, then angles his body toward them.

"Hey, Mom, Dad. I just…I just wanted to let you know I really miss you. I think about you every day. Sometimes, it's like I'm just waiting for you to walk through the door and tell me it was a misunderstanding and the police got it wrong. I…"

I press a kiss into his hair as more tears roll down his face.

*I'm still here. I've got you.*

"I wish I had hugged you more. I wish I had hugged you tighter that day you said goodbye for the last time. I'm sorry I didn't tell you how much I loved you more often. I wish I could go back and tell you that every single day, and Alex—I know he loves you so much. Dad, he's dating a hockey player—can you believe it?" He lets out a choked laugh and leans back into me.

"He's so happy and in love. They've got a dog; his name is Ernie. Blaine named him after Grandpa. He's so cute, but he's got them both wrapped around his little paw. I think they'll get married, and I think both of you would have loved Blaine. He looks at Alex the same way you looked at Mom, and their love reminds me a lot of yours."

I hug him a little tighter.

He's silent for a moment, and his next words tear my heart in two.

"I hope to have that one day. Someone who loves me so much he never wants to be away from me. Someone who can be my favorite hello and my hardest goodbye, but most of all…I hope you're proud of me. I hope that wherever you are, you're happy together and that you'll keep watching over us. Knowing you're with me keeps me going when getting up and facing the world is too hard. I hope I can keep your memory alive by living my life to the fullest and knowing you're in my heart every step of the way."

*You're my favorite hello,* I silently tell him.

A larger bird lands, startling the two robins, and the second they fly away, Jacob crumbles in my arms. Harsh sobs rack through him, and my own eyes fill with tears.

I want to be worthy of him.

I believe I can be worthy of him.

I just need to silence the voice of fear in my head and take the leap.

And I hope that Jacob will catch me when I land.

## Chapter Twenty-Two

*Ethan*

I gently caress Jacob's fingers, curving around his knuckles, and draw a circle on the back of his hand before repeating the pattern. His soft, shallow breaths tickle the hair on my chest.

And possibly for the first time in my life, I'm completely and wholly content.

Lying here in bed with Jacob, with our legs tangled, and his body curled against mine. His head resting on my chest like I'm his own personal pillow.

I didn't know it was possible to find such peace just by being in someone's presence. Listening to the sound of his breathing, inhaling the sweet scent of his hair. The soft thud of his heartbeat against my rib cage.

I didn't know it was possible for someone to feel like home. It's a strange sensation.

For the last decade, I've put my career first. I've repeatedly told myself that I didn't need someone in my life. That I was perfectly fine on my own without risking my stupid damaged heart by getting involved with someone, when in reality, it was just that I hadn't met Jacob yet.

I suppose sometimes you need to spend time in the rain to really appreciate the sun when it comes out. He made me understand that my emotional scars don't make me unlovable, just selective over who I allow behind my barrier.

Or, as Jacob likes to call it, my protective shield.

For the first time, I believe I can do it. I believe I can have a loving relationship because it's Jacob.

He's stable. Solid. He's there, whether standing by my side or rooting for me while I tackle my mental demons on my own. He's supportive in ways I've only ever experienced with my mom, and for once, I don't feel afraid.

I'm out in the water, and he's the lighthouse, guiding me to safety.

Maybe it was seeing the way he crumbled in the backyard, showing me that whatever strength keeps him upright despite the darkness in his life isn't always there. But even with the tears streaming down his cheeks, he was still the most beautiful person I've ever laid eyes on.

When I first met him that gloomy January day, I couldn't help but notice the sparkle in his eyes was diminished.

But now? Now he's shining.

Really shining. Sparkling brightly like the Eiffel Tower on a clear night, and it makes my heart soar.

Pressing a kiss to his head, I blink away the wetness from my eyes. My heart feels so full with this man in my life. It makes everything else seem so...superficial.

I don't need another Stanley Cup ring in my collection to know I'm worthy. I don't need another championship title to my name to prove that my career has been commendable. I don't need external validation from anyone.

No.

What I need is for this man to love me until my very last breath.

To love me despite my flaws. To love me *because* of them.

To stand by my side as I face a new chapter in my life.

To wake up every morning and see his gorgeous face next to me.

Only then, will I truly be a champion.

I just hope I can find the words to tell him that I'm falling in love with him.

Glancing over to the nightstand, the clock reads nine a.m. We only have a few hours until we need to leave for the airport, and I'm not ready. My mom is coming over soon to say her goodbyes, at least until she flies to Chicago for the holiday season.

Slowly slipping out from beneath Jacob, I move my pillow and gently lay his head on it. He curls his arm around the pillow before his soft snores continue. I stand there for a beat, just watching him sleep so peacefully. His blond hair sticking up in all directions, his lips parted.

He's extraordinary.

Managing to pull myself away, I quickly shower, get dressed, and throw everything into my suitcase. Luckily, I tend to pack light as I keep clothes here, so it doesn't take me long to get everything packed. Once I'm done, I head downstairs and make a start on breakfast just in time for Mom to walk through the door.

"Good morning, sweetie," she greets me.

Placing the pancake batter next to the stove, I open my arms, wrapping them around her. "Hey, Mom."

"I can't believe you're going back already." She frowns before turning to get a cup out of the cupboard and making herself a coffee. "I wish you could stay longer."

"Me too, but we've got to get back for Jacob. Maybe you could come out before the season starts? You know I'll pay for your flights whenever you want to come."

She gives me a warm smile. "Thank you, darling. I'll see if I can work something out." Taking a sip of her coffee, she eyes me over the rim of the cup. The steam does nothing to disguise her pointed stare. "Are you going to tell him how you feel?"

"What do you mean?" I grumble, pouring some of the pancake batter into the pan.

"Ethan, don't play dumb. It doesn't suit you," she chuckles, rolling her eyes. "I meant, are you going to tell Jacob how you feel about him? I really like him. He's a good one, and I can tell you really care for him."

I sigh and run a hand through my hair. "Yes, but I don't know when. I figured maybe on the plane?"

She shakes her head. "No, you've got to do something romantic. Tell him when you land back at O'Hare; let him know that you want to see how things go now that you're back."

I chew on my bottom lip.

"Ethan, you need to be the one to do this. I know what you're like. You're guarded like a vault, and Jacob doesn't know what's going on in your head. Or maybe he does, but he still needs to hear it from you." She takes another sip of her coffee. "You're going to have to fight every instinct that's been ingrained in you for so long and use your words, sweetie. He's not Ian or your father. He's a good man with a good heart. You're both very well suited for one another, but you need to be the one to take this step. You need to give yourself a chance."

I run a hand down my face and sigh.

I know she's right. I've allowed fear to consume me for more than a decade. I've allowed others to take away my chances for too long.

"Good morning, sweetie." Mom greets when Jacob appears, looking rumpled from sleep.

He walks over to her and wraps his arms around her in a tight hug. "I thought I wouldn't get the chance to say goodbye."

"Never. I would've run down the street waving if I had missed you," she says with a laugh. "Plus, I need to get that recipe from you! Don't forget."

Jacob's laugh hits me square in the chest. "I'll email it to you the second I get back to the bakery."

My mom gives him another hug and looks over his shoulder, then mouths, "Tell him."

As hard as it's going to be, I know I need to be the one to bring up the topic of where we go from here when we get back to Chicago. Jacob might change his mind once the season starts, and he realizes how hectic my schedule is or how regimented my day-to-day life is.

But I know I'll regret it if I don't try.

Picking up the last suitcase from the conveyor belt, Jacob is practically bouncing on his toes.

"I'm so excited to see Alex again." Jacob beams, there's a bright smile on his face. "I feel like I haven't seen him in forever."

I force a smile.

It's not because I'm not happy that he gets to see his brother again; I am, but I'm fucking nervous. Anxiety is eating away at me as we get closer to the doors, knowing that Alex is on the other side waiting to pick up Jacob, and I still haven't spoken to him about how I feel.

Yep, I spent the nine-hour flight from London to Chicago trying to think of the right words to say. The right way to express how I feel about him. That this trip was the most incredible time of my life, and it was all because of him.

Feelings don't come easily for me. I'm fine when it comes to my captain duties because it's not about *me* per se. It's about the team. A united front. The focus isn't on me and my fucked-up emotions when we're talking hockey. I can easily talk strategy or about ways to improve our gameplay.

To make it worse, it's this place. This airport. Where I ended up with my heart in pieces last time. It's causing my brain is going into overdrive.

I can't focus. My stomach is in knots. My palms are sweating on the handle of my suitcase as I drag it along beside me.

It's now or never. I need to do it now, or I'm going to miss my shot.

"Jacob—"

"Ethan—" he says at the same time.

We both laugh.

I hold my hand out. "You go first."

He stops on the other side of the arrival doors, moving us out of the way of the other passengers. Those gorgeous blue eyes gazing up at me with such warmth and admiration.

"I just wanted to say thank you. For everything. For helping me in a time of need, for inviting me on this trip of a lifetime. It's been truly magical." He leans up and presses a kiss to my cheek. "Thank you for being such an incredible friend. I can't thank you enough."

*Friend?*

My heart plummets. Did I completely misread the signs? I know I said at the beginning that I couldn't offer him anything more than just the time we had in England, but I felt the change. That simmering chemistry between us turned into something more.

I couldn't have imagined that. Surely not? It was too powerful, too visceral for it not to be real.

Suddenly, I can't breathe. My chest feels painfully tight, like an invisible weight is pressing down against my lungs. I open my mouth to speak, desperate to find the words I've been wanting to say, but they get lost on my tongue.

My mom's words come rushing back to me, *use your words, sweetie.*

"J—" I croak.

"I'll cherish the time we spent together more than you'll ever know." He smiles, his voice dripping with sincerity.

I fucking need to say something, but my throat closes up.

The sound of the noisy arrivals terminal becomes distant, and I'm just left with the frantic pounding of my heart.

"Jake!"

Jacob turns at the sound of Alex's voice and takes off in a jog, dragging his suitcase behind him. There's nothing I can do except stand and watch as they embrace, Jacob's face lighting up with happiness and relief in his brother's arms.

"Hey, Ethan. Thank you for taking care of him," Alex greets me, wrapping his arm around Jacob's shoulder and squeezes.

I grunt, jutting my chin in acknowledgement. Both brothers are staring at me as I just stand there. Jacob eyes me, his brows slightly furrowed in confusion, but then Alex says something that snaps him out of it, and he takes hold of his suitcase.

He looks back at me one more time as they wave goodbye and leave.

The anxiety rushing through my veins is replaced by a wave of numbness. The proverbial walls that Jacob helped knock down slam back up, surrounding me. The back of my eyes burn at the sight of Jacob leaving.

"Fuck!" I pull at my hair.

I'm such a fucking idiot. I've done exactly what he said and allowed the ghosts of my past to control me in the present.

I need to do something. I need to find a way to tell him that I don't want what we had to be a cherished memory. I want what we had to be real.

I don't want to be his friend.

I want to be the person he's been waiting for. I want to

be the one who's worthy of him, who'll love him the way he yearns to be loved.

I'm in love with him, and I've fucked it all up by not letting him in.

# Chapter Twenty-Three

*Jacob*

I'm not usually one who mopes around feeling sorry for myself. I like to keep myself busy, my mind preoccupied with anything and everything, so I have less time to think.

But since I got back to Chicago a week ago?

God. This week has been hell.

I would give anything to go back to England and go back to the cocoon that Ethan and I had wrapped ourselves up in.

I miss him.

I miss the soothing sound of his steady breathing in the morning, the feel of his warm body blanketing mine. The way he would hold me—so protective and strong—the world could crumble around us because, as long as I was in his arms, I would be safe and sound.

I promised myself that I would be okay with putting a lid on our summer fling as soon as we boarded the plane in

London, but I don't think I am. I don't think I can stuff my feelings for Ethan into a box and just forget about them.

But he shut me out, like our time together meant nothing. He essentially stopped talking to me the moment we boarded the plane in London. His replies came in grunts and grumbled answers. There was no holding my hand or reassuring caresses during takeoff. His arms stayed locked, crossed over his chest, his body angled toward the window. He seemed lost in thought.

I wanted to tell him how I felt. I wanted to ask him if he would consider giving us a chance here. Taking things slowly while he focuses on his career and I still focus on the bakery. Showing him that I'm nothing like his ex-fiancé, begging to be made a priority.

But his silence and closed-off body language told me everything I needed to know.

It was just for the summer.

He did warn me, after all.

*Ugh!*

I know I need to talk to him. I need to stamp down my fear of having my heart broken and just *talk* to him. Otherwise, I'll never know.

Why is it so terrifying to put yourself out there when all you ever want is to love and be loved?

Alex flicks the closed sign on the door and twists the lock. He turns back to face me, arms crossed over his chest and a scowl that could rival Ethan's.

"Okay, I'm done tiptoeing around you. Talk to me, Jake. You've been miserable as hell since you got home, and it's really stressing me out." He takes a few steps before stopping in front of me, placing his hands on the counter. His eyes are laced with worry. "What happened? I thought you had a great time in England, but since you've got back, things have been…different, and not in a good way."

The backs of my eyes start to burn as I stare at Alex's concerned expression. I've buried my head in the sand, only giving vague answers whenever I'm asked about my time there, letting them know it was lovely and great and fun.

"I did what I said I wasn't going to do," I admit. "I fell in love with him."

If Alex is surprised, he doesn't show it. His face softens, those kind eyes that are an exact replica of our father's looking at me with love, not pity.

"Oh, Jake," he says softly. "Does he know?"

I shake my head, quickly swiping my fingers under my eyes, my breath coming out in a shaky exhale.

"Jake…" Alex sighs.

"Please don't tell Blaine," I quickly add.

He blinks, his mouth gaping open. "You want me to lie to him?"

"No, I just… I don't want him to know. I don't want to drive a wedge between them because they play together. There's no need to involve anyone else because it was a vacation fling." The words burn my stomach like acid at the admission. "It's done. Ethan said it would only be while we were there. A summer romance, just like Blaine suggested."

Alex frowns. "From what you told me, it was more than that. Have you heard from him since?"

"No," I say as I shake my head.

He runs a hand through his hair before placing it back on the counter and tapping his finger against the smooth surface. "Maybe I could speak to him."

"Please, Alex. Just…let it go."

Done with this conversation, I turn and begin unloading the empty trays from the counter and carrying them into the kitchen for cleaning. Alex is right behind me.

"No, Jake. I'm not gonna just *let it go*. Is it scary to put yourself out there and hope they feel the same? Abso-fuck-ing-lutely, but you know what's worth it? When they do, and Ethan?" He points at the door, even though there's nobody there, the tone of his voice becoming more frustrated with each word. "Ethan has looked at you like you're special for months. I've seen it every time you two were together in a room. I saw it the day he came in here and made that deal with you. He looks at you the same way Dad looks at Mom in all the photos. Like you're his favorite person in the world. Isn't that worth the initial fear of laying your heart out there?"

A tear rolls down my cheek. I sniff, glancing up at the ceiling as I blink, trying to ward off a waterfall.

Alex's hand lands on my shoulder, spinning me around. He gives me a reassuring smile. "Jacob, you deserve so fucking much. You deserve more than this world can give you, but Ethan…I think he'd do a pretty good job at trying. Talk to him. Let him know what your heart is telling you. If he doesn't feel the same, we'll deal with it, but he might be just as afraid as you are."

My throat goes thick. "What if he says no?"

"Then I might have to kick his ass." Alex grins.

I snort a laugh.

"Okay, maybe not me, but Blaine would. Elliot, too, probably. Although he'd probably just slap him like a turtle." He bats his hands in the air in quick succession.

I let out a small laugh.

"There's another reason why I don't want you to tell Blaine. Ethan, he…" I sigh. "I think he's got some things he wants to work on with the guys, and I don't want to get in the way of that."

"I get that. I won't. But if, for some crazy reason, Ethan doesn't want to give things a shot, then that's okay because you've got us. We love you, and you'll find your someone."

The following day, I spend the day hiding away in the kitchen working on custom creations while Alex and Daniel man the front.

I was so emotionally drained last night when I got home that I had a little cry into a glass of wine before I passed out on the couch while watching an old Hallmark movie.

Despite Ethan's behavior on the flight and at the airport, there's still this part of me that thinks…what if he *does* feel the way I do but is just afraid of putting himself out there?

It's kind of funny. I harped on about taking chances, and loving loudly, and I did the opposite. I didn't tell him how I feel because I was afraid of getting my heart hurt when I should have taken my own advice. I could have spent the night wrapped up in his arms instead of crying pathetically into a glass of rosé.

When I walk out after closing, they're sitting in a booth, scribbling something on a notepad.

"Hey," Alex says when he spots me. "Would you like a coffee?"

"No, I'm good, thanks." I shake my head, taking a seat next to him. "What are you working on?"

"I'm planning a small get-together next week for Blaine and Elliot's birthday," Alex replies. "Just some of the guys from the team and their partners. I was going to invite Nate, too. Obviously, you two are invited."

Daniel holds his hand up for a high five.

I forgot it was the twins' birthday next week.

"Is there anything I can do to help?" I ask.

"I was going to ask if you could help me with the cakes." He rubs his forehead, his shoulders sagging slightly. "I've been getting a little stressed out about food because they eat a lot, and I don't know what everyone likes or how much to make…but Daniel suggested having a theme."

"Yeah, so each person could bring something that reminds them of one of the twins. We can randomly assign them a name, and maybe like sweet or savory," Daniel explains.

"That sounds like a great idea."

Alex nods. "Yeah, it does. It's kinda fun, and also that way I don't get stuck with doing everything."

"Are you thinking one big cake, then a few dozen cupcakes?"

We talk through amounts, writing down what ingredients we'll need to order in, along with flavors.

All the while, I'm trying to mentally prepare myself for seeing Ethan in person again.

# Chapter Twenty-Four

*Ethan*

Peyton: BBQ at mine in an hour.

Peyton: Don't try and evade us, Parkes.

Peyton: I know where you live.

Peyton: Don't make me come over there and sic Elliot on you.

Peyton: He'll sit on you and tickle you like an annoying Tickle Me Elmo.

Ethan: You do the tickling with Tickle Me Elmo, not the other way around.

Peyton: Whatever. The threat still stands.

Looking down at my phone, I huff out a laugh and shake my head. The group chat has been blowing up since I returned home a week ago, but my mood has been shit. I've avoided them all, not wanting them to see that I was a mess, but I should have known I couldn't hide forever.

As I see the other messages there, my thumb hovers over Jacob's name. I almost text him to tell him I miss him, but there's something I need to do first.

Jonathan Peyton lives in Lakeview, a few doors down from Adam Kendrick and his wife Maria. The Kendricks are usually the hosts outside of our dedicated boys' night, but since Peyton and his wife are currently living apart while they work through their marriage trouble, I have a feeling Peyton is hoping for some company.

I quickly shower and change, then make my way over. The circle drive is already filled with cars when I pull into the gates. I walk inside the large entryway and come to a stop at the sight of Elliot sitting on the kitchen floor with Jackson Wilde's three year old daughter, Isabela. They're both surrounded by boxes of colored beads. Elliot's tongue peeks out the corner of his mouth in concentration as he threads the beads onto some string. Between his backward baseball cap and Pokémon socks, he looks like an overgrown child.

"Ethan!" Isabela shrieks when she spots me.

Her sudden outburst startles Elliot, and the beads in his hand scatter onto the floor in clinks and pings.

"Aw! Izzy, my girl! Why did you do that? Now I've gotta start over again," Elliot whines, scooping everything up from the floor.

She ignores him and quickly gets to her feet, rushing

over to me. I scoop her up into my arms, placing a big wet kiss on her cheek, causing her to burst into giggles.

I walk over to where Elliot's sitting with his legs stretched out in front of him. "What are you doing?"

"I'm making friendship bracelets." He grins up at me proudly. "I've decided yours is going to say 'grumpy pants'."

I glare at him. "No, thanks."

Isabela giggles again.

"See, she likes it. It's locked in; no going back now, dude."

Isabela hides her face in my neck before wiggling to get down. I place her back on her feet, and she takes a seat next to Elliot, carefully going back to handing him the colored beads with one hand while the other lays protectively on his forearm.

"Where are the others?" I ask.

"Outside by the grill. My brain was having a bit of an overload, so I came inside to unwind, and Izzy ended up showing me her bracelet-making kit. I decided I'd make one for everyone."

"Ethan." Isabela taps my leg. "Sit."

"If I get on the floor, sweet girl, I won't get back up, but you look after Elliot, okay? I'll go and find your dad."

She nods firmly, seeming happy with that answer.

I make my way outside and see Kendrick manning the grill with Jackson. They both wave when they spot me. Blaine and Mitch are playing knee hockey with Jackson's son, Ryan, and Peyton is relaxing on a sun lounger, sipping on a beer.

"You made it!" Peyton throws his hands up, causing beer to slosh onto his hand . "I was starting to think I'd have to break into your apartment and force you to come have a hot dog."

I chuckle and shake my head. Taking a seat next to him, he hands me a beer from the cooler, and I lean back.

"I didn't want to risk being tickled by Elmo," I deadpan.

He grins. "Knew that would scare you."

I roll my eyes, then glance around the backyard.

"No Zach?"

"Nope. Dude's still in Denver. I don't know how they don't get sick of each other spending all that time together. It's like they're a married couple or some shit."

I don't even know how to answer that.

Zach and Carter's friendship is…complex. They've been friends since they were six and have done everything together up until they were both drafted by two different cities. I can't lie and say I'm not concerned about the code-pendency they've got going on, because that kinda connection often leads to one of them getting hurt, and I just know in my gut it will end up being Zach.

Not that Carter is a bad guy, but Zach is too nice for his own damn good.

Peyton's vizsla, Daisy, comes bouncing over, her tail wagging like crazy. She takes one sniff of me, then looks at me with an almost perplexed expression. Instead of sitting next to me like she normally does, she moves to Peyton's other side, curling up with a huff, and gives me sad eyes.

"Dude, your vibe is making my dog sad," Peyton states. "What's going on?"

I look at him out of the corner of my eye and shake my head. "It's nothing."

"Clearly it's not nothing, 'cause even the dopey dog doesn't want to be near you." He points at Daisy.

Not that I blame her. I'm a miserable motherfucker at the moment, even more than usual.

Knowing I need to start opening up more to these guys, I look over to where they're standing around the grill. I don't know if I'm ready to confess everything to all of them, especially Blaine, considering he's dating Jacob's brother, but if I talk to Peyton, it's a start.

Baby steps, right?

"I'm having trouble with some things," I begin.

"Such as?"

"I can't stop thinking about this guy, and I'm not sure how to handle it."

Peyton's silent for a moment, then his face breaks out in a stupid grin. "Dude, I was worried you were gonna sprout some bad shit, like you're sick or something. Wait, unless you're getting back together with Ian." His brows furrow. "Please don't tell me you're getting back with that fucker."

"Fuck no." I quickly shake my head.

He lets out a relieved sigh. "Then what is the problem?"

Rubbing my hand over my face, I mumble, "I fell for Jacob."

"I'm sorry? What was that?" He cups a hand around his ear mockingly. "I don't think I heard you right because it sounded like you just confessed to having feelings for someone," he teases.

"I'm in love with Jacob."

"Jacob?" Peyton wonders for a second. "Alex's brother, Jacob?"

I nod.

"That's awesome!" He punches my bicep. "He seems like a great guy from the few times I've met him, so I don't understand why the long face? He doesn't feel the same or something?"

"I said that we could have a 'what happens in England, stays in England' kind of arrangement, so when we landed back in Chicago, he thanked me for everything and then said I'm an incredible friend."

Peyton looks dumbfounded. "O-kaaay…And you didn't think to tell him how you felt before you went your separate ways? That you didn't want it to end?"

I shake my head.

Peyton blinks at me, looking at me like I've grown two heads. "Did you at least give him any indication that you have feelings?"

I shake my head again. "No. I was going to, but then I spent the entire flight trying to figure out how to say it. By the time I was ready, he'd already spoken, and it was too late."

"Fuck's sake, Ethan," he groans, rubbing his face with his hands before giving me an exasperated look. "He was probably assuming nothing had changed. That whatever you had really stayed in England. I mean, if you didn't say anything, he probably presumed he was nothing to you. A one and done. The whole 'friend' spiel was probably to protect himself or give you an easy out."

I reel back like I've been struck.

What we had wasn't *nothing*. He's not *nothing* to me. He's so far from *nothing*.

Our time together—and him—became everything I didn't know I needed. But I convinced myself that I couldn't bare my soul to Jacob, just in case it was simply a summer romance to him.

I allowed the one man who understood me to slip away.

*He hasn't gone anywhere.*

Fuck. I had a whole week to go talk to him instead of wallowing in self-pity. Hell, I haven't even checked in to see how he's doing—if he's struggling with the jet lag he was so worried about. If things at the bakery are all good.

How was he supposed to know he owns every fiber of me when I didn't have the balls to tell him?

"I saw Ian at the wedding. Told me he left because I was never home. He said that I was difficult to love and he couldn't compete with hockey," I confess to Peyton, as if this somehow excuses me.

"What a fucking prick," he spits. "Don't tell me you believed his shit, Ethan. You know better."

"I have a season left in me—two at most. I started thinking that I wanted another cup before I retired, which would mean putting in a lot of work. Long days, strict routines—you know how it goes." I suck in a breath, my voice going quiet as I confess, "And I don't want Jacob to end up resenting me. I don't want to end up pushing him away."

Peyton's fingertips dig into his brow bone as he processes my words. He's silent for a beat. When he looks up again, his expression is serious.

"I think you should speak to him. Open up. Unlike that fucking asshat Ian, Jacob has a business. He has other interests besides you. He has Alex. A home. Other stuff going on in his life that has nothing to do with you to keep him busy while you're doing whatever you're going to put yourself through—which, for what it's worth, I think is insane. But you need to take this to him. Don't make the decision for you both."

"Yeah, you're right," I grumble, staring out across the lawn to where Blaine mock celebrates with Ryan. "I'll talk to him."

"Good. Thank you for talking to me about it, though. I appreciate it." He stops for a second. "And don't think I didn't notice you said you *wanted* another cup. Like maybe that's not all that matters anymore."

I rub the back of my neck as I think about Jacob and his idea for when I retire. Since that day in the museum, ideas have been flowing on how I could make my foundation great.

When I don't say anything, he continues, "You know, the guys went crazy when you sent that text saying you missed us."

My eyebrows lift in surprise. "Really?"

He nods. "Yeah. They've always felt a little…unsure, I guess. You're here, but you're not very open. Kendrick and I get it 'cause we've known you for so long, but the younger guys?" He looks over his shoulder before looking back to me. "They're desperate to know you, Ethan, but as a person, not just their captain. If this is going to be your last season, maybe…I don't know…let them in. Show them a part of your journey that got you where you are today."

I'm stunned into silence. Jacob mentioned the barrier I've inadvertently created between me and them, but I think I didn't realize the extent of it. Or how they felt about it— or me.

I thought I was only protecting myself, but I was hurting other people in the process.

They're my teammates. My brothers.

The guys who would ask how high if I told them to jump.

Then I hurt Jacob.

The guy who understood me so seamlessly. Who opened his heart to me in such a beautiful and tragic way. Who made me look at life differently.

"Since when are you this keen on dishing out advice?" I grumble.

"Couples' therapy." Peyton shrugs. "I can't say it's going to save my marriage, but it's given me a different perspective on things."

That causes me to look over at him with a frown. "You don't think it's helping?"

"No, it is helping, but not us as a couple. I fucked up—a lot—then got mad because she slept with someone else. I didn't stop to think about the times I hooked up with other people on the road while still wearing a wedding band on my finger, and it wasn't because I didn't love her. It was just because I could. If anything, these sessions are showing me she's better off without me. She deserves a lot more than what I can give her, and I think she's realizing that too."

"You want a divorce?"

"Honestly? I don't know. I want her to be happy, and I don't think she will be while we're together, but I want it to be her decision. And I know I have a lot of growing up to do."

While I've thought that for quite some time, it was something Peyton needed to realize on his own. There's only so much guidance I can give these guys before they have to deal with it themselves.

"Food's ready!" Kendrick shouts, waving a hot dog sausage in the air with the tongs. The sausage breaks in half and flies onto the floor. Daisy scrambles off the sun lounger to grab it as Kendrick grimaces. "Shit! Sorry, Pey!"

Peyton rolls his eyes and laughs, waving him off before looking back at me. "We worry about you, man... I've always wondered whether you were lonely up in your ivory tower, so talk to him, 'kay?"

"Yeah, I will," I reply as we stand.

Kendrick piles a mountain of food on our plates, and we head over to the table to eat.

Elliot comes outside with Isabela close behind, wearing beaded bracelets up to her elbows. She goes around the table, handing over bracelets to each of the guys. They thank her and slip the bracelet on their wrists, but when she gets to me, she crooks her finger to come closer.

Leaning down until I'm at eye level, she cups her small hand around my ear and whispers, "Yours is my favorite."

There's a tug at my heart at the joy in her sparkling brown eyes, and when I accept the bracelet, I have to swallow down my emotion. The beads are red and black, like our jerseys, and it has 11—my number—a heart, and my last name. I put it on next to my watch while she watches me.

"It looks awesome, Isabela. I'm never going to take it off."

She preens, the apples of her cheeks turning pink.

"Isabela, come get some food," Jackson calls.

She quickly runs off to her dad before taking her mini

plate to where there's a blanket laid out on the grass, where she sits next to her brother and Daisy the dog.

"So, how was England?" Kendrick asks.

"Good." I nod. "I think Jacob enjoyed himself."

Blaine eyes me warily. "Did he? He's been kinda quiet since he got back. He said he had a great time, but he doesn't seem like himself."

Fuck. I never wanted that to happen. It pains me to know he's hurting, and it's all because of me.

"I think he did…" I trail off. "Look, there's something I need to tell you."

I need to do this. I need to open up, let them in.

I watch as they gather around me without even thinking about it, and, taking a deep, steady breath, I tell them everything.

I tell them all about my dad leaving when I was seven, about my mom struggling to keep me playing hockey, about my name change and the pressure from scouts when I was only fourteen.

I tell them all about Ian and the way I've protected myself ever since, even by keeping them at a safe distance. By the time I'm finished, no one says anything for a while, but they all look shocked.

"Fucking hell, man," Blaine says, breaking the silence. "I had no idea."

"Kendrick and Peyton were the only ones who met Ian. I worked hard for you to see me as a decent captain, a good teammate. I didn't want you guys to see me any differently or feel sorry for me." I run an aggravated hand through my hair.

I'm not annoyed at them.

No, this is all on me.

"I'm sorry for not letting you guys in sooner. For allowing you to feel like you never really knew me. I wanna get better at being more open. It's tough, especially when I've been keeping everyone out for most of my life, but you guys mean the fucking world to me."

"You know we wouldn't have looked or felt any differently about you, right?" Elliot says, worried.

"I suppose I always knew, but it was hard to trust that feeling. My past really did a number on me. Jacob was the one who helped me see things a little differently—that I've been allowing the ghosts of my past to dictate my future."

Blaine's eyes widen slightly. "Jacob knows all this?"

"Yeah." I nod. "I told him everything while we were in England. He even met Ian. And I also fell in love with him in the process and then fucked it all up when I couldn't tell him how I feel."

Elliot's jaw drops open. Everyone seems to be in shock.

"Holy shit," Kendrick blurts out.

Peyton sits to my right, grinning like the Cheshire cat.

"The real question is—what are you going to do about it?" Jackson asks.

"I'm gonna get him back," I confess.

Blaine and Elliot share a look, mirroring bright smiles.

"I think this calls for an Olsen plan of action."

# Chapter Twenty-Five

*Jacob*

With summer having well and truly arrived in Chicago, I'm making the most of my day off and enjoying the warm weather. I wiggle my freshly painted toenails, watching as the dark purple glitter sparkles under the bright sun, and take a sip of the frozen pineapple and cranberry mocktail I just whipped up.

Leaning back into the sun lounger, I let out a contented sigh and close my eyes.

This week was crazy.

From carrying out interviews for another member of staff as Aria is heading back to college in the fall, to completing some incredible wedding cakes and juggling my ever-evolving emotions when it comes to Ethan, it's easy to say my brain has been feeling a little overwhelmed.

I know the pace I've been going at is unhealthy and that burying my head in the sand is only effective for so long.

One day, I'm going to need to bite the bullet and confront Ethan. I can't believe I haven't heard from him at all since we returned home ten days ago. He hasn't stopped by the bakery at all or even sent a single text saying hello, but then again, I haven't tried to reach out either.

I want to regret going to England. For getting on that plane, for agreeing to be his fake boyfriend, for meeting his mom and standing up to his asshole ex—but I can't.

As much as I'm hurt and upset right now, it was still one of the most incredible trips of my life.

"No point crying over a real man when you can lose yourself in a fictional one," I mumble to myself as I open my book where I left off, losing track of time until a loud knock at the door steals me away from the chapter I'm reading.

Slipping my bookmark inside to keep my place, I make my way inside. When I open the door, the last person I expect to see is standing there.

Holding the largest bouquet of flowers I've ever seen.

His eyes trail down my body before making a slow perusal back up, taking in my tank top and shorts.

"Hey." Ethan smiles when his eyes finally meet mine. He rubs the back of his neck with his free hand, all unsure and lacking confidence. "These are for you."

He holds out the flowers, and I take them in my arms. They're heavier than I expected and nearly take up the width of the door frame.

A mix of dark and light peonies and roses. Some of the peonies have started to open, and I bring them to my nose to sniff.

My stomach swoops, and my heart flutters like there's a

kaleidoscope of butterflies in my chest. I can't believe he remembered they're my favorite.

When I don't say anything, he shoves his hands in the pockets of his jeans and gives a small shrug. "I just…" he trails off. "I miss you."

My breath hitches in the back of my throat.

Well, I wasn't expecting that.

But this was what I wanted, right? For Ethan to realize that we're good together. So why am I starting to feel frustrated? Does he think that he can just waltz in here and expect things to go back to the way they were after over a week of radio silence?

*You know him better than that.*

I thought I did. I thought he wouldn't shut me out the second we left English soil, so now I'm not sure what to think.

"Thank you, Ethan; these are beautiful." This is awkward. He's just standing there, looking at me, and I don't want to regret not saying what I feel. So I add, "I've missed you, too."

The smile he gives me makes the dimple in his left cheek pop out.

"Would you like to come in?" I finally ask, stepping aside.

He nods, stepping inside and closing the door behind him. He follows me into the kitchen in silence while I find a vase for the flowers and put them in water. I offer him a drink, then lead him outside, where he sits on the patio chair next to the sun lounger.

"So, how have you been?" he asks, taking a tentative sip of soda.

I glance over to him, shielding my eyes from the sun with my hand, even though my sunglasses are on my head. I don't want to shield my emotions this time. I want him to see everything.

"Honestly? Not great."

His face falls, but I'm not going to give in. I'm not going to pretend everything's fine when he's pissed me off. He opens his mouth to speak, but I cut him off.

"I thought we had something special, but the way you shut me out the second we boarded the plane?" I shake my head. "It hurt. It was like you just dismissed everything we had, closed the book on that chapter of your life, and moved on." I stop talking and take a shaky breath. "I know what our deal was, but you just let me walk out of the airport without a word."

Ethan leans forward, resting his elbows on his knees. His hands twist as his forehead creases with a deep frown, in his jaw ticking with tension. When he looks up, sorrow is written all over his face.

"It wasn't like that at all, and I'm so sorry I made you feel like that was the case," he begins. "I was racking my brain trying to find the right way to ask if you would like to give things—us—a chance when we got back. Not as a friends-with-benefits arrangement, but actually dating, and I know it sounds fucking ridiculous because all I needed to do was *ask*." He runs his fingers through his hair in distress. "I know I didn't need to make a big thing out of it, but my anxiety convinced me that I needed some sort of grand gesture for you to take the leap. Then, by the time I stopped being an idiot and getting myself so worked up over it, it was too late."

I chew on my bottom lip.

I want to believe him. I really do. But while my heart is yelling at me to do this, my brain is questioning how long it will take until his anxious thoughts take up space in his head. How long until he shuts me out again.

The only way this is going to work is if we both put everything on the table for once and for all.

Including the painful truths.

"If we give this a chance, how do I know you won't just end things the second the season starts? How can I trust that you're all in and that I'm not just someone for you to spend some time with between now and when you're playing again? That I'm not a stepping stone for someone else?"

His gaze remains fixed on mine, those chocolate brown eyes boring into me, unwavering as he speaks.

"I wouldn't do that to you," he states. "This last week without you only cemented the fact that I don't want what we had to be a fond memory. I don't want to wake up in the morning and not see you next to me. I understand your fears, and I'm so fucking sorry that I caused this."

I swallow the lump in my throat. He's saying all the right things, pulling at my heart strings in ways he doesn't even know, but I need to be sure he's serious, and that isn't going to happen overnight.

"I want to be better, J. I don't want my past to control me any more. Can we just take it day by day?" he asks. "Let me prove to you that I'm not going to run from this. From us. I want to be with you, and I'll wait as long as it takes for you to believe me. You're not a stepping stone to me."

I sigh, smiling softly. "Okay."

His returning smile causes my breath to catch. Oh, how I've missed those fucking dimples.

"Would you like to do something this afternoon? Like an impromptu date?"

My eyebrows raise in surprise. "What do you have in mind?"

"Maybe the zoo?"

My resolve falters a bit, and I answer, "I'll go get ready."

An hour later, we're standing in front of the lion's den at Lincoln Park Zoo. Ethan has his hand on my lower back as we watch two male lions basking in the sunshine on a rock. One is grooming the other lovingly while the other sleeps.

Ethan's words keep running through my mind in a loop. I want to believe that he is serious, that he won't run at the first sign of struggle, or during our first fight, but I know how long he's allowed his fear to control him.

And I'm not naive enough to think that it would simply disappear.

I don't want to lose him. But I also don't want to fall so madly, deeply in love only to find out it was mostly one-sided. Only for him to hurt me somehow.

And while I know it wouldn't be intentional, it would destroy me, nonetheless.

"I told the guys about my dad and Ian the other day," Ethan announces.

I turn to face him, shocked. "How did that go?"

He laughs quietly under his breath, slightly shaking his

head. "They were great. Supportive as ever. It made me feel like a fucking asshole for being so closed off for so long."

I know how difficult it has been for him. This means something.

*Maybe he does want to change.*

"I'm proud of you."

He looks down. Behind his glasses, there's a slight bashful glint in his eyes. His lips part as if to speak, but he remains silent.

"I mean it. I know how hard it must have been to open up to them, but they love you. They want the best for you and to support you in any way they can." I place my hand on his bicep, squeezing the firm muscle gently. Oh, I missed his arms. "It'll take time to unlearn all your coping mechanisms, but it'll be worth it, I promise."

As we continue to make our way around the zoo path, he tells me all about what happened with the guys. I find my hand gravitating toward his, my heart slowly filling with joy as he speaks. Slipping my hand into his, I lace our fingers together. He stops in his tracks and looks down at our joined hands before looking back up at me.

I give him a reassuring smile.

I know in my heart he's genuine; I'm just being cautious. But I don't want him to think I don't care because I do.

A lot.

We make our way past the penguins and stop in front of the polar bears when Ethan announces, "I've also spoken to my lawyer about setting up the foundation. You know, getting the ball rolling."

I gasp, turning to face him. "Ethan, that's amazing!"

He smiles coyly. "Maybe, but I couldn't have done it without you."

"Yes, you could. You just needed a little nudge in the right direction. A bit of self-belief. I know it's a cliché, but you can do anything you set your mind to, E."

He wraps his arm around my waist, bringing me close to his side, and I can't help it. I lean into him, loving the feel of his body against mine. The woody scent of his aftershave.

"Hey, guys!" The loud voice startles me, and I turn to see Elliot rushing toward us with ice cream in hand and a large grin on his face. "We're gonna go see the otters! Wanna come?"

Close behind him is a young guy with shoulder-length hair who can only be Mitch Henry, based on what Ethan told me, followed by Blaine and Alex.

A flash of hurt rushes through me as Ethan quickly drops his hand from my waist. When I glance at Alex, I assume he saw it too, based on the scowl he's sending Ethan's way.

We follow the others, but Alex lets go of Blaine's hand to take hold of my elbow, pulling me back slightly so we fall behind.

"What's going on?" he whispers.

"He showed up at the house with a big bouquet of flowers and told me he missed me," I start before telling him everything else.

"That's amazing, right? So why do you look so…blue? Is it because he let you go when we arrived? Because I saw that, and I'll kick his ass for it."

"Yes." I sigh, running a hand through my hair to push it off my face. "I'm scared, Alex. He just did that in front of you, so what will happen when the season starts? Will he remember all the bullshit his asshole ex said and end things before giving me the chance to show him I'm not anything like him?"

Alex frowns. "I can understand your worries, but I don't think Ethan does things on impulse. He wouldn't have come to you if he wasn't serious about it, or about you."

"I know. I'm just afraid."

"I get that. Just…don't write him off just yet. Give him a chance," he smiles.

"Didn't you want to kick his ass a minute ago?"

"I'm going to give him a chance too. For now."

When we reach the otter enclosure, Elliot is already up against the glass. I can see his bright smile in the reflection.

I stand next to Ethan. His fingers brush against mine in a gentle caress. When I glance over to him, I realize that I need to start taking my own advice.

If I'm going to do this—if we're going to do this—I can't let *his* past affect how I live my life going forward either.

And I would be a fool to deny this man a chance.

# Chapter Twenty-Six

*Ethan*

"I'm really sorry about this," Jackson says, running a hand through his hair. "I wouldn't ask if I wasn't desperate."

"It's okay," I say reassuringly.

Jackson called an hour ago, asking if I wouldn't mind looking after his kids for a couple of hours. He was traded to the Thunder back in February to be closer to his parents following an amicable divorce, and I've kind of taken him under my wing ever since. I don't like seeing people struggle.

Plus, his kids are pretty cool, so I have no problem with him dropping them off with me.

"Take as much time as you need. I don't have anything planned today, so it's fine."

Jackson rubs his face with his hand. He looks exhausted, but I guess becoming a single dad while still playing professional hockey will do that to you.

"Thank you," he answers with a grateful smile. He turns

to speak to the kids. "Be good for Ethan, okay? Do what he says. I'll be back soon."

"Okay, Dad." Ryan waves, then takes his little sister's hand. "I'll look after Izzy."

She wiggles her hand free from his and clings to my leg like a koala. "I want Ethan."

Ryan rolls his eyes. "Whatever, Izzy." He looks up at me. "Ethan, can I watch Sports Network?"

"Sure." I barely have time to nod before he runs off into the living room and jumps onto the couch.

Jackson hesitates at the door. "Call me if they give you any trouble."

"I'm sure they won't, but I'll call you if there's an emergency."

"Bye, Daddy!" Isabela sings, waving her hand so hard her entire body shakes.

Jackson sighs, gives another small smile, and nods. "Okay, bye. See you later."

The door clicks shut behind him, and I look down at the little curly blonde girl hanging off my leg.

"So, what do you wanna do?"

She shrugs. "Color?"

"Uh, yeah, okay."

She takes my hand—or more like she grabs hold of my fingers—and drags me into the living room, where she's dumped her pink backpack. She empties the contents out on the floor and collects an assortment of colored pens. I sit down next to Ryan, who's engrossed in the hockey game highlights showing on the screen, his eyes wide.

"How's hockey camp going, Ryan?" I ask.

He nods slowly, not taking his eyes off the TV. "Good."

"Did you go this morning?"

He nods again. "Yeah, scored two goals."

"That's awesome, dude."

He aimlessly sticks his thumb up at me, making me laugh. I don't think he's blinked once since he's sat down. He's following in his dad's hockey footsteps, and from what Jackson has told me, he seems to be thriving in the U8's.

It's wild to think he's now the same age I was when my dad left.

Isabela climbs onto the couch next to me and settles on her knees, popping the lid from one of her pens before starting to color one of my tattoos.

My brows furrow in concern.

"Uh, Isabela, are those permanent markers?"

"What's perm-an-ent mean?" She looks up at me curiously.

"Like, this will come off, right?"

"Dunno." She shrugs, then continues to color, completely unfazed.

I turn to her brother. "Ryan? Do you know if these pens wash off?"

"I think so." He shrugs too. What's with these kids shrugging all the damn time? "Can we have snacks?"

I look down at where Isabela is holding my wrist with one hand while she concentrates on coloring with the other. Her tongue peeks out of the corner of her mouth, just like Elliot's when I walked in on them making bracelets.

"Sure, yeah, go help yourself."

Ryan jumps off the couch and sprints into the kitchen, returning minutes later with a big bag of chips.

I guess he found the stash I keep for whenever Elliot raids the pantry.

"Don't eat them all or your dad will go crazy on me."

"Yeah, okay." He shoves a handful into his mouth, laughing when the presenter shows fight highlights from last season.

Considering I'm unable to move, I relax back on the couch and allow myself to imagine my life like this. Sitting in front of the TV, watching the world go by outside the window as I watch the kids doing their stuff and just being there with them.

Would I stay downtown or get a house in the suburbs?

Would Jacob want kids?

Fuck. I'm getting ahead of myself. I told him we'd take things slowly, and here I am, jumping feet first into a possible house with possible kids.

It's been a few days since our mini-date to the zoo, and I tried to give him space. I sent him a couple of texts, called a couple of times, and it seems fine.

Except I want more. But at the same time, I understand his fears completely.

Hell, I deserve it.

It's going to take time for him to see I'm serious about us and that I won't leave him behind as soon as the season starts.

No matter what it takes, I'll make him see I want to be with him.

I'm not sure how much time has passed when the door buzzer sounds. Slowly prying myself out of Isabela's hold, I ignore her pouting frown and get up to head to the intercom.

"Hey, what's up?" I say as I answer.

"Hello, Mr. Parkes. I have Mr. Lowry here to see you," Andrew, my doorman, responds.

My heart squeezes.

Jacob's here?

"Please send him up. I'll leave the door open," I say quickly. "Also, please add him to my approved visitors' list."

"Of course, Mr. Parkes."

I hang up and turn around to see Isabela standing next to me. She holds her arms up, doing a grabby motion with her hands, and because I can't say no to her, I pick her up. She curls her hand around the back of my neck and plays with the hair there.

"Who that?" she asks timidly as we watch the door for Jacob to appear.

I tilt my head to look at her.

"A man who is very special to me." *The man I'm in love with.* "Are you going to be nice to him?"

She pouts again. "I'm nice. I get stickers at school."

I laugh under my breath.

A moment later, the door opens, and Jacob peeks his head around the door.

"Hello? Ethan?" he calls out.

The second I see him, it's like a rush of warmth fills my body. He's dressed in some faded jeans and a light gray V-neck t-shirt, and his hair is perfectly styled. When those blue eyes land on me, my breath hitches slightly.

He's so fucking beautiful.

"Hey." I smile.

"Hey," he replies, his eyes flicking to Isabela and then

back to me. "Sorry, I didn't know you were busy. Blaine said you needed my help with something."

*Oh, did he now? The sneaky little asshole.*

I manage to swallow my laugh at my teammate's meddling antics.

"I'm just looking after Jackson's kids for a few hours while he's at a meeting. This is Isabela," I introduce her. She gives him a shy smile and waves before hiding her face in my neck, her fingers still twirling the hair on the back of my head. "Ryan's watching TV. Can I get you a drink?"

He shakes his head, rolling his lips inward as if he's unsure. I don't like how guarded he's become around me. It's like we've gone back to when we first met. When he was hesitant and unsure around me. When he didn't trust me.

*This is all on me.*

My behavior and my actions caused this, and I fucking hate that I've dimmed the light of my sunshine.

"No, I'm fine, thanks."

Leading him into the living room, Isabela still hanging onto me, I carefully sit down, pulling her into my lap. I glance down and see she's eyeing Jacob.

"She's adorable." Jacob smiles, causing her to go all shy again and hide her face in my neck.

"Yeah, she is. I don't know why she's taken to me the way she has."

He looks startled. "Why wouldn't she?"

I shrug. Clearly, the Wilde shrugging has rubbed off on me. "I don't know. I didn't grow up around kids, so I don't really know what I'm doing most of the time."

"She probably knew you secretly had a fun side behind that grumpy exterior," he grins.

"Maybe," I grumble. "She's a big fan of Elliot too."

At the sound of his name, Isabela raises her head. "We go see Elliot?"

I chuckle. "I don't know if he's home."

She huffs, her shyness suddenly disappearing and Jacob laughs.

"I don't think you have anything to worry about," he proclaims.

"What do you mean?"

He motions between me and Isabela. "You said you weren't sure whether you would make a good father. I don't think you have anything to worry about. You're a natural."

I glance down at the little girl in my arms. Her big, brown eyes shift from Jacob to look up at me. She instantly liked me when we first met, and she was the first kid who ever did that. She seemed nervous and shy around everyone except me and Elliot.

Ryan was a little…startled at first, and he kept asking Jackson if I was really me, but as soon as he realized that I was just a regular guy, he relaxed. Now I always try to join Jackson on their scrimmage, and I've kind of taken on the Uncle role.

I guess I never really noticed how easily that happened or how much I like it.

"Do you mind just keeping an eye on them for a minute while I try and wash this off?" I point to my arm.

He eyes the colorful ink, his lips twitching. "How did that happen?"

I point a finger at Isabela. "*She* happened. She decided her coloring books weren't good enough."

"You have pictures?" She asks Jacob, pointing to his arm.

"No, I don't." He shakes his head. "But I think you've done a beautiful job coloring in Ethan's pictures."

She giggles and slides off my lap, immediately grabbing hold of her coloring book and pens and climbing back onto the couch next to Jacob. She shoves a pen in his hand and points at an empty page.

"Help?"

Knowing she's in good hands, I get up, ruffling Ryan's hair as I pass on my way to the bathroom. I fill the sink with some soapy water, and I'm scrubbing my arm hard with a washcloth when Jacob calls out.

"Ethan?"

His voice sounds weird, so I head back out into the kitchen with my arm still wet. I notice there's a carton of orange juice on the side, along with the plastic cups I keep here for the kids, but my eyes lock on him. He's holding a piece of paper, his brows are furrowed in confusion.

*Oh. Shit.*

"What's this?" he asks, his voice cracking slightly.

He's holding the "Thank you" letter I received this morning from the charity I donate every one of his repayments to. I don't know why I haven't told him this before, and with the panicked look on his face, I realize I should have.

"What is this, Ethan? It has my name on it. It says I've paid over three thousand dollars to this charity."

His words come out in a rush, and I go over to stand next to him. I place my hands on his shoulders, angling his body to face me.

"When I lent you the money, I didn't want you to pay me back, but I knew you wouldn't take it otherwise. I had no hidden agenda—I just didn't want to see you and Alex struggle anymore. It was something I could easily fix, and I was an outsider for you, so it was fine. I mean, if Blaine had offered the money, it would have become complicated if something happened between him and Alex. I donated all the money you repaid me to a charity that funds research and cares for those diagnosed with leukemia, in honor of your grandma."

His eyes turn glassy with unshed tears, his chest starting to tremble with his ragged breaths. The letter in his hand begins to shake.

Shit.

*Please don't be mad at me,* I want to beg.

"I'm sorry if that was out of line. I didn't mean to—"

Jacob drops the letter back on the counter, then reaches up to take my face in both hands and presses his lips to mine in a passionate kiss. I wrap my arms around him, bringing him close and holding him as I feel his tears hitting my cheeks.

I don't know how long we stand like that. Peppering of gentle kisses, just a silent communication of love and gratitude. When Jacob pulls away and rests his forehead against my chest, his body shudders slightly as he quietly sobs.

Quickly glancing over my shoulder to make sure the kids are okay, I place my fingers beneath his chin, I gently lift his head. Those blue eyes are shining like the ocean.

"I hope you're not angry at me or think I've overstepped, but I don't regret doing it. I know how much you wish you could've done more for your grandma, so this was my way of honoring her and the wonderful job she did—they did—raising you and Alex."

He shakes his head a few times, wiping his eyes. He gives me a wobbly smile as he croaks, "Thank you."

"You're not mad?"

"No." He laughs softly. "Of course not. How could I be mad, Ethan?" He places his hand on my chest, smoothing his palm over my heart. "It's the nicest thing anyone has ever done for me."

I raise my hand, brushing his hair off his forehead before cupping his cheek.

"I don't want you to pay me back, J. I don't care about that at all. I want to be with you. What's mine is yours. I just want you to be happy, and hopefully your happiness will include me." I give him a lopsided grin.

His choked laughter is like music to my ears. I can't help but grin wider.

"I'm sorry I doubted you."

"No." I shake my head. "Your feelings were completely valid, J. I was an asshole—"

"Bad word!" Isabela interrupts from where she sits on the couch.

Jacob smothers his laughter with his hand as I grimace.

"Sorry, kid," I say over my shoulder before focusing on Jacob again.

"I was an idiot, and I let my negative thoughts win. I'm sorry for shutting you out when all I wanted to do was let you in. I'm so fucking sorry." This last bit is more of a whisper in case Isabela is still paying attention, which I'm pretty sure she is.

"Ethan, I need you to remember I'm not them. I'm not

your father or Ian. I'm not going to demand you give me all your time or make you choose between me and your career. I want to be there *with* you. I want to be there when you come back from your games so you can tell me about your day and I can tell you about mine." He pats my chest once. "I want to be your partner. I want to support you in every way, just as much as I want you to rely on me, but you have to let me in. We have to be in this together."

Leaning down, I take his lips in a gentle kiss, telling him without words how fucking incredible he is, how much he means to me, and how much I want to be his.

How much I want *us*.

"Aw!" I hear Isabela giggle. I knew she was listening, the tiny eavesdropper. "Cute!"

"Kissing is so gross," Ryan grimaces.

I glance over my shoulder to see her with her head in her hands, Isabela's nose scrunching up adorably, looking like butter wouldn't melt. "You're lucky you're so cute."

"I know!" she answers gleefully.

Jacob bursts into laughter. "She's really adorable."

I kiss his nose.

*I love you,* is on the tip of my tongue. But I swallow it down.

It's too soon for that.

One step at a time.

A little while later, we're lazing on the couch watching a movie that Isabela picked out. She's snuggled up against my side and struggling to stay awake. Ryan's sitting on the other side of Jacob, playing a game on my iPad. Jackson called ten minutes ago to say he's on his way to pick them up, and I can't stop myself from smiling.

I'm just so fucking happy right now. I can see this in my future—Jacob and I together, our kids sitting next to us. A family of our own.

As if he can hear my thoughts, Jacob tilts his head up to look at me, a knowing smile on his lips. I lean down, pressing a soft kiss to them before whispering, "Will you stay?"

He nods.

I glance down at Isabela as the intercom beeps. She's fast asleep, her mouth hanging open.

"Can you get it, please?" I ask Jacob. "It's Jackson."

He kisses me gently and gets up. I hear him talking to Andrew, and the door clicks open moments later. I slowly pry Isabela's hand off my stomach and scoop her up in my arms. She's like a rag doll, her limbs all floppy.

"Wow," he whispers as he laughs quietly. "You've gotta teach me how you managed that because the only time I can get her to nap is in the car."

I jut my chin toward my arm, where the pen didn't wash off. "I was the canvas."

Jackson shakes his head. "Oh shit, I'm so sorry."

"It's no trouble, as long as she had fun." I transfer Isabela over to her dad as Ryan shows up behind me. He gives both me and Jacob a high five, then heads to the door.

"Thank you for this. I really appreciate it," Jackson emphasizes.

I wave him off. "Anytime. If you ever want a day to

yourself to sit in your boxers and watch baseball, give me a call. We'll take them out for the day."

Jackson looks between me and Jacob, a slow smile spreading on his face. "I'm happy for you—for both of you. I'm glad you finally pulled your head out of your ass, Parkes."

I guffaw and flip him the middle finger. "Fuck you, Wilde."

Jackson grins, returning the gesture with his free hand.

We say our goodbyes, not before I promise Ryan we'll have a scrimmage next week, and when the door closes, I turn to face Jacob, pulling him against me.

"So, Blaine said I needed your help?"

He grins, wrapping his arms around my shoulders. "I think he was meddling."

I hum. "It sounds like it, but I'm glad you came today."

I run my fingers through his soft hair, admiring the delicate lines of his face. His high cheekbones, the slope of his nose. The dip in his cupid's bow. The smoothness of his skin.

He's so fucking perfect. How am I so lucky that this man, with the biggest heart I've even known, wants to be with me?

Would he want us to live together?

It feels too soon for that, but this apartment has never felt like home to me. It's been a landing pad, a safe space for me to hide away from prying eyes and the pressure of my job, but Jacob has a home. The home he grew up in. It has seen some monumental moments, both joyous and sad, but Jacob's home is a *home*.

And wherever he is, is my home.

"Stop thinking so hard," he tells me, running his hands up my chest.

"I'm not."

He tilts his head. "I can practically hear you thinking."

"I guess you know me too well." I huff a laugh.

"Tell me. Whatever it is. If this is going to work, you need to be open and honest with me."

Chewing on the inside of my cheek, I brush a strand of hair from his face and take a deep breath.

"In time, I mean, not right now, as I know it's too soon, but eventually, maybe…Would you like to move in together?"

His eyebrows raise slightly. "Oh, wow. I mean, of course." He frowns. "Is that what you were worried about? That I would say no?"

I shrug.

Jacob smiles, sighing. "Ethan, if we're in a relationship, it would make perfect sense for us to move in together eventually. Why would you even doubt this? It would just take me some time to come to terms with leaving my home."

"That's the thing—what if you didn't?"

"What do you mean?"

"What if I moved in there with you and sold this place? We could redecorate or renovate. Whatever you want."

His eyes widen. "You'd do that? But this apartment is gorgeous."

"It is. It's good for what I needed it to be, and it made sense to me. But Peyton described it as my ivory tower the other day, and it's exactly that. It's not a home, not really, but your house is."

Tugging his bottom lip between his teeth, Jacob eyes me for a moment before his face morphs into the sweetest smile.

"You are an incredible man, Ethan Parkes. Did you know that?"

I wrap my arms around his waist and lean down, kissing his mouth with abandon.

"Mmm, I'm not sure. Maybe you can tell me that a few more times," I say against his lips, grabbing his ass to lift him up, and carry him into my bedroom where I plan to lose myself in him.

# Chapter Twenty-Seven



Jacob's hand gently pushes my shoulder, urging me to roll over onto my back. I go willingly, pulling him with me. He straddles my waist and rolls his hips, brushing our hard dicks together, and groans my name deliciously.

Our mouths have been fused together since the second I picked him up in the hallway and carried him into my bedroom. I'm not even sure how much time has passed; we're just lost in each other.

Making up for lost time due to my stupidity.

Fuck, I've missed him.

I've missed his kisses. The soft mewls he makes when I suck on his tongue. The way he lights up every inch of my body with a single touch.

His bright smile and how he feels in my arms.

I've missed every fucking thing about him, and I hate that I nearly lost him.

But there's no time to dwell on that now.

Jacob trails his lips under my jaw and down the column of my neck, his teeth grazing over my pulse before he sinks his teeth into the juncture of my neck.

"Fuck, J," I growl.

My cock throbs behind the zipper of my jeans, begging to be freed to be reunited with Jacob.

But it seems Jacob is in the mood for some torture.

He snickers, rolling his hips in a teasing rhythm, causing me to let out a sharp hiss.

I'm having a difficult time reining myself in, and it's taking every ounce of my control not to throw him onto his back and bury myself inside him. But I also don't want to rush this.

I want to show him how much I've missed him by exploring every inch of his incredible body, letting him know we have all the time in the world now.

I might not be good with words, but this isn't pretend, and I'm all in.

Stroking my hands down his sides, I reach around to squeeze the globes of his ass, halting the hypnotic grind of his hips.

"You're gonna make me come if you keep doing that."

I feel his smile against my lips. He nips at my bottom lip before sitting up and grabbing the hem of my t-shirt. He pulls it up and over my head, tossing it onto the floor before shifting down until his ass is resting on my thighs.

His hands go to my chest, kneading the firm muscles of my pecs. Fingers circle my nipples before flicking them. My breath hitches, my abs tightening under his traveling hands. When he reaches the waistband of my jeans, he pops the button, and a heavy sigh escapes me as Jacob drags the zipper down. My cock stirs inside my boxers, and Jacob licks his lips.

"May I?" he whispers, motioning to my jeans.

I nod.

Wordlessly, he crawls off my body. He removes my jeans and tosses them aside before curling his fingers into the waistband of my black boxer briefs, but instead of taking them off, he pauses.

"You know, when we were in England, there were times where you were fully clothed and I was completely naked."

My dick jerks at the memory. "Yeah, I remember."

"There I was, naked and exposed, and you made me feel like I was the sexiest man in the world. I've never felt so… seen. I felt so happy, so ecstatic every time, and I *loved* it." He pulls my boxers down, finally freeing my thick, heavy cock. He flashes me a wicked grin as he throws them over his shoulder. "Now it's your turn."

Jacob wraps his fingers around my throbbing shaft, stroking me in a soft, languid glide. My head tips back on a moan as his other hand smooths up my thigh to my balls, flirting with the heavy sac.

"Move to the edge of the bed," he demands.

My eyes widen slightly, taken aback by the unfamiliar tone in his voice, but I don't argue. Shifting to sit up, I shuffle down until my feet touch the floor. He kneels down between my parted thighs, those bright blue eyes locked on mine as he wraps his lips around me and takes me into his mouth.

"Holy shit," I murmur, reaching out to take hold of his head, but he bats me away and releases me with a pop.

"Hands stay on the bed. I've missed the way you taste, and I don't want to be rushed." He tongues the slit, licking the bead of precome before taking me back into his mouth.

I grin. "Someone's feeling bossy today."

He hums in agreement around the head, and stars fill my vision.

"Fucking hell, J." I hiss, gripping the sheets with my fists.

While one hand grips the base of my cock, the other flirts with my balls, massaging and squeezing with just the right amount of pressure. He sucks my cock like a dream, taking me deeper, inch by inch, with each passing slide of his warm, wet mouth. The tip of his tongue traces the pulsing vein with every upstroke of his lips, and then he swallows around me, and I lose my everloving mind.

"Fuck!" I curse, my toes curling into the carpet.

I reach for him, cupping his face with my hands, and this time, he doesn't stop me.

"As much as I'm fucking loving this right now, J, I want to be inside you when I come."

He lifts his head, wiping the saliva with the back of his hand, and it's a good thing I'm already sitting down because the smile he gives me knocks the breath from my lungs.

How did I get so fucking lucky?

Taking his chin in my hand, I angle his head up to me and capture his lips in a scorching kiss. Jacob places his hands on my thighs and stands, sucking my bottom lip between his teeth before pulling away.

I watch as Jacob takes off his t-shirt and jeans, kicking off his briefs before he climbs into my lap and wraps his legs around my waist.

His fingers comb through the hair on the back of my

head as we exchange sweet, lazy kisses. Wrapping my arms around him, I gently turn him so he's leaning back against the pillows. I sit back on my haunches between his legs and take him in, grazing my fingers lightly down his side, over his abdomen, and down the outside of his thighs.

"You're so beautiful," I whisper.

He sucks in a breath.

"I wish I was good with words, so I could tell you every day just how magnificent you are."

"You don't have to tell me." Adoration shines in his blue eyes. "Show me."

So I do.

I trail featherweight kisses from his ankle to the juncture of his thigh, following the same pattern on the other leg. When I reach his erection, I nuzzle my nose into the soft, groomed blond curls at the base, inhaling his heady scent.

My name is a chorus of soft moans as I pepper kisses along his length and take his balls in my mouth. I massage each heavy sac with my tongue and up the underside of his shaft, then engulf him in one gulp.

"Fuuuckkk!" Jacob cries, his back arching off the bed.

His body trembles as I swallow around him. I grind my own aching cock against the sheets, desperately seeking relief.

"Please," he begs, raising his legs to rest over my shoulders.

I take him to the back of my throat until his muscles quiver around my ears, then release him with a wet pop to reach over to the nightstand for the lube. I move to retrieve a condom, but Jacob shakes his head.

"I'm negative," he whispers. "I haven't been with

anyone since you, and I was tested before we went to England."

My breath hitches. "Me too."

"I want to feel you." He squeezes my cock and smirks. "All of you."

Coating my fingers, I rub two against his taint before ghosting over his hole. I trace the puckered rim, then gently press the tip of one finger inside.

I thrust my tongue into his mouth as I slowly ease my finger inside him, eagerly claiming each whimper and groan as he takes another digit.

"Ethan," he murmurs against my mouth. He's riding my hand, his hips squirming as he tries to get closer, wanting it deeper. His fingers are tangled tightly in my hair, keeping me where he wants me.

I slick up my length and press the head against his hole. He's ready for me. With one hand steadying the base of my dick, I lift one of his legs and bend it toward his chest, the angle opening him up for me to gently push inside.

I bare my teeth in a hiss as I pass that first ring of muscle. He's so fucking tight, my feet tingle. Slowly thrusting my hips, I raise his other leg and rest his ankles on my shoulders. I move, my elbows bearing all my weight as I slowly rock my hips, inching inside him as I cover his mouth with mine.

Jacob grabs hold of my shoulders, letting out a long, breathy moan when I'm all the way in.

I don't move. I simply bask in the way he feels with nothing between us, but he soon squeezes around me, urging me to move. I rock my hips, stroking my tongue into his mouth in slow, unhurried caresses that match my rhythm. I adjust my hips so I can reach that magical spot with every thrust, and I'm rewarded with Jacob's moans of ecstasy.

There's a burning ache in my chest. I didn't know it could feel this way. To love someone so much it consumes me.

His cock jerks between us, leaving precome against my abs.

"Oh, God! Ethan!" Jacob pants, his fingers digging into my shoulders. "I'm gonna come."

Pleasure pulses down my spine as I chase Jacob's release with my own, hitting his prostate in a frantic rhythm. His back arches, and warmth seeps between us. He squeezes around me as he comes, and that's all it takes. I come inside him, a ferocious roar escaping my throat. I'm unable to hold myself up any longer; my limbs shake and collapse on top of him.

Jacob runs his fingers through my hair, pushing it from my face. Taking hold of his wrist, I press a kiss to the center of his palm before raising my head and pressing a kiss to his chest, right over his heart.

"I'm not letting you go this time," I whisper. "This is the start of forever."

# Chapter Twenty-Eight



"Am I doing this right?" Ethan asks, holding his flour-dusted hands up.

I peer around him to look at the dough he's been mixing to make Elliot's favorite cookies ahead of Blaine and Elliot's birthday get-together tonight.

We decided to close the bakery today so Alex could focus on getting everything ready and so I could use the kitchen with no interruptions to make the selection of cakes I will be bringing with me.

As Ethan got Elliot and a sweet dish in the random generator Alex created, he spent all of yesterday in a slightly stressed state over what to do, until I suggested making his favorite cookies.

He looked at me, completely perplexed, but I reassured him I would help him. It took some convincing, as he didn't want to rely on me to help him when I had to make the cakes, but I promised it wouldn't be a bother.

"Yeah, that looks fine. Just make sure the chocolate pieces are spread evenly throughout."

He grunts, pouring more crushed-up M&M's into the mixing bowl.

I shake my head, grinning.

Over the past two weeks, we've settled into a relaxed routine. On the nights I'm working late, he lets himself into my house and gets dinner ready for when I get home, and when I have days off, I stay at his downtown apartment. We've gone on double dates with Alex and Blaine and slowly weaved our lives together.

Ethan's been gradually lowering his guard every day. I can still sense it's difficult for him at times, especially when he's spent the majority of his life being a vault, but his actions tell me how he feels.

He's so kind and attentive, that he doesn't need to tell me with words how he feels.

As I place the sponge cakes on a cooling rack, I get to work mixing up the cupcake batter when I hear a knock on the door.

I lift my head, looking over to Ethan. "Did you hear that?"

He looks over his shoulder and takes a step toward the door. His brows lift in surprise.

"It's Zach," he announces.

Wait…What? He's supposed to be in Denver for at least another month. Worry prickles in my stomach.

"Go let him in."

Ethan disappears. I hear the jingle of the bell above the

door and the muffled sound of voices. Zach appears, looking a little worse for wear. Dark circles emphasize his tired-looking eyes. Tendrils of long, dark hair have escaped his bun.

"Hey, Jacob," Zach says, smiling weakly.

"Hey!" I round the counter, wiping my hands on a cloth, before giving him a hug. "I'm surprised to see you back so soon. I thought you were spending the summer in Denver."

His shoulders drop as his entire demeanor shifts. "Yeah, I…uh…I had to come back earlier."

Ethan's back stiffens. "Did something happen with you and Carter?"

I slide one of the stools across the floor and motion for him to sit down. Ethan crosses his arms over his chest, his jaw ticking as annoyance flares in his eyes as he leans back against the counter opposite.

Zach lets out a heavy sigh. I notice the skin around his nails is red, like he's been biting them anxiously.

"Me and Carter…Well, you know we've been best friends and inseparable since I was six. I guess you could say we're kinda…codependent. I know it's bad. I don't really know how to live without him in my life, but…" He takes in a deep, shuddery breath, and when he looks up, his eyes are filled with so much heartbreak that I feel the ache in my own chest. "I'm in love with him, and I've made my peace with it. I've always known he didn't feel the same and that he won't. I told myself it would be fine, that as long as I could still have him in my life, I would get over it. But I haven't. I don't think I can, and I don't think I can sit by and watch as he meets other people anymore."

"Oh, Zach." I wrap my arms around him. His head falls

onto my shoulder, and I'm engulfed in one of his lovely big hugs.

I stroke my hand in soothing circles on his back. I catch Ethan's eye over the top of his head, a mix of anger and sympathy written on his face.

"Have you thought about telling him?" I whisper.

I feel him shake his head, his words mumbled against the fabric of my t-shirt. "No. I can't. If I tell him and he gets mad, I could lose him completely."

I squeeze him a little tighter.

"I don't think you would lose him, Zach. You two have been thick as thieves for so long. What if you told him and he feels the same?" Ethan suggests.

Zach looks up, but remains silent.

"I nearly lost this guy because I was too afraid to put my heart on the line." Ethan places a hand on my shoulder. "It's fucking terrifying, but it worked out. I think you should talk to him. He can't do anything about it if he doesn't know."

A smile spreads across my lips as Zach eases out of my hold. His light blue eyes dart between us before landing back on Ethan. "You did it then?"

"Did what?" Ethan asks.

"You finally pulled your head out of your ass and admitted you have feelings for Jacob."

Ethan groans. "Fuck you and Jackson for saying the same thing." He gives him the double bird. "Yes, I did pull my head out of my ass, thank you very much."

I let go of Zach and wrap my arms around Ethan's waist, resting my chin on his pec as I peer up at him. "He's alright. I might keep him."

Zach snorts a laugh, and Ethan shakes his head, tsking

under his breath, but his lips quiver as he tries to hide his smile.

I turn back to face Zach. "Seriously though, Zach, talk to him."

"I will." He nods solemnly. "But not today. Will you help me make something for the twins?"

"Of course." I give Ethan a quick kiss, then turn back to Zach. "How about donuts?"

"Better make some extra for me, I've missed your donuts so much."

"What the fuck is this?" Blaine points to the expansive cheeseboard in Adam Kendrick's hands.

He's been quizzing every person as soon as they walk through the door as to why they brought the food they did and the meaning behind it, but Kendrick's might be the best one yet.

The wooden board is filled with blocks of various cheeses, along with chopped apples and red grapes, and a selection of crackers.

"A cheeseboard," Kendrick says with a roll of his eyes. "Duh!"

"I gathered that, Einstein," Blaine drawls sarcastically. "But why a cheeseboard?"

Kendrick snorts. "Because, my dude, you're the cheesiest fucking sap I've ever met. You're cheesier than The Cheesecake Factory."

"They don't technically sell cheese there," I point out, chuckling, as I take the wooden board from him.

"Semantics." Kendrick waves me off before slapping Blaine's shoulder. "The point is, Blaine, my bro, you are a major simp for Alex. You've turned into a walking gouda, so it's only appropriate to bring the dish that resembles you best." He moves to stand beside me and does jazz hands at the cheeseboard. "Ta-da! Cheese!"

Blaine rolls his eyes, irritated, and flips his teammate off, but his mouth betrays him, the corners of his lips kicking up in a small smile.

Kendrick puts Blaine in a headlock, and the two of them begin to wrestle like children, so I quickly sidestep before they can knock the board out of my hands and place it on the kitchen counter next to the other dishes.

"He was so pleased with himself for this." Kendrick's wife, Maria, laughs, pinching a grape from one of the containers.

"I think it might be the best one yet," I admit.

She grins, then holds out her hand. "I'm Maria, that idiot's wife." She jerks her head in Kendrick's direction. "It's lovely to finally meet you. I've heard a lot about you from Alex, but I've never seen you at a game. We'll have to change that."

I shake her hand. "It's lovely to meet you, too, and thank you for everything you've done for Alex. I know it means the world to him."

At the start of the year, Alex received a high number of unpleasant messages from "fans" who weren't happy that Blaine was off the market. Thankfully, Maria understood exactly what he was going through, having experienced it firsthand, and became a beacon of support for him. They've since become good friends, and I've been looking forward to meeting her thanks to all the great things Alex has said about her.

"You haven't seen me at a game because I'm not that much of a hockey fan, to be honest. I doubt you ever will." I laugh, shaking my head.

*Although I would go if Ethan asked me to.*

"What?" she gasps, holding her chest mockingly. "I'm kidding. It's fairly common for significant others not to attend games."

Glancing over my shoulder, I search for Ethan, and his eyes are already locked on me in a possessive stare as he listens to Peyton. My heart races at the sight of him.

My big, grumpy, gorgeous man.

Maria takes a step forward, placing her hand on my arm.

"I've never seen Ethan look at someone the way he's looking at you. The only time I've seen a look remotely similar was when they won the Cup. But that face?" She juts her chin in his direction and lowers her voice, winking at me. "That's the face of a man in love."

*Is he in love with me?*

We haven't said those three little words yet, but I can't deny that I'm stupidly, head over heels in love with him. I think I've been in love with him since he talked to the two robins in his backyard in England.

Talking to them as if they were my parents. Helping me find comfort and being there for me while I pushed through it.

"Have you met everyone?" she asks.

Giving Maria my full attention again, I shake my head. "I've met some previously, but not all of them. I've been a little busy so far making sure Alex doesn't have anything to worry about."

"Let's change that."

She takes my hand and leads me through the group of people. She introduces me to a few of Ethan's teammates and their wives and girlfriends and Blaine's agent, Hayden. Then she points at Jonathan Peyton, who gives a goofy grin and wiggles his fingers in a wave.

Ethan rolls his eyes and shoves him.

"Jonathan Peyton is married to Katy, but they're currently going through some stuff. He never used to show up at events like this. I don't know the ins and outs of it, but he's been a lot more present with the guys recently."

I turn at the sound of the door opening. Jackson appears, equipped with a casserole dish filled with tacos. Excusing myself from Maria, I head over to Jackson and take it from him.

"Hey! Thanks for coming."

"Hey, I'm sorry I'm late. Isabela wasn't too happy about me leaving her with my parents for the night," Jackson replies.

"Hey, man." Ethan approaches, giving Jackson a one-armed hug, then moving to stand behind me. He wraps his arms around me and rests his chin on my head. "How's my girl?"

Jackson snorts. "She does not shut up about you. I'm tired of hearing 'Ethan this and Elliot that' all the freaking time."

The three of us laugh.

Ethan gets Jackson a drink, and the second Jackson walks off, Ethan cages me against the counter with his arms.

"I feel like I haven't had a minute alone with you tonight," he grumbles.

I ghost my hands up his obliques before coasting back down. "I've been busy playing host to your friends."

"Well, let's tell them to go home so I can have you all to myself instead."

"This isn't our house. You will have to be patient."

His eyes widen slightly, lips parting with an unspoken question. I know he's been desperate to bring up us moving in together since he first asked a couple of weeks back. I've even caught him looking at home décor inspiration boards on his iPad.

Cupping his face with my hands, I rise up on tiptoes and steal a quick kiss.

"To answer the question you're thinking right now, yes, I think we should move in together before you start training camp."

"Really?"

"It makes sense, and I have to admit, I like having dinner cooked for me every night."

"I'm offended that you only want me for my cooking skills," he says, grinning. "But I'll cook for you morning, noon, and night, as long as I get to wake up with you every day."

"Well, you have other interesting *skills* too, but we can talk about those in detail later."

"Sounds." He kisses me. "Like." Kiss. "A." Kiss. "Deal."

"Will you two stop making out? It's time to eat!" Elliot calls out.

Ethan takes my hand, lacing our fingers together, and leads me to where I've placed all the dishes everyone brought with them. Once everyone's plates are full, I take a seat next to Ethan at the dining table, resting a hand on his thigh while he talks to Blaine. My fingers flirt along the seam of his pants on the inside of his thigh, edging higher and higher. He grabs hold of my wrist, and the look he gives me is laced with desire.

I bite down on my bottom lip and smirk.

"If you don't fucking stop, you're going to see those particular *skills* earlier than expected. And in public," he whispers.

Alex looks at me from across the table, a knowing smile on his face. Blaine throws his arm around Alex's shoulder, and he leans into him. I love the way they love each other.

Ignoring Ethan's threat, I pick up one of the cupcakes and use the tip of my finger to scoop some of the frosting off and bring it to my mouth. I let out a low hum as I suck my finger clean from the sugary goodness.

Ethan growls under his breath, so I do it again. He turns slightly on his chair and angling his body toward me. He spreads his legs, reaches down to grab hold of my chair leg, and pulls until I'm seated between his spread legs. His hand goes around my throat, fingers pressing under my jaw, and he turns my head until his lips hover over mine.

"Stop being such a goddamn tease, or you'll be in a world of trouble."

A shiver runs down my spine, and I'm about to tell him to put his money where his mouth is when someone coughs.

*Oops!*

Ethan drops his hand, and my face heats when I raise my eyes to see several people watching us wide-eyed with their mouths gaping.

"This is the best birthday ever!" Elliot hoots, knocking off the party hat he's wearing. "The only way you could top this is if I had a pet otter in a top hat."

"That's not gonna happen, El," Zach says.

Elliot lets out an exasperated sigh. "Dude, it's my birthday. Just indulge me."

"Actually, there is something I'd like to say," Ethan announces.

He pushes his chair back and stands up, taking my hand in his. Anxiety swirls in his eyes, and his breath comes out a little shaky, but his words come out smooth.

"J, seven months ago, this dumbass," he starts, pointing at Blaine, "brought you into my life, and I didn't realize how much of an impact you would have on me. You're like sunshine. I wanted to be near you all the time, to feel your warmth. I felt comfortable around you, and I didn't really understand why until we spent time together in England."

Everyone is completely silent as he continues.

"You made me look at life differently. I was so jaded for so long, allowing ghosts to rule me when there was no reason to be afraid. I have a family around me, and they love me, no matter my flaws. They loved me even when I couldn't let the fuckers in," he admits with a chuckle, motioning around the table, and they all laugh.

"You made me see that I'm not broken. I'm not unlovable. I have a purpose away from the ice. You made me see that I want to be worthy of *you*. I want to grow old with *you*. I know this is too soon, but you've taught me life is short and we need to live each day to the fullest, so I'm telling you, Jacob Lowry, I want us to live together. I want us to have a family. I want to invite these crazy fools to *our* home in

England on vacation and watch as they tear up the place. I want to watch you grow into an even more amazing human being than you already are."

He cups my cheek with his hand, wiping away the tears I didn't realize had fallen.

"J, you told me in England you wanted to be someone's favorite person. And you are. *Mine*. You're my favorite hello and my favorite notification on my phone. Your eyes and your smile are my favorite. Your hug is my favorite, and yours is my favorite hand to hold. Your kiss will always be my favorite, and your love is the only thing I want. My favorite days are the days I spend with you. But you're not my hardest goodbye because I never want to say goodbye to you."

I rush to my feet. Grabbing his face with both hands, I pull his head down and slam our lips together. I'm aware of the hoots and cheers around us, but all I can think about is this man in front of me.

This man, who not long ago couldn't show his feelings.

This man, who was too afraid of letting these very people in enough to know *him*.

This man, who confessed his vulnerable side to those he loved for the first time.

This man, who just told me everything I wasn't sure I'd ever hear.

"I love you," I whisper against his lips.

"I love you, too," he declares. "I mean every word, Jacob, and I'll be showing you how much every day for as long as you'll let me."

## Chapter Twenty-Nine

*Jacob*

*5 months later - December*

"Oh. My. God," I mumble under my breath, gazing around the arena. "This place is insane!"

Alex rocks on his heels, a broad grin on his face. "I know, right? It's amazing."

I'm not quite sure what I was expecting, but this wasn't it. I didn't know it was this huge. I've watched Ethan's games on TV, but you can't fully appreciate the sheer size through a screen. It's kinda crazy to think this is Ethan's workplace. This is his *job*, and as I look around, watching people find their seats, a small smile crosses my face at the thought they might be here for the same reason as me.

Because it might be my first hockey game, but this game marks an incredible milestone in Ethan's career.

This will be his 1600th game played in the NHL, including playoff games.

When I asked him how he was feeling about hitting such a monumental record, he downplayed it. He just shrugged and asked what I wanted to eat for dinner, but I wasn't going to let him get away with it.

He doesn't know we've booked dinner for tomorrow night with all his teammates and their partners, or that his mom, Jennifer, has flown out to watch it. She's sitting up in a box with Kendrick's wife, Maria, who is currently five months pregnant, and a few of the other players' families. But I've decided to sit with Alex a few rows behind the home bench.

We take our seats, and I glance up at the rafters. There's all the championship banners, along with retired players' names and numbers. I can't help but wonder if Ethan's will be up there one day after he retires.

It will, right? Twenty seasons with the same team is rare, according to Alex, and he's been so influential for this team. He deserves a place up there with the legends.

"How are you feeling?" Alex asks.

"Nervous," I admit. "I'm excited to see him play but also really nervous. What if he gets hurt?"

Alex laughs softly. "I get that. I knew it was a dangerous sport before I met Blaine. When they step on that ice, they're not thinking they might get hurt, but it is a possibility. It's fast-paced, sometimes it can be quite brutal. But since I started dating Blaine, there's an added sense of…fear, I guess, every time I watch a game. Because to others in this arena, he's just a player, but to me, he is my fiancé. He's my lover, he's my everything, and if he got hurt, they wouldn't feel it like I would. So I get you're feeling nervous, but you've got to remember that if anything does happen, Ethan is in great hands."

I rub my hand over my face. I know he's right, but it doesn't stop the wave of nerves pooling at the bottom of my stomach.

Since the season started, it's been a learning curve for me. I was aware of the hectic schedule because of Blaine, but living it with Ethan is different. There's days where we hardly see each other. Sometimes I leave for work before he wakes up for practice, or he's left for an away game before I get home. I was a little worried that when the season started, things would change, but they didn't. If anything, they got better. Our relationship became stronger. The time we spend apart has allowed our hearts to grow fonder.

Whenever he's on the road, we FaceTime every night, and he makes sure to set his alarm to wake up to talk to me on the phone while I'm preparing the day's bakes, then sends heartfelt texts throughout the day. Then, on the nights when he returns home late, he whispers, "I love you," before wrapping me up in his arms.

Any worries that I had about him succumbing to the negative thoughts in his brain disappeared, because I know without a doubt he loves me with every fiber in his body.

He moved into my house a week after the twins' birthday and sold his downtown apartment. We redecorated and made it ours, but Ethan made sure to showcase certain memories so they wouldn't be forgotten. I had mentioned my grandma's garden in passing and how all her flowers died because I didn't know how to take care of them, and then one day I came home to him deep in concentration on his iPad, his notebook beside him. He was researching what soil to buy to grow peonies, roses, and hydrangeas, as well as movable planters so we could bring them inside when winter hit.

I cried happy tears; I couldn't believe he remembered, but I was so touched that he did.

He also built a bookcase to store all my grandpa's records and sat with me for hours while we organized photo albums.

He may not be good at *telling* me, but he's incredible at *showing* me, and actions speak louder than words.

The lights go up, illuminating the ice, and the players step out. Alex hoots and claps his hands when Blaine steps onto the ice. I search for Ethan as they appear one by one, but he steps out last. He's so graceful, skating like it's as natural as breathing. I suppose it would be, as he's been doing it for so long.

I tried during family skate day at the start of the season, but I wasn't any good. My legs wobbled like a newborn calf, and I held onto his arms for dear life. Thankfully, he didn't drop me, but that was my first and probably last time.

Blaine skates over, throwing himself into the boards before squishing his face against the glass.

Alex tips his head back and laughs.

"He's such an idiot," he sighs happily. "But he's my idiot, and I love him."

Elliot is doing a little dance, and when he spots me, he waves his glove comically before hitting Ethan on the butt with his stick. My man turns around, his eyes scanning the rows, and when they land on me, he knocks the breath out of my lungs.

I will never get over how beautiful he is when he smiles. Those dimples. How the fine lines around his gorgeous eyes crease. He's so damn handsome, and he's all mine.

When warmup finishes, he gives me a wink before stepping into the tunnel. When he comes back out, my stomach churns with nerves.

The lights dim, and the announcer's voice booms through the speakers.

"The Chicago Thunder are proud to announce that tonight, your captain, Ethan Parkes, will play his sixteen-hundredth professional hockey game. Hailing from Toronto, Canada, Ethan was drafted to the Thunder at eighteen, when he was the number one draft pick twenty years ago. He has delivered the Stanley Cup to Chicago five times, and we are honored to call him our captain. Please direct your attention to the video board as we look back on Ethan's career so far."

Images and videos of a fresh-faced, eighteen-year-old Ethan appear on the jumbotron from the night he was drafted to his first NHL game. The footage spans across his career with the Thunder and each time he lifted the Stanley Cup. It even included some of his rare fights, which I'll be having words with him about later. Tears fill my eyes as I watch, my heart swelling with so much pride I could burst.

Alex wraps his arm around my shoulders, bringing me in close as I suck in a shaky breath.

Once it's over, the camera shifts to Ethan, and the twitch in his jaw tells me he's trying to rein in his emotions. His beautiful dark eyes are glassy, but he's saved by Elliot throwing himself onto him, followed by the rest of the team surrounding him as the fans erupt in cheers.

When he found out this would be happening tonight, he informed his head coach that he didn't want them to make a fuss.

"I don't like being the center of attention," he'd grumbled.

So the team held a private presentation in the locker room before warmups, giving him an engraved silver hockey stick and framed photo of his most memorable moments.

I clap until my hands burn. I'm so freaking proud of him, of everything he's achieved.

I knew he was afraid of retiring, but I didn't truly understand it until now. Seeing that footage, seeing his legacy on the screen spanning across two decades, I can fully appreciate his reasons. His professional career was such a prominent part of his life for so long, and I'm sure he'll mourn it in a way when he hangs his skates up.

I'll be there for him. Whatever he needs.

The game gets underway, and I'm a bundle of nerves. Alex chuckles every time I suck in a breath when someone gets close to Ethan. I don't know how he does this every time Blaine has a game because I don't think my heart can cope. When the game ends with the Thunder winning 4-2, we make a quick stop at the team's store where I pick up Ethan's jersey, before Alex leads us toward the area where we wait for them to shower and change.

I quickly slip it on, smoothing it down my stomach.

"It looks so good! He's going to love it," Alex grins.

I chew on the inside of my cheek. I know how much Blaine loves to see Alex in his jersey, so hopefully Ethan likes seeing me in his too.

When Ethan appears, my heart flips in my chest,

because one thing I didn't know I'd enjoy this much about hockey is game-day suits.

Ethan fills out a suit like a dream. His navy blue tailored pants fit his strong legs, hugging each muscle perfectly. A few buttons of his white dress shirt are left open at the neck, giving a peekaboo to his chest hair underneath, and when he spots me, his chocolate eyes sparkle from behind his black-framed glasses.

I meet him halfway, and he scoops me up in his arms, wrapping them around me as he captures my lips in a toe-curling kiss.

Wolf whistles echo down the corridor, but nothing could tear me away from the most magnificent man I've ever known.

"I'm so proud of you," I murmur against his mouth.

"Yeah?"

I nod, peering up into his eyes. "I'm so freaking proud; seeing you out there was…" I shake my head, tears welling in my eyes. "I love you."

He cups my cheek with his hand, wiping a stray tear away with his thumb. Pressing a gentle kiss to my lips, he whispers, "I love you, too, baby."

Taking a step back, he tries to suppress his smile by rolling his lips as his eyes trail my body, but it only causes his dimples to pop.

"Turn around," he mumbles.

I turn so my back is to him, and when I cast a glance over my shoulder, he's biting down on his bottom lip.

"I like this a lot," he confesses, grabbing hold of my hip, spinning me around, and pulling me toward him. His hands slip under the jersey, and he grabs my ass.

"I've never fucked someone while they're wearing my name before. Think you might wanna wear that later?"

I reach up to wrap my arms around his neck, nipping his lip with my teeth.

"Do you even have to ask?" I whisper, before sliding my tongue into his mouth.

"Yo! Parkes! Quit the PDA and come for drinks at Gino's," Jonathan Peyton calls out.

Ethan shakes his head but doesn't take his eyes off me. "No, you guys go. I'm going home with my man."

*Home.* I love every time he says that.

"Ready to go?" Ethan asks, slipping his hand in mine.

"With you?" I lean in to kiss his lips. "Always."

# Epilogue

PART ONE

*Ethan*

*June - Six months later*

I glance up at the jumbotron as the clock winds down in the third period. There's just under six minutes left, and we're currently up 3-1. We might be dominating Boston at the moment, but we can't get too complacent.

A lot can happen in six minutes, and we can't let our hard work be thrown away by getting comfortable.

Without taking my eyes off the third line battling for puck possession, I pick up my bottle and squirt some water into my mouth. My knee is bouncing non-stop as Mitch poke checks one of Boston's wingers before he's heading toward their goalie on a breakaway, skating like his ass is on fire.

"Come on, Mitchy!" I'm on my feet, voice hoarse.

When he sinks it between the goalie's legs, the energy on the bench is indescribable.

"Fuck yeah!" we all shout, and the arena goes wild.

My blood is vibrating with adrenaline, but I'm remaining focused. We're looking good out there. Really fucking good. If we keep putting those pucks in the net, being strong on the defense the way we are, and if Elliot keeps making those unbelievable saves...

Fuck. I might actually cry.

But I don't have time for emotions right now.

Mentally shaking them away, I jump over the boards for my shift once the whistle blows.

Taking my spot for the face-off, I keep my eyes focused on the linesman's hand but grunt at the Boston winger next to me.

"Ran out of shit to say, eh?"

They've been the chirpiest team I've known in a final, but as the games have gone on, they've become quieter and quieter.

"Fuck off, Parkes."

"Nah." I shove the young player slightly with my shoulder, causing him to lose his balance. "I'm good, thanks."

He grumbles something else under his breath, but I don't catch it because the linesman drops the puck, Blaine passes it straight to me, and I one-timer it into the top right corner of the net. For the second time in the space of a minute, the goal horn sounds, and the guys crush me against the boards, hollering and whooping.

"Fucking yesss!" someone screams.

We make our way back to the bench, and I can't help the smile that takes over my face. My eyes burn with unshed tears as the clock counts down. It's the final minute of the game, and Boston looks like they're ready to throw in the towel. The bench vibrates as we begin to celebrate. Some of the guys are jumping up and down and hugging, but all I can do is focus on the timer ticking down.

Five...

Four...

Three...

Two...

One...

The buzzer sounds, not only declaring us the Stanley Cup Champions but also signaling the end of my NHL career.

I informed Coach Harris and management last week that this would be my last season, but we agreed not to tell the rest of the team until after the Finals.

I didn't want them to lose focus or worry about me. We had too much at stake, and it's not like I'm moving away from Chicago. I'll still be living here because it's where Jacob is, and my home is wherever he goes.

The confetti cannons go off. Helmets, sticks, and gloves are thrown into the air as we swarm the ice, huddling together as we celebrate. Some of the guys let their tears fall. Blaine and Elliot are in a tight embrace as Elliot's tear-streaked face lights up with a bright grin.

We did it.

We fucking did it.

We're Stanley Cup Champions.

Our hard work and dedication have finally paid off, and I couldn't be prouder of all of us. I hug everyone, telling them how proud I am of them and how amazing they played.

They deserve this so much, and I'm so honored to be a part of this incredible achievement.

Glancing out toward the family seats, I search for the person who makes my heart beat, and when I see him, a wide grin splits my face.

He's jumping up and down next to my mom, his hands on his cheeks, like he's trying to hide that wide grin. When our eyes catch, he blows me a kiss and waves, fresh tears rolling down his beautiful face.

I skate back to the boys, and we line up to shake each of our opponents' hands. I thank each of them for a great series, and when the carpet is rolled out, I'm physically shaking.

This is what we work for.

We sacrificed so much for this moment.

Long days, nights away from our loved ones.

Blood, sweat, sometimes losing our teeth, or injuries that could cost us our careers.

At that thought, I glance over to Zach, relieved that he's able to be with us. And as if hearing my thoughts, he looks up, giving me a watery smile and a tip of his chin.

I'm so fucking glad he's here.

The announcer's voice booms over the sound system as the Stanley Cup is carried to the podium. I bite the inside of my cheek, sniffing back my emotions.

"We're delighted to present this trophy to your Chicago Thunder captain, Ethan Parkes!"

I skate over to the League Commissioner, shaking his hand and posing for the standard photo. When he hands over the Cup, I lift it over my head and skate toward the boys before skating a lap around the rink, relishing in the screams and cries of loyal fans, bringing the cool silver to my lips, and kissing it.

A year ago, I was an empty shell. I was looking at my time here with an expiry date, when I only needed to remember that there's more to me than hockey.

I've dedicated twenty years to the league, almost thirty-five years to the game, and now I'm ready for the next chapter in my life.

My foundation is nearly ready to go, and I can't wait to help those kids. To give them the chance to be in the position I am now where they can share the ice with their best friends—the family they'll create when they play the most incredible sport in the world.

I hand the Cup over to Kendrick and watch as each of my teammates lifts it over their heads, taking their lap of honor.

My heart fills with so much fucking pride that it feels like it could burst through my chest protector.

Once we finish taking photos, all the family is allowed onto the ice. I spot Jacob and my mom, and I immediately skate over to them, taking Jacob's face in my hands and kissing him like he's my next breath.

"I'm so proud of you," he sobs, tears falling into his beautiful smile.

When he steps back, my mom practically jumps into my arms, and I have to grab hold of her so she doesn't fall. She squeezes me as hard as she can around my protective gear, her cries filling my ears.

"I'm so fucking proud of you," she chokes out.

The lump in my throat thickens, but I still snort at her dropping the f-bomb.

"I knew you would do it. I knew it," she declares with a nod. "You played phenomenally, and I'm so over the moon you got to become champion again in your final season."

"This is just a bonus." I grin at my mom before looking at Jacob. "I became a champion in the off-season when Jacob handed over his heart to me."

# Extended Epilogue

## PART TWO

*Jacob*

*One year later - July*

"Do you need help with anything?" Alex asks.

"No, I think we're all good." I pick up the numbered candles, carefully placing the four and zero on top of the cake we finished decorating this morning.

"It looks beautiful, Jake." My brother is beaming as he wraps his arm around my shoulders and gives me a squeeze.

I thank him, leaning into his embrace, and glance out of the window that overlooks the backyard of our British home.

It still feels a little surreal that this is my home too. The same home where I fell in love with the most wonderful man. Only this time, it's filled with our closest friends—our chosen family—for the first time to celebrate Ethan's fortieth birthday.

It's hard to believe two years have gone by since Ethan and I were first here, but it also feels like everything is new because this time we're here as a married couple.

Yep! Ethan proposed on Christmas morning. We both decided we didn't want anything elaborate, so a few days later, on New Year's Eve, we got married at City Hall. Ethan's mom, and Alex and Blaine were our only guests, along with their dog Ernie, who came dressed in a bow tie.

After that, we all went to the Kendrick's, who threw a big New Year's Eve slash wedding party at their Lakeview home with all our friends.

It was perfect for us.

After Ethan hung up his skates and retired last year, he hit the ground running, launching his foundation to help underprivileged kids. Seeing him come into his own made me so proud. Not that his hockey-playing days didn't, but knowing how much it means to him that he's able to help a child in need—a child like he once was—is something else entirely. And seeing the joy on his face when he receives an email from a thankful parent, knowing it means the world to him, is all I could ever ask for.

Now the backyard is buzzing with activity.

Elliot is playing monsters with the kids. Jackson's daughter, Isabela, although a bit older, still hangs on to his leg like a spider monkey as the dogs chase them, making them giggle and squeal.

When I suggested inviting everyone to England to celebrate his birthday, Ethan was nervous they wouldn't want to come. Because while the carefully constructed walls have come down, Ethan still worries he hasn't done enough.

Sometimes it takes time to change deep-seated habits, but seeing him now, all bright-eyed and smiling widely, laughing with his closest friends, makes my heart swell. He may not think he's come that far, but I know he has.

He might love quietly, but he loves fiercely.

But he wasn't the only one who had to get used to change.

The bakery is now one of the most successful bakeries in Chicago. Alex has taken a back seat, working more behind the scenes, and I started giving myself a break. Daniel is now the bakery manager, and Aria is with us full-time now they've finished college. They've taken over the commission orders, and we've added a few more members to the team.

Plus, when we started planning this trip, we decided to close the bakery for two weeks so Daniel and Aria could join us.

It's been a big learning curve for me. I'm learning to put myself first and that it's okay to have sad days, and with Ethan by my side, it's been easier.

Alex twists the white gold band around his left ring finger. It's still crazy to me that him and Blaine have been married for nearly a year now.

I hear him sniff, then let out a shaky breath.

"It's wild, isn't it? Not too long ago, it was just the two of us. We were barely keeping our heads above water, and now look at us. We've got this incredible family that keeps growing—hopefully more soon."

For the last nine months, Ethan and I have been going through the process of surrogacy. We met Willow, who has become one of our closest friends, but we haven't succeeded yet. She keeps telling us not to give up, but I see Ethan becoming more and more withdrawn with each negative test. I wish there was something I could do, but sometimes you've just got to leave things for the universe to figure out.

I take a deep breath.

"Maybe. Hopefully." I nod, not wanting to get my hopes up.

Maria Kendrick steps into the kitchen with Paisley on her hip, her other hand resting her growing baby bump. Since meeting her at Blaine and Elliot's birthday party two years ago, Maria has become one of my best friends. She found out she was pregnant with Paisley shortly after we met, and seeing her blossom as a mom has been special.

"Ready for the cake?" She grins.

"Cake!" Paisley giggles, reaching out with grabby hands.

"I think so!" I grin.

Alex lights the candles, then I carefully pick up the cake from the counter and carry it outside.

Jennifer is the first one to spot me and begins to sing "Happy Birthday". Everyone joins in, and when my eyes land on Ethan, he's hiding his smile behind his hand. Those dimples I love so much pop in his cheeks more often now.

Placing the cake down on the table in front of him, I take the empty seat next to him.

"Make a wish!" Blaine hollers when the song comes to an end.

Ethan closes his eyes for a moment, then blows out the candles. We cheer and clap. Whistles pierce the air before the celebration is interrupted by Ethan's phone ringing. He casts me a concerned look as he slips it out of his pocket.

Frowning at the screen, he angles it toward me. Willow's name flashes on the caller ID.

"Answer it," I say, trying not to let my panic show.

Ethan swipes his finger across the screen to answer, and everyone goes quiet.

"Hello? Willow? Is everything okay?"

I rub soothing circles on his back as he listens, the crease between his brows deepening, and then I see it. Relief washes over him, and tears begin to pool in his gorgeous brown eyes.

"Really?" he croaks. "It worked? Are you sure?" He looks at me with another dimple-worthy smile on his face, and my heart swells in my chest.

I cover my mouth with my hand, my own tears falling down my cheeks.

"I'm here with him now; I'll tell him the good news. Thank you, Willow. Thank you so much." He ends the call and pulls me onto his lap. His hands cradle my face. "It worked. The test is positive. She's just had a scan to confirm and it shows a healthy heartbeat."

A choked sob escapes me. I wrap my arms tightly around his neck as he holds me close, hiding his face in my shoulder.

I'm aware our friends erupt in celebration around us, but all I see is Ethan.

All I see is the man I love with every fiber of my being.

I kiss him, wiping his tears away from under his eyes with my thumb.

"This is what I wished for," he whispers.

"For it to work?"

He nods. "When I blew out my candles, I wished for it to work this time."

I steal a kiss from my man before our friends surround us. Getting up from his lap, I accept every embrace. Maria cries happy tears, along with Jennifer. Alex engulfs me in a tight hug, and when Blaine wraps his arms around me, he says, "I think the baby should be named after me."

"Why?" I laugh.

"Because if it wasn't for me interfering, you two would still be pining for each other from afar."

I snort, but he's right. If it weren't for Blaine subtly—well, not so subtly—pushing us together, and planting the fake relationship idea in Ethan's head, we might not be here.

Ethan pulls me into his lap again, peppering kisses against my temple.

"I'm going to be an uncle!" Elliot punches the air, and I laugh as his partner shakes his head with an adoring smile.

"Don't think it works like that, baby," he says, patting Elliot's shoulder.

But I don't care about the technicalities. Every person around this table is family. This is the family we found—the one we chose.

I press a kiss to Ethan's forehead and glance over his shoulder. There's two robins sitting together on a branch, almost like they're watching it all unfold. One tilts its head, looking right at me, and I know—my parents and grandparents may no longer be with us in person, but they're still with me.

With us.

Supporting us and loving us through every moment.

I trace the outline of the two orange-breasted robins

Ethan got tattooed on him two years ago, just before the season started. I will never stop missing them, but I learned that a grieving heart can love and grow, and mine has never felt fuller than it is now.

Surrounded by the people who love me, with a man who would do anything for me, knowing I would do the same for him, and a tiny version of us on the way.

It feels perfect.

"So, Ethan, can I call you Daddy now?" Elliot grins.

## THE END

Want a little more of Ethan & Jacob?
Visit my website for bonus scenes
https://www.jodioliver.com/bonus-content

# About the Author

Jodi Oliver is a British author who writes MM sports romance, happily ever after guaranteed. She loves donuts, dogs and ice hockey, and when she hasn't got her head in a book or hiding in the writing cave, you can find her at an ice hockey game.

She lives in England but dreams of living in the Canadian countryside, with some highland cows and otters.

You can find her on Instagram @JodiOliverAuthor
Sign up to her mailing list: https://www.jodioliver.com/newsletter

Join my FB reader group for the latest updates:
Jodi Oliver's Sin Bin

# Also by Jodi Oliver

Trade Deadline (Chicago Thunder #1)

Blaine & Alex

Off Season (Chicago Thunder #2)

Ethan & Jacob

Defensive Zone (Chicago Thunder #3) - coming Fall 2024

Zach & Carter

# Acknowledgments

When I started writing Off Season, I knew I wanted to touch on Jacob's grief. To dig that little bit deeper behind his sunshine exterior to those sore spots he keeps hidden away, but little did I know that halfway through writing, I would be grieving myself. I was completely blindsided by my loss, and struggled to know how I could possibly write about two people falling in love when my own heart was broken.

But then one of my lovely friends said, "Why don't you channel your grief into Jacob's?", so I did. And wow, talk about cathartic! I cried and cried, but it helped, and now Ethan & Jacob are incredibly special to me for that reason.

And on that note, I couldn't have asked for a better support system while writing this:

My parents for not letting me give up when life became too hard after we lost Ollie.

Rachel, not only for alpha-ing and proofreading, but also for putting up with my constant overthinking stress-head, and for listening to my million voice notes and ramblings.

Leticia, I could not live without you! Thank you for everything.

Ella and Brooke, thank you for being my biggest cheer-leaders. I love your faces so hard.

Lottie, Colleen, Emma, Janette, Jo, Steve, Willow & Lark - thank you for being the best friends a girl could ask for.

Ollie - my angel, my little prince, I miss you so much. There's not a day that goes by where my heart doesn't hurt, but I know you're still with me, by my side. I'll love you always.

Most of all, YOU! Fabulous readers - thank you for all of your support, your love, and your messages and comments. It means more to me than words can describe. I'm so incredibly grateful for every single one of you!

www.ingramcontent.com/pod-product-compliance
Lightning Source LLC
Chambersburg PA
CBHW051246210726
48287CB00002B/365